SURVIVING
Life

❧

A NOVEL

JEANNE SKARTSIARIS

ACKNOWLEDGMENTS

For my daughter Alexandra, who inspired this book. My husband Terry, who patiently puts up with my writing. To my fabulous critique group: Jean Reynolds Page, Ian Pierce, Mary Turner, Kathy Yank, Lou Tasciotti, Chris Smith, Helen Roth and Rachel Simeone.

Editor Alicia Street, book cover artist Erin Dameron-Hill, and formatter Amy Atwell.

Readers: Regina Cabrera (a bright YA reader with cool insights). Karen Huston, Donna Holmes, Lynn Dickson, Cherryl Duncan, Brigitte Kelly.

The Surviving Life Book Club: Mary Misdom, Sally Harvey, Cheryl Seager, Jean Waddle, Jill Thomas, Kathleen Hickman, Maureen Mixtacki, Maureen Luby, Lisa Clark, Susan Weliik, Anne Darrouret, Cindy Grimshaw, Fran Schmehl.

For Mary Lynn Vaughan and my sister, Julie Dee who always supported me.

And pretty much everybody I've met in my life!

Thank you.

Frog

Shahaley —

live your dreams!

— Jeanne Skartsiaris

SURVIVING
Life

For Alexandra

Enjoy life – and buckle up!

PROLOGUE
Hide-and-Seek

"Nice paper, Harper."

"Carson." Carson corrected her high school English teacher.

"Of course, *Miss* Harper." Her teacher placed the paper on Carson's desk and turned away quickly.

Carson Harper, the invisible girl, Carson thought, folding her essay. She looked out of the classroom's open window. A small drift of spring air scented with honeysuckle carried her back to happy times when she wasn't invisible.

When she wasn't fat.

When her mom wasn't a safety freak.

When her dad was alive.

"Ready or not, here I come," Carson's daddy's voice echoed. He was still too far away to find her. She giggled and crouched lower into her hiding place.

These were the best days ever. Summertime, when all the neighbors were out and the kids played hide-and-seek until way after dark. The smell of honeysuckle so thick Carson thought if she opened her mouth she could taste the sweet air.

"I see you." Her daddy laughed and took chase.

Carson heard Trevor scream. She stole a look from her hiding place and saw him run for the big oak tree in her yard, which was base. Trevor was always the first one caught, the first one to run home to his mommy if he got hurt. He was such a chicken all the time, afraid of finding the best hiding spots because he got too scared. And he was already seven, almost a whole year older than Carson.

"I know you're here." Her daddy headed to the old shed next to the garage. He threw open the door and two more kids ran squealing for base.

"You're next, Cars. I'm going to find you this time."

This time. Because all the other times Carson was the last to be found. Her hiding spots better than anybody else's. She was going to win tonight, too. Carson peeked from under the tarp that covered the firewood. Her daddy walked into the shed.

"Come out, come out wherever you are." Some of his voice was lost inside the walls.

She giggled and ducked under the tarp. Carson loved playing in the dark because it was easier to hide. She hugged her knees close and felt the scab pull from the scrape she'd gotten earlier racing Trevor. She'd been winning too, almost at the finish line when she'd tripped and landed on her knee. Probably because, as usual, she'd been barefoot. Her mother had given her an "all better" kiss—which worked more for the sting inside than the sting outside—then sent her back out to play.

"Go have fun," her mother had said. "It's just a little boo-boo."

Dry grass crunched near Carson's hiding place. She curled her dirty toes into the soft dirt and tried to be as still as a statue. She couldn't be found until she was officially declared the winner.

"Come out, come out." Her daddy was close.

"Maybe she's over here." By now all the kids tagged out were looking too. "You win Carson."

Carson wasn't ready yet. Not until Trevor said it.

The footsteps crunched grass again. Started to walk away. Carson tingled and tried not to dart out.

"Okay, you win," Trevor whined.

Carson threw back the tarp and jumped out to claim first prize, running full speed into her daddy's big hug.

2

CHAPTER 1

"Look at the beautiful butterfly." Bet Harper pointed through the windshield at a yellow-and-black butterfly dipping in and out of view.

"I'm not four years old." Carson sighed, not looking up from her iPod. "Geez. Is this the longest stoplight ever?"

"I know you're not four anymore. But no matter how old you are, you'll always be my baby." Bet smiled and patted Carson's leg.

The butterfly swooped near Bet's window. "Wow. How graceful. I think it's a tiger swallowtail." She touched Carson's arm. "Look how pretty it is."

Carson glanced up just as the butterfly flitted in front of a moving bus. Its whimsical flight stopped, crunched against the hot grill of the bus.

"Yeah, pretty." She turned back to her tunes. "If you like smush."

A car horn sounded behind them.

Carson shook her head at her mother. "*Green* usually means *go.*"

Bet hit the accelerator. "I'm going." They merged into traffic.

"Can you drive any slower?" Carson said. "This isn't a school zone."

"I'm going the speed limit." Bet had both hands on the steering wheel in the ten-and-two position.

"Then why is the whole world passing you?"

Bet sighed. "This is why I don't want you to start driving. I worry you'd go too fast."

"Fast? If you call going the speed limit fast." Carson plucked an iPod speaker from one ear. "I'll be seventeen in two weeks, and you still won't let me get my permit. I'll be wearing Depends when you finally let me drive."

"Carson, driving is a huge responsibility. It can be..."

"*Dangerous*. I know! But I'll be a good driver. Give me a chance."

"Honey, I don't know." Bet glanced at her daughter. "Working at the insurance company, I see so many terrible claims. Accidents that could have been prevented. I just worry."

"*I know*. You saw a case where someone ran a red light, or their brakes went out, or they were steering with their big toe, *whatever*. I'll be careful."

Bet looked ahead.

"Just because dad died in a car accident doesn't mean I will, too," Carson pleaded. "Trust me. I'll be a good driver." More than ever she missed her father. Ever since he died, her mother micromanaged her every move.

"We'll see."

"You won't let me do *anything*. I'm going to die of boredom."

"Carson! Don't talk like that." Bet put a hand on Carson's shoulder. "I don't know what I'd do if anything happened to you."

"I know I'd like *something* to happen to me. *Anything*."

CHAPTER 2

The next morning, Carson stood in the middle of her room. "Mom," she yelled, "where're my jeans?" Carson was, as usual, late getting ready for school. She hated school. She hated the kids that made fun of how fat she was. She hated that everybody thought she was a stinking nut case because she was the fat kid.

"Your jeans are in the dryer, still wet," Bet called to her. "Wear something else."

"I want to wear my jeans!" Carson tossed a big handful of clothes from her dresser to the floor and tried not to cry. She didn't want to admit that she needed to wear those jeans because everything else was too small.

Her mother wouldn't let her play sports. Not that she'd be any good at them anyway, but her mom, especially since her dad's accident, worried that Carson would get hurt, especially since her dad's accident. The only thing Carson was allowed to do was watch TV and eat. And even *that* worried her mother—what if she choked on something when no one was home?

The kids at school made no secret that they thought Carson was a pimply blob. Even the teachers, while scolding the moronic taunters, ducked their head as they tried not to laugh at the mean jokes. Especially the coaches. Carson *hated* the coaches. During gym they often used Carson as an example by trying to make the fat girl skinny. She seemed to be their personal charity case. If they could get her to lose a few pounds, the world would be a better place to live, and the coaches would have done something good for: (pick one) the environment, pollution, humanity, cancer prevention, global warming. Carson ticked off the list. Yeah, the world would rotate better, and there'd be peace on earth if she could only chuck a few pounds.

"Carson, we have to leave now," her mom called down the hallway.

Carson sat on her bed and didn't answer.

"Carson?" A pause. "Cars, you okay?" Footsteps rushed to her door. "Carson!" her mom said, flushed, the usual look of worry in her eyes. "Why didn't you answer me? I thought you'd fallen in the shower and hit your head or something." She took a deep breath. "Get dressed; you'll be late."

"I don't want to go."

Her mom thought for a minute. "You've only got one more week of school."

"I know. It's a freaking eternity. Please can I stay home?"

"I don't think so, honey." Bet walked to the window. "Besides, the neighbors are having work done on their house. I don't want you here alone with those workers next door."

Carson fell back on the bed, put a pillow over her head, and moaned. One week. Only one more week till school let out and she would be free. Really free. A pang of guilt whipped through her when she thought of the plan. Her plan. The one that would change everything. Where she would be in control.

Sure, her mother would miss her. But Carson had to do it. She'd spent too much time organizing and promising herself that she'd go through with it. So far, everything was in place.

It would happen.

Only one more week.

Then the rest of the world would feel bad for making fun of her. She'd show them.

CHAPTER 3

Bet worried about her daughter. Okay, maybe that was an understatement. She did want her daughter to grow, to be happy, but if anything bad happened to her, Bet knew she couldn't stand the pain. She'd already lost her husband to an accident. Her heart would be shattered if Carson...she couldn't even think about it.

"Mom, let me walk home today. I want to stop at Starbucks. It's not that far."

Bet knew Carson was embarrassed to be the only high school student who rode the bus.

"I'll take you there later, after work." Bet patted Carson's knee as they waited at a stop light near the school.

"No. I want to go by myself."

"Why?" Bet gripped the steering wheel tighter. "I don't have to go in with you, but I don't want you walking alone. Someone could try and hurt you. Even though most people are good—"

"You never know which person is some psycho-kidnapping-murdering-sicko. I *know*! You've told me a million times."

"Oh, honey, I don't know."

"Fine. Forget it."

"Can you find someone to walk with you?"

"Who? I have no friends; I'm not allowed. One of them might hurt me." Carson put her forehead against the car window, her breath fogging the glass. With her fingertip, she wrote "freedom" in the sweaty glass—then quickly smeared it.

Bet's breath caught when she saw Carson's scribble. *Freedom.* Was life that bad for her?

No. Bet allowed Carson some freedoms, and certainly if Bet

was there supervising her. Carson's safety was more important than anything. *She'll understand when she's older,* Bet thought as she looked lovingly at her daughter. "Maybe you and I will take a nice long walk later. How does that sound?"

"Like a barrel-full-of-monkey fun. Just freaking peachy."

Later, in her room, Carson put everything in its proper place. She didn't want anybody going through her stuff after she was gone and find something that would embarrass her. She waited until her mother ran to the grocery store before pulling out the shredder to demolish the pages of her diary. She plugged in the shredder, and her mother's warning echoed in her head as she pushed the paper through: *Don't get too close to the blades. You could lose fingers.* Carson stuck as many pages as would fit into each pass.

A few pages made Carson sad. *I 'heart' Dylan.* An entry she'd made last year. She'd had a huge crush on oh-so-cute Dylan since elementary school. The cutest boy in school, his smile seemed meant for her and her alone. Though he hadn't glanced her way since fourth grade. She'd known him since kindergarten, when he got laughs by blowing booger-bubbles. How did he outgrow that and become popular, while she turned into Invisible Girl? She studied her pudgy face in the mirror and then her apple body. Disproportionate, she thought. Like someone stuck an air hose in her belly button and filled her tummy and just the top of her long arms and legs. Sort of like a Macy's parade float. She sighed. *If Dylan could just get to know me, he'd like me.*

Her crush was crushed when, one day in the cafeteria, he laughed the loudest when one of his jock friends squeezed an éclair, saying this was what would happen to the fat kid if someone squished her. Carson looked away as the creamy goo spilled over the cafeteria table. She didn't know what was worse, the éclair demonstration, or the fact that none of them, especially Dylan, seemed to know her name.

The last few pages of her diary spoke of her plan. She paused before running them through the shredder. Everything she needed was hidden now. Ready for takeoff, she thought as she looked to the heavens. She whispered a short prayer. *Please, God, give me the strength to go through with it.*

Only a few more days.

After emptying the shredder and taking the paper to the curb for trash pickup, Carson went back inside to start on the note, no, letter. This would be the most important letter she'd ever written, detailing everything. It had to be perfect.

A small tear balanced on her eyelashes when she thought of her mother finding it. Carson didn't want to hurt her mom, but she knew deep down there was no alternative. No other way. Carson *had* to do this. She needed to prove to everybody that she could do it.

She took a notebook and started writing.

Bet pulled into the driveway and glanced at the overflowing trash can. Did Carson walk out to the alley to take the garbage out? *She knows I don't want her out here alone.* Bet looked around cautiously to make sure no one hid in the shadows before pulling into the garage.

She stepped inside the kitchen from the garage. "Carson, I'm home." Bet heard shuffling as Carson's door shut.

"Hi. I'll be out in a minute." Carson's voice sounded muffled through her closed door.

"What are you doing?" Bet walked to Carson's room.

The door opened. "Nothing. Cleaning." She was breathing hard.

"Did you finish your homework?"

"Yeah, well, you know, we don't have much since school's almost out."

"Shouldn't you be studying for finals?"

"I did." Carson looked away and cringed as she thought, *Why bother?*

"Did you still want to walk to Starbucks? I'll walk with you." Bet smiled. "We can even grab dinner out."

"No, I'm okay."

"We could both use the exercise." Bet patted the tiny roll around her abdomen.

"So we walk three blocks for a five-hundred-calorie frappucino?" Carson snapped.

Bet turned toward the kitchen. "Okay, maybe we can take a nice walk after dinner." She worried about Carson's weight gain. Now that her daughter was seventeen, the "baby fat" or the "big boned" excuse didn't cut it. Bet had recently joined the Y, intending to take aerobics classes. She'd encouraged Carson to go, but Carson balked every time Bet mentioned a workout.

She hated to see her daughter get as big as she had, but other than school, Bet was afraid to let her out of her sight. Her daughter was a beautiful girl, maybe a little plump, but what if she went for a walk alone and someone tried to kidnap her? Sure, team sports would be a good way for her to get in shape, but sports could be dangerous. Head injuries were a big fear. Bet had considered a treadmill or bike for the house, but what if Carson used it, and she fell and hurt herself when no one was home?

Bet sighed. "I'll start dinner."

Tonight, what Carson wanted more than anything was to eat a meal of comfort food like her mother's macaroni-and-cheese, the noodles and cheese melted into a brick with the cheese crispy-browned on top. That, paired with the meat loaf her mom used to make, all juicy and delicious, before her mom started putting bran and rice and all sorts of weird healthy stuff in it. Then Carson wanted to curl up on the couch. Be comfortable and enjoy the moment. She only had a few more days.

She mindlessly flipped through TV channels, not paying attention to the shows. Her mind kept going over the letter she'd started. She'd almost had a heart attack when her mother came home early. In a panic, Carson had stuffed the paper and pen between the mattresses, using the bed ruffle to swipe sweat off her brow.

The smell of onions sautéing wafted to the den. Carson closed her eyes and savored the aroma.

Home cooking.

She already missed it.

Dear Mom, the note started. *I don't want to hurt you, but this is something I have to do. Please try to understand.*

Carson knew her mom would freak but eventually would know it was for the best.

I'm tired of people always laughing at me and calling me fatty.

Her mom had constantly supported and loved her. Carson glanced at her mother working in the kitchen. Bet was movie-star pretty but with softer, more rounded edges. Someone you could hold on to, like a life preserver.

I do love you, Mom. You'll see. It'll be best for everybody. I won't be a burden anymore.

Carson hadn't had a chance to finish the letter before her mom had come home. Tomorrow, she'd finish writing it—and the next day, after school, she'd do it.

CHAPTER 4

Cheyenne Mountain, Colorado–NORAD

The computer monitor blinked, its screen glowing a clear 3D image of Earth. Small flashing lights danced around the shimmering planet like a shaken snow globe. Mark Cooke, his first day on the job at the Space Defense Operative Center, leaned in for a closer look at the monitor.

"Wow, this is so cool." Mark pointed to the dancing lights. "Is each light really a piece of space debris?"

"Yup," said Mark's training officer, Steve Vann. "Some are as small as a paint chip. There are tools, old rockets, inactive satellites, even astronaut gloves. Each one is assigned a number so we can track them if they head toward mama earth. We're Vandenberg AFB's backup watch in case one piece hits another and creates a cascade effect." He balled his hands together then exploded them out. "Kaboom! Don't want any of the big pieces to get through and crash."

"How many have fallen?" Mark continued to watch the monitor sparkle.

"A few," Steve answered. "Texas, South Africa, Saudi Arabia. Don't worry, Chicken Little, you're safe here. If one does get through the atmosphere, most burn out anyway. And we'd have plenty of warning since it takes hours or even days to crash to Earth." Steve wadded up a paper ball and shot it at a trashcan. "Missed. Man, this is not my night."

Mark turned away from the screen. "Sorry you got stuck

training me on my first day."

"I sure got the short straw." Steve looked at the new trainee. "I get the squeaky clean newbie. And on my birthday."

"Happy birthday." Mark fiddled with a roller ball on the console. "So, how old are you?"

"Twenty-seven. Almost over the hill." Steve wadded up another ball of paper and shot at the trash can. The wad landed near a pile of missed shots.

Mark remembered his twenty-seventh birthday, three years ago. He and his buddies sat around a fire on a perfect California beach after a perfect day of beach volleyball and crashing waves. He missed San Diego terribly but not his dad for always harping on him and calling him a "drop-out."

"Look, do me a favor." Steve stood. "Don't touch anything. I'm going out for an hour. My girlfriend's going to bring me a birthday surprise in about five minutes."

"But Officer Coffey said we're not supposed to leave the monitors unattended."

"They're not, dufus. You'll be here." Steve ran his fingers through his military cut hair and checked his image in the computer monitor. "Just watch all the bouncing balls on the screen. If one breaks off and the computer starts beeping, call me." He turned to go. "Believe me, this is the most boring detail ever. Nothing exciting ever happens." His cell phone chirped. He answered, "Hey, baby, I'm on my way down. Did you bring my present?" He winked at Mark as he spoke. "Meet me by the side exit. I already told the guard to let you in." He hung up and smiled. "I love birthdays."

"I don't really feel comfortable," Mark said. "I'm not sure what to look for if something goes wrong."

"Just don't touch anything." Steve pointed to his phone. "Call me if you need to. I'll be back in an hour." He patted his crisp uniform and checked his pockets. "Oh man, I left my key pass in my car, and I've already been written up for that. Let me borrow yours."

"I was told not to..."

"I said I'll be back soon. Chill, okay?" Steve held his hand out. "You don't want to start out here as a dork-head, do you?"

"No, but..." Mark fidgeted.

"Believe me, the guys at this station will eat you alive if you're wimp-for-brains. Just give me the pass and take a nap. Badda bing." Steve reached out and grabbed Mark's pass and unclipped it from his starched shirt. "Thanks, dude."

Almost two hours passed before Mark's bladder began to get uncomfortable. He needed to get to the restroom but couldn't get back in the surveillance room without his pass. He picked up the phone and called Steve again. The phone rang five times before rolling to voice mail. *Where is he?*

Mark stood and went to the door. He grabbed a wad of paper from the missed-shot pile and stuck it in the heavy door to prop it open. *This should hold for a few minutes.* He took one last glance at the monitor before trotting down the hall.

If he'd known how to read the data on the computer screen, he wouldn't have missed a large chunk of debris break away from the orbiting trash around Earth just before he ran out. Instead, after his potty break, he went to the kitchen for coffee to help himself stay awake. He didn't realize the chunk of paper hadn't been strong enough to hold the heavy door until he came back fifteen minutes later.

Mark tried to open the secure door. The wrinkled paper was squished flat between the locked door and its frame.

No! He looked at his watch. *Steve better get back before we both get busted.*

Steve would be back soon. *Had* to be back soon.

Mark sat outside the door. Maybe I *am* a screw-up, he thought. His family had been on him to follow his father's military-medical-school path and quit being a "beach bum" as his father called him. He wanted Mark to grow up and get a "real job." No matter how hard Mark worked, or how well he did in college, it was never enough for his father.

I hope they're happy now because I'm completely miserable, he thought. Mark longed to feel the sand on his feet, instead of sitting at a stupid desk during the graveyard shift. He sipped his coffee and fought to stay awake. This night shift's rough, he thought, before nodding off to sleep.

In a restless dream, he thought he heard a faint beep, like a warning, through the thick metal door.

CHAPTER 5

The bell rang.

Carson's heart jumped. It was time.

Amid the sea of celebrating last-day-of-school kids, Carson rushed to her bus. She needed to call her mother to let her know she'd made it home safely before she began the plan.

On the bus, Carson took her regular seat near the front. Ignored, as usual, by the other kids, she looked as the familiar neighborhood passed by. *How many times have I been by here and not really seen the houses or streets?* She bit her lip and squeezed her backpack close to her chest. *Do not cry here.*

Carson finished the letter, rewrote it about a hundred times before she finally got it right. She'd hidden it between the mattresses in her room and hoped her mom didn't decide to change the sheets this morning. Nah, Bct had dropped Carson off at school and had gone directly to work.

Besides, if her mom had found it, she would have had the National Guard and the Texas State Troopers at school making sure Carson was safe.

Carson jumped off the bus at her stop and walked home. She let herself in, dropped her backpack, picked up the phone, and dialed.

"Hey," she said, as her mom answered. "I'm here."

"Good. How was your last test?"

"Okay, I guess. Kinda hard."

"I'll try to leave early, and we'll celebrate your last day of school. You can pick the restaurant, okay?"

A small sob escaped. "Uh, okay."

"Are you all right, honey?"

"Yeah. I coughed and talked at the same time."

"It sounded like you were crying."

"Oh, yeah. For school. That's it, I already miss my friends and teachers." She fiercely wiped her eyes.

After she hung up, Carson checked the time. She ran to her room and pulled the note from her bed.

A hot rush of tears started again. *Don't dweeb out. You can do this!*

Carson ran to her closet and took out the backpack she'd packed weeks ago. She grabbed the note and put it on the kitchen counter. No not the counter—the table. No not there either—the living room. Nothing seemed right. Now watch the whole plan crash because Carson couldn't decide where to leave the stupid note. She finally went to the entry and placed the letter, folded, on a small table under a potted orchid.

Her mom would see it as soon as she walked in the door.

Carson gathered her backpack and took a deep breath.

She opened the front door and looked around, her eyes falling on the letter last. "I'll miss you, Mom. I love you," she whispered.

And she left.

CHAPTER 6

Bet sat at her desk and held the tickets to Carson's birthday and end of school present. A week's vacation to New York City. Carson had always wanted to go and would be thrilled when Bet handed her the tickets. Bet indulged in a daydream imagining Carson's ecstatic reaction. It was getting harder to make her daughter happy these days.

Beach vacations used to be Carson's favorite, until wearing a bathing suit became an issue.

The trip was scheduled in three weeks. Bet thought if Carson was excited enough, she might join her at the Y, where they could take classes together. It wouldn't take much for Carson to lose weight, but if she didn't do it soon, Bet feared she'd fight it for the rest of her life.

The city's emergency alert sirens sounded. That's odd, Bet thought as she stood and went to the window. It was Friday, not Wednesday when the alarms were usually tested. The sirens stopped.

Bet went back to her desk and opened a file, another tragic car accident. Her job at the insurance company was to pay claims on these cases and sift through other layers of insurance. Working amid walls and walls of filing cabinets filled with accident claims made Bet a nervous mother. Maybe a little too nervous, Bet admitted, but it took only one accident, one injury, one mistake for a life to end or a person to be seriously injured. Carson was all she had now.

Bet remembered the phone call from the police the day she lost Carson's father. She was getting Carson, then seven years old, ready for bed. Carson snuggled next to a pile of goodnight books, saving her favorites for her daddy to read to her when he came home.

Bet picked up the phone, thinking it was her husband calling to say he'd be late.

"Is this Mrs. Harper?"

"Yes."

"Mrs. Harper, this is officer so-and-so." Bet could never recall his name. "I'm afraid I have some bad news. There's been an accident."

"I'm sorry, what?"

"There's a police officer at your door. You need to talk to him."

Bet gripped the phone. "No. I don't want to go to the door. Please, don't make me go to the door."

The rest of the memory was like a film clip. Some images slow motion, blurred, others rapid, clear and sharp.

Sharp enough to still hurt after ten years. She'd taken Carson to a neighbor's then rushed to the emergency room. To make sure it was really him.

It was.

Bet stuffed the airline tickets into her purse and went back to the car accident file. She had to stop rewinding that memory every time she had a bad case to review. She looked at the phone. Maybe she should check on Carson again. What if the neighbor still had the workers next door? She needed to make sure Carson shut the blinds.

She heard a muffled *boom*. The emergency warning sounded again.

Bet closed the file and looked out the window again. Moments later, sirens sounded in the distance. She stood and looked outside. Fire trucks sped down the street. Police cars raced behind them. She pushed her head against the glass to see what was going on.

That's a lot of emergency vehicles, she thought, straining to see where they were headed.

She left her office to look out another window. More vehicles and now helicopters rushed toward her neighborhood.

Bet couldn't actually see her house, but she liked this office because it was close enough for her to keep an eye on the immediate vicinity, especially since Carson was there alone after school. It looked as if all the police cars, fire trucks, ambulances and helicopters were headed straight there.

A plume of black smoke billowed above the treetops.

She ran to her office and dialed Carson.

The phone rang and rang. Voice mail picked up.

Bet dialed again. Then tried Carson's cell phone.

No answer.

More sirens passed. Bet's throat tightened around a ball of panic.

Carson, where are you?

Bet slammed the phone down, grabbed her purse and ran.

CHAPTER 7

Carson ran.

Ran away from the kids that laughed at her when she tried to keep up in gym. Ran from her mother's oppressive rules. Carson ran from the teachers who preached healthy lifestyles to the whole class, yet stared only at Carson through the lecture. She ran from people telling her how pretty she *could* be. From the whispers and snickers of the students when she walked past. But mostly, she ran from Dylan. From the time in second grade when they were friends and he told her he wanted to marry her because she had such pretty eyes and was faster and stronger than he was—to now, him not even remembering her name.

Carson huffed and wiped sweat from her eyes. She didn't have far to go, but she'd gotten so lazy and overweight, moving her body any distance was hard. She hated herself for that.

She wanted to keep running to prove to everybody that she was a real person. To have a boy look at her in a way that made her feel special. And most of all, to show everybody that she was capable *and* smart *and* pretty.

She only wished she believed it herself.

CHAPTER 8

Colorado

It was almost five o'clock in the afternoon on Friday, hours before Mark and Steve's graveyard shift. They'd been called by Officer Coffey to come in early.

"Too bad we don't offer a moron medal of honor. You both would be first in line for one." Coffey stood over Mark and Steve, who sat side by side in the monitoring room. "Why don't you tell me how you missed a huge chunk of satellite debris? A satellite big enough to make it through the atmosphere and crash to Earth?"

Mark, his second day on the job, tried to think of another career to pursue, one that, hopefully, didn't include being incarcerated. He looked at Steve. Officer Coffey got his face next to Steve's. Mark sensed the heat radiating from Coffey's sweaty, crimson brow, didn't envy Steve getting the direct attack.

"Well?" Officer Coffey sprayed as he talked.

Steve flinched from the spit-and-sweat shower. "Well, sir. It was his first day here. I was so busy training him we missed the alarm."

Officer Coffey straightened and crossed his arms. "You missed the alarm?"

"Yes, sir." Steve glanced at Mark. "I was showing him the other departments."

"You left the monitor unattended?" Coffey spewed.

Mark felt a few splatters on his cheek.

"Not for long."

"Is that what happened?" Coffey turned to Mark. "You both were playing office *tourista* and looking at all the different departments?" He bent closer and growled, "Leaving yours alone?"

Mark turned to Steve and answered Officer Coffey. "Sir, I'll speak for myself. I did leave the monitors unattended."

Officer Coffey's wet face came closer. "And it shows that you left the property and came back using your key badge. Oh, let's see." He took a document from his desk. "You came back three hours later!" He screamed the last part. "Where did you go?"

Shaking, Mark sputtered. "Um, the kitchen, sir."

"What kitchen? One in Texas?"

Steve sat straighter. "I tried to tell him, sir. But since it was his first day...you know."

Coffey didn't say anything but continued to stare hard at Mark.

Mark's face reddened. *That creep! What about the truth?* He turned to Steve. "I'm sorry, what did you try to tell me?"

Steve gave him a 'let me do the talking' look. "I said you weren't allowed to leave. You remember."

Mark shook his head and kept quiet, unsure what to say without being labeled a tattletale.

Officer Coffey took a handkerchief from his pocket and wiped his face. He sat at his desk and turned to his computer, slipped in a DVD, and hit play.

"Do you think we're completely stupid?" Coffey looked at Steve.

Mark looked at the screen and saw both him and Steve in the control room from an aerial view. Like the camera that caught them was mounted on the ceiling.

Coffey's eyes bored into Steve. "You better start talking."

CHAPTER 9

Bet sped frantically to get home but was stopped before she got to her subdivision by a crush of emergency vehicles and police officers directing traffic away from the neighborhood. She screeched to a halt and jumped out of the car.

"Ma'am." An officer held her back. "You can't go there."

"My daughter, my house. I live there." Bet pushed past.

Another officer let her through and fell in step with her. "What's your address?"

Bet rattled off the number. "My daughter was home alone. She called me. I need to find her."

"Did you say 6804 Maplewood, ma'am?"

"Yes, why?" Bet froze. "Is my daughter all right?"

"Ma'am, I need to have someone talk to you."

"Talk? About what?" Bet's voice was high-pitched and loud; her heart pounded nearly out of her chest. She began running toward her house. "Carson? Did you find Carson?"

"What time did your daughter call you?"

"Why? What's happened? *Carson!*" Bet screamed and took off at full speed. When she rounded the corner to her street, she got disoriented. The scene was wrong. Everything was wrong. The big oak tree was gone. A charred cavity with scraggly roots shooting out every which way was all that was left. Fire trucks, ambulances, and police cars were everywhere. Thick black smoke rose, puffed around tendrils of flame. The grass was gone. Other trees had fallen, ripped from their roots.

Was this her street? Bet was confused, shocked. Someone touched her arm.

"Is this your...your address?"

The person couldn't have asked 'is this your house' because her house was no longer there. Gone. A smoldering, fiery pit was all that was left of their home.

No! She sank to her knees. *No, this can't be!*

"Carson!" she screamed. Screamed from her heart, her core, her soul. From the big hole of pain inside her.

"Carson!"

CHAPTER 10

Bet had no control over her shaking body. A paramedic had given her a blanket even though she wasn't cold. She'd refused any treatment. They had no medicine for the cavernous ache she felt. She needed to find Carson. She'd overheard people talking about the "accident," saying things like:

"It just dropped from the sky."

"It came so fast I couldn't tell what it was."

"I swear it was a UFO."

She sat on the bumper of an ambulance. A few police officers tried to offer comfort. One female officer stayed near, not saying much, but kept offering Bet water or coffee.

"I overheard that someone named Officer Coffey, from NORAD, is coming from Colorado to see...it." The officer handed Bet another bottle of water.

Bet absently took it and set it next to the other five unopened bottles on the wet street.

Bet turned to the woman. "*It* was my home. My daughter..." A wave of pain hit her. She didn't finish her sentence. "I need to find her."

"I understand, ma'am. Maybe she left before the...the crash."

"Are you trying to locate a signal from her cell phone?"

The officer looked away. "We're still checking."

"She wasn't allowed to go outside." Bet began crying. "I wouldn't let her go out alone." She wiped tears with the coarse blanket. "Maybe she heard the plane before it crashed and got out."

The officer wouldn't look at her.

Bet stood. "What kind of plane was it? Why didn't it damage any other homes? The wingspan, I don't understand."

"I'm not sure it was a plane."

"Then what?" Bet couldn't take her eyes off the smoldering gap that had been her house. *Carson? Please, Cars, be okay.*

"I overheard someone say it's from outer space."

"Aliens? A flying saucer?" Bet felt like she did when she'd had a bad reaction to pain medicine. Like her body wouldn't sync with her brain. "Please tell me this is a terrible dream."

"No, it's real." The officer held out another bottle of water. "Talk is that a chunk of space debris came through the atmosphere. Like a fallen satellite or something."

Bet turned away from the offered water. *Space debris?* "Couldn't they have known it was falling?"

"They said it wasn't supposed to fall here." The officer shrugged. "It was supposed to burn up or land in the ocean. You'll need to ask Officer Coffey."

In the dusky light, Bet noticed a few neighbors walking along the street, assessing the damage. She jumped from the bumper of the ambulance, the blanket falling from her shoulders, and ran to the group. "Has anybody seen Carson? Did you see her this afternoon? Did she come home?" Bet was frantic. "Maybe she went to Starbucks or something." Bet tried to control her body from shaking so hard.

"Bet." Her next-door neighbor put an arm around her. "I'm sorry."

A young girl who lived two houses down stepped up. "I saw her. The bus dropped her off over there." The girl pointed to the black hole. "Then she went home."

CHAPTER 11

Carson was alone.

For the first time in her life she had to find her own way. So far she hadn't gotten lost, but there was an underlying fear of not being able to turn and see someone you trust telling you you're doing okay. Not to mention going against all the rules, something Carson rarely did.

She'd almost chickened out, considered staying home and blowing off the whole plan. After calling her mother that afternoon, Carson almost had a heart attack, running with her heavy backpack to a nearby Radisson hotel. It was so hot, and she was too fat and out of shape. She'd walked in a back door and gone to a restroom to freshen up so she didn't look like a sweat ball. Then she approached the bell stand.

"I need a shuttle to the airport." She tried to act like a hotel guest.

"Which airport?"

"D/FW," Carson answered.

"Good timing. He's loading now. Can I take your bags?"

"No, thanks." Carson grabbed her backpack, the only thing she was allowed to bring on the trip, and jumped on the van. She could see her mother's office building from the window.

She checked her airline ticket and her watch. She'd barely make it even if there were no traffic delays.

As the van merged onto Central Expressway, Carson was startled by a huge bang behind the hotel. Before they exited onto the Tollway, Carson heard a bunch of sirens. She turned but didn't see anything except an elderly couple in the back of the van going over their travel brochures. For an instant, she thought she glimpsed a spiral of smoke rising from the line of trees near her neighborhood, but the shuttle sped over a hill and she lost the view.

She almost missed her flight because of the stupid security agent. Carson had used "Casey" on her airline ticket, which didn't match the name on her student ID.

"This says Carson, not Casey." The uniformed woman glared at Carson as an announcer called that her flight was boarding.

"Casey's my nickname. You know. Carson's a weird name. I hate it." She felt a trickle of sweat streak down her back.

"Why don't you have a driver's license?"

"My mom. She won't let me."

"I need to talk to my supervisor, take a seat over there." The agent waved Carson to a bank of blue plastic chairs. "The names need to match the ticket."

"Final boarding for fight 2435 to Denver," came across the loudspeakers.

Carson stood. "That's my flight. Can I please go? My mom'll be worried if I don't get on."

The guard whispered something to another agent and then said to Carson, "Here, bring us your backpack."

Carson stood and handed it over.

Both agents opened it and looked inside, talking between themselves. "Yeah, it was a piece of a rocket or something. Almost shut down flights here."

"That's scary. How'd they know it wasn't a UFO? I mean, it is the government telling us what they want us to hear."

"It was some piece of space garbage. My grandmother lives near there. I can't wait to see the crater it left." The agent looked at Carson. "Are you camping?

"Yes, sir. For Outward Bound."

"Okay, go on. Have fun."

"Thank you, sir." Carson grabbed her pack and dashed to the gate, momentarily slowed by a cluster of people watching something on TV. Carson had no time to see what was so interesting; she barely made it before the door to the gate closed.

And now, in Denver, she waited in the cold air at an airport she'd never been to, for a bus full of strangers, so she could start her plan.

She really missed her mom.

CHAPTER 12

A week later, Bet sat on the uncomfortable hotel bed, a box of hotel-issued scratchy tissue at her side, still not believing what happened. That Carson was gone.

God, she missed her.

She looked around the dark hotel room she'd been living—no staying—in for the past week. Living was something she did when Carson was here. She had an urge to crawl into the lumpy bed and never wake up. She wanted to dream of Carson. To be with her child. She hated this. Her own soul was shattered like broken china.

I'll run. Keep running until my broken heart gives out.

There was nothing left to live for.

Bet knew what she had to do.

She wiped her raw nose with another tissue and decided the best way to end this pain was to die. She'd start taking risks. All the dangers she'd warned Carson about, Bet would now do. Ride a huge roller coaster, go to a bad part of town, bungee jump, sky dive, and swim in the ocean far away from shore. Drive fast.

That way, she wouldn't really kill herself. God would take care of that part. She'd just make it easier for him to bring her to Carson. Even though she was mad at the world and at God for letting this happen, she had to keep her faith. If not, where was Carson now?

She wished she would have let Carson get her driver's permit. Let her know what it felt like to be in control behind the wheel. She regretted not allowing Carson to play sports. Maybe she would've been at practice or a game that afternoon instead of at home.

What if?

What if the *human* that made the *error* had been the one under the rocket debris? That made perfect sense. Bet took a breath. No, that wasn't right either. She didn't wish anyone else to get hurt.

The pain was unbearable.

She stood, put on a pair of new tennis shoes, part of the clothing ensemble that she'd gotten because she had nothing left of her own. Not even a pair of old socks. Not even one of Carson's soft sweatshirts.

Nothing.

She grabbed her purse and left the sterile room.

Heading nowhere.

CHAPTER 13

Mark sat in his small room and watched the darkness come. The sharp edges of the Rocky Mountains softened during dusk, turned purple with the changing light. A girl had died because of his stupidity. Because he let someone walk over him. The night of the crash, Vandenberg AFB tried to call NORAD, who was supposed to contact NASA in Houston to determine if the damned satellite was really going to hit earth. How he and Steve landed on the bottom of the domino-effect-screw-up pile, he wasn't sure. But someone had to take the fall for it, and they were the least experienced and easiest targets.

And then, if the piece of debris made it through the atmosphere, it was supposed to burn up on entry.

He pounded a fist into the hard mattress.

He knew little of the girl or her family, but he wanted to contact them to apologize. He wished he could turn back the clock. To bring that kid back. It was eating him up inside.

CNN covered the story, said the girl's name was Carson Harper. She lived in Texas, where she'd just completed her junior year of high school. She and her mom lived together. Her father had been killed in a car accident ten years ago. CNN kept showing one grainy high school yearbook photo of her.

The news occasionally cut to the same video of the girl's mother sitting on the back of an ambulance, a cluster of water bottles at her feet. It broke Mark's heart to see the woman's face. Her countenance was the sum total of despair and hopelessness.

For the past week, the reporters talked of space debris falling and the chances of it happening again. They interviewed experts about space, or people who thought they were experts. The news reporters talked to people who knew the girl, people who knew that something like this would eventually happen. They were all on camera ad nauseam.

He turned the TV off.

Officer Coffey had told him to stay put in Colorado while he took care of business in Texas. As soon as Coffey came back, he'd "deal with Mark and Steve."

At least the video showed that Steve had been the one who pushed Mark that night. Mark got a measure of satisfaction watching Steve squirm while the video played.

But he was still wrong to let Steve push him.

He longed to go back to San Diego, to days and nights on the beach. Go back to being a "beach bum" as his father called him. As soon as he could, he'd quit the whole program and head home.

But he wanted to at least apologize to the girl's family first.

CHAPTER 14

Wow. The mountains really do turn purple, Carson thought as she watched the last light of day fall over the Rockies. And the stars, they were so clear and so many! Carson had never seen the sky so blanketed with them. She'd already wished on two shooting stars.

Her first wish was that her mother wasn't too worried.

Her second wish was that she would be strong enough to get through the solo hike of the Outward Bound course she'd signed up for.

She sat huddled around the campfire she and her group had started. The warmth of the fire took the chill out of the crisp air. Today's trek was easy, her group leader, Dana, had said. She told them to relax and enjoy it because the hike tomorrow would test their physical limits.

Carson was already sore and tired from the "easy" part of the hike. They'd been practicing for the big trek for days, preparing each camper to go out on their own for a week. When she'd first checked in to Outward Bound, Dana had looked her up and down.

Fat kid, Carson could almost hear her thinking.

"You going to be up for this?" was all Dana asked.

Carson nodded and watched Dana look over the medical releases that Carson had fudged. She'd gotten them herself, signed her mother's signature on all the documents, and put her name down as Casey. Close enough to be called a typo but hopefully not enough to be picked up by the police.

Carson knew that Outward Bound hadn't called her mother before Carson got on the plane, since the only phone number that

35

Carson left was for her own cell phone. The phone that she'd accidentally left at home while she tried to find a place to leave the letter.

The campfire made her sleepy. It was beautiful out here. Man, her mom would be so proud that she'd done this all by herself. Worried, yeah, but she'd have to be proud, too.

She thought of the note she'd left and hoped her mom didn't freak out too much after she'd found it. It didn't say where exactly Carson was, but it said she couldn't be contacted for two weeks.

The wood from the campfire popped sparks. Carson pulled her sleeping bag around her shoulders and breathed the cedar-tinged mountain air. The five other kids in her group were sitting close to the fire as well. A few spoke to each other, but during the week nobody had introduced themselves to Carson. Nothing new, she thought.

It occurred to her that maybe she could be the one to make the first move. She didn't know these people and wouldn't see them again after the camp. What did she have to lose? She started to get up, but hesitated. The cutest boy, Seth, looked at her and crossed his arms, but he smiled.

Before Carson could work up enough nerve to talk to Seth, Dana called the group together. They gathered in a circle, Carson sat with them, her sleeping bag still wrapped around her shoulders.

"You all have a long hard day ahead of you. Make sure you check your equipment and supplies. Take only what you can carry." Dana glanced at the faces around the fire, all lit by the dancing flames. "This hike is hard; that's why we've been training all week. You will depend on good skills to stay on the path and with the group. Find your inner strength." She cast a glance at Carson. "It will help prepare you for your individual excursion. You must be strong for that."

Carson could feel her face flush, and she looked away. She was supposed to have been training these past months. But she never found the time or had the energy to get out and run. Plus, her mom would've freaked if she'd left the house alone.

She took a deep breath. I will do this. I'll show mom that I'm strong, that I can do things on my own.

A wave of homesickness hit her in the gut and tears filled her eyes.

"Have you ever hiked before?" One of the more fit hikers, Torey, stood over Carson.

Carson shrugged. "A little." She thought of the little nature hike her fourth grade took at a bird sanctuary along a well-worn path. The Rice Krispy treats they got at the end of the hike were shaped like birds with M&M eyes.

"Don't slow us down. We didn't pay good money to babysit," Torey said as she adjusted tight hiking pants that hugged her fit thighs.

Just like school, Carson thought. She swallowed a dose of courage and said, "Keep your waffle stompers laced and don't worry about me." Even though she wanted to crawl into an empty log and hide.

"We got your back." Seth stepped near Torey but spoke to Carson. "You can do it." Then he turned and walked into the darkness.

Whoa, did that just happen? A cute boy realized that I was on planet earth? Carson looked into the dark woods, trying to see him. She smiled and sunk into her sleeping bag. *I can do this.* She closed her eyes and recalled the line from Peter Pan— "Clap if you believe." She put her hands together and clapped silently, then said a quick prayer for strength.

CHAPTER 15

A week after the explosion, a service was hastily put together. Not a memorial, since Carson's remains had not been found, but a service to "honor her life." Several neighbors called the school, which contacted students. The few that hadn't left town or had other plans came.

Bet walked into the cool, dark church where the priest greeted her.

"Mrs. Harper. I'm so sorry." He took her hand and held it between both of his. "You'll see Carson again." He looked to the ceiling. "She's in a better place now." He patted her arm.

Bet stifled a sob and allowed the priest to escort her to a front pew. A smattering of people sat throughout the church. No one was crying. Bet overheard two mothers complaining their children's summer camp lasted only two weeks. Envy worked into the sadness in her chest.

News reporters had tried to call Bet until her cell phone battery died. She didn't want to talk to anybody or to see it replayed and rehashed on TV.

The meager turnout disappointed Bet. Carson was so special. She deserved a standing-room-only crowd. By the altar, a table stood draped in white cloth. On top, a few anemic bunches of flowers drooped near a grainy eight-by-ten print of Carson's high school picture.

In the picture, Carson wasn't smiling, and it hurt Bet's heart more. Carson glared at the camera lens, her hair pulled back in her trademark ponytail. Bet dabbed her eyes and tried to remember the last time she'd seen Carson's hair down. Was it third or fourth grade? Carson started wearing her hair like that years ago, and only took it down to wash it and get an occasional trim. She even slept with it pulled back.

Bet couldn't provide any photos of Carson for the service, since everything in their house had been destroyed. No pictures, no videos, no T-shirts that still held her scent. Not even any of Carson's cute "I love you mommy notes" that she'd made when she was younger. Bet cherished each scribbled letter and had kept every one of them. But nothing was identifiable in the wreckage.

Nothing of Carson left. Not even a fingerprint. It was as if she'd never existed.

Everything that was their life together had been destroyed. *Vaporized,* Bet had overheard someone say. The crash was bad enough, but the final blow was the gas line exploding and incinerating everything.

An Officer Jack Coffey from Colorado had spoken to Bet that first night. Offered a few insincere apologies, and said something about human error and a piece of space debris managing to get through to earth, past all the monitors and safety nets. Then the debris didn't disintegrate like it was supposed to when it hit earth's atmosphere, and then it landed in a populated area. The odds were a gazillion to one. It wasn't supposed to happen. A mistake.

She wasn't even able to see her home—or the hole that was her home. After the gas line to their house exploded, there was no gas or power for blocks. Plus, the government wanted to examine the "rubble." The whole neighborhood had been moved to a nearby hotel.

Bet chose one farther away.

Office Coffey left a number, said to call if she had any questions. Yeah, she had a million, like how could this have happened? Of everything she worried about, everything she'd tried to protect Carson from, space debris had not been on the list of possible risks.

Human error.

The minister started talking. A few people came in. Some left. The numbness that encompassed Bet kept her sitting there. Quiet. Even though inside, she was dying. Was Carson really gone? It hurt too much to think about.

"Mrs. Harper?"

Bet looked up at a young man Carson's age.

"I'm Dylan. I'm really sorry about this. It's so weird, you know, especially... a rocket." He squirmed a little.

Bet was grateful that he'd taken the time to talk to her. "Yes. It's terrible." Bet took a Kleenex and wiped her face. "Thank you for coming."

"I didn't really know her, but I remember she had really pretty eyes." He backed away. "Sorry, again." He retreated and went to a woman Bet assumed was his mother. By the way he acted Bet could tell that she'd made him talk to her.

Dylan's mom stepped in front of Bet. "I'm sorry for your loss. I can't imagine what you're going through." She held Dylan's arm. "We'll certainly miss Carter."

"Carson," Bet whispered.

"Carson. I'm sorry." She hastily turned and pulled Dylan with her. They walked out.

The church emptied. People offered small condolences. The minister told Bet to take her time, but she wanted to leave. He handed her the photograph of Carson as he walked her to the door.

The harsh glare of sunlight contrasted with the dark quiet church. Bet stood outside for a moment, the minister near. A small breeze lifted Bet's hair off her neck and it went through her like needles. Then the air wisped through leaves on a nearby tree, like a soul on their way to heaven, letting their presence be known once more before leaving earth for good. Her knees buckled and she held the door for support.

The priest took hold of her elbow. "Do you want to sit?"

"No, thank you," Bet said, regaining her balance, and stepped into the thick air, holding the photo close to her.

Can I send someone to your house"—he stopped—"to where you're staying, to keep you company?"

Bet shook her head and descended the first of too many stone steps. She didn't want to talk to anyone, but she didn't want to be alone either. Besides, the priest probably had a wedding or bingo scheduled. He'd go home later and chalk this day up like all the others. Funerals, blessings for the sick, baptisms. Then he'd take off his robe, sit in his recliner and watch TV, while Bet had to live with the pain.

Bet waved to him and continued to her car. All she wanted to do was crawl into the scorched pit that had been her house and die. Her only reason for living was gone. Carson was the energy that fueled Bet. Without her, life was impossible.

Why go on?

Bet looked at the church, stone and stained glass shimmering in the late afternoon sun, and considered that thought. Considered a way to end her pain. Dark thoughts entered her mind. What about carbon monoxide poisoning with her car? Would it work with a hybrid? *I don't even have a garage anymore.*

As much as she wanted to, she couldn't take her own life. That would be wrong, a sin.

But how else would she see Carson again?

CHAPTER 16

After an agonizing afternoon of sitting in the lonely drab hotel room, Bet buckled herself into her car and turned onto the service road of Central Expressway. The car seemed to drive itself; Bet couldn't think where to go. The minister's voice echoed in her head. *Carson's in a better place now. You'll see Carson again.*

Before she realized it, she was heading toward home.

She hit the brakes and turned away.

No, I can't go there. Bet drove through a neighborhood near her own. She fingered her seatbelt nervously as she cast glances in the direction of her house. Big tears blinded her, but she wouldn't wipe them away. She couldn't breathe and unbuckled the binding seatbelt. She choked through the biggest sob of her life and sped through a stop sign, needing to run away from everything.

She must've been going thirty or thirty-five through a residential zone. It was oddly exhilarating and held the pain at bay for a fraction of a second. For the first time in a long while, she'd broken the rules.

She jumped when a honking siren broke her thoughts. Flashing lights pulsed in her rearview mirror.

"Pull over." A loudspeaker crackled from the police car.

For an instant she considered speeding up.

The siren chirped, and the voice again told her to pull over.

Bet sighed and pulled to the curb. She fumbled for her license and reached into the glove compartment for her insurance papers. An officer approached the car and Bet rolled down the window.

"Afternoon, ma'am." The officer was brawny, fit and stern. He leaned to the window. "License and insurance, please."

Bet handed him the documents.

"Do you know why I pulled you over?"

"Was it because I ran that stop sign or for speeding?"

He smiled at her. "I wish everybody were as honest. Why aren't you wearing your seatbelt?"

"It was too tight."

He looked at her license. "You are Mrs. Harper?"

"Yes." She stared ahead.

"Excuse me for a sec." He strode to his car, and Bet could see him punching buttons on a keyboard then he got on a cell phone.

After a few minutes, he came back to the car and handed her the papers.

"You're the victim of that space debris accident. I'm real sorry about that, ma'am." He paused. "Especially about your daughter."

Bet nodded and tried to look at him, but tears blinded her.

"Look, considering everything, why don't you just go on. I'm not going to give you a ticket. I think you've been through enough."

"Thank you." She glanced at his holstered gun.

"I'm a parent, too. I'm sorry for your loss." He looked down. "Losing a child... I can't imagine."

Bet continued to look at his gun. "You ever get a chance to use that thing?" she asked.

"My gun?" He touched the handle. "Target practice mostly."

Bet's heart started beating faster and her hands began shaking. She leaned out the window and reached for the snap on the holster.

The officer looked down as if she was trying to brush a bug off his body. "What are...?

She flipped open the snap and lifted the gun in one move. It was so much heavier than she'd expected. Her hands fumbled it.

"Hey!" The officer tried to grasp the falling gun.

In a weird slow-mo instant the revolver spun in the air and knocked against her car door before clanking to the ground. It didn't go off.

"You want to use it today? On me?" Bet threw the car in drive and jammed the accelerator. The tires of her little Honda screeched and blew a puff of black smoke as she fishtailed away from the officer.

"Hey!" He jumped back, almost fell, then scrambled on all fours to get his fallen gun, and ran to his car.

Bet hoped she hadn't hit him and looked quickly in her mirror. *Come on, hurry. Take that gun and shoot me.* She slowed down a little so he could catch up.

He turned on the lights, sirens full blast, and sped after her. She could see him on his mic and imagined him calling for backup. Backup—for her!

She hit the accelerator again and sped through a neighborhood. Oh, dear. I don't want to run over any children. Bet turned on to a busier street then shot into an empty church parking lot. She made a figure eight until he got close enough. Her open window blasted hot summer air through her hair. Sure enough, more police cars raced into the lot. *This was exciting!*

"Pull your guns out and shoot!" she yelled.

"Stop your vehicle." A disembodied voice crackled the air.

"No, you'll have to take me down." Bet laughed at the absurdity of it all. *Carson, here I come.*

Suddenly, she saw a young boy on a bike, riding wobbly as he tried to stay on two wheels while his father lunged toward him, reaching to grab him before the crazy woman ran him over. Bet screeched to a stop. "Oh, I'm sorry!" She jumped out of the car as the father lifted the child from the bike and ran the other way. "I didn't mean to scare you." She waved frantically.

The police were on her like a pack of wild dogs. They threw her face down on the hot pavement and handcuffed her.

"Are you out of your mind?" The officer that had pulled her over knelt next to her.

"What happened to 'shoot first, ask questions later'?" She raised her head, felt the sting where she'd skinned her cheek on the rough concrete. "I only wanted you to shoot me," she whispered. "I'm sorry for all the trouble."

"What did you say?" The officer leaned closer. "Ma'am, do you need a crisis counselor?"

Bet shook her head and laid her head back on the scorching pavement. The driveway grit stung her cheek, but that hurt far less that the burning tears.

CHAPTER 17

Dana led the hikers back to camp. Even Torey limped in pain after the grueling walk. Carson hobbled behind, blisters screamed on her feet, and every inch of her body throbbed with pain. She'd almost given up hours ago, but Seth had fallen in step with her and cheered her along.

"You're doing good," he encouraged. "One foot in front of the other. Think about other things." His smile rejuvenated Carson.

"Thanks for the support. I know I'm out of shape—" Carson tripped on a tree root and didn't finish her sentence.

"The more you do, the faster you'll get in shape. You're already stronger than when you first got here." Seth cleared a branch for her. "I used to be overweight."

"You?" Carson stopped and hungrily gulped the thin air.

"Come on." Seth kept going. "We don't want to lose the group."

Carson shuffled behind him. "How did you lose weight?" She couldn't believe she was actually talking to a hot guy. And that he used to be fat.

Seth shrugged. "Exercise. Better diet." He flashed a quick smile. "And I had to figure out why I ate so much. It was like I needed to fill a hole."

Carson was breathing too hard to answer, but she thought of all her "holes." Her father's death, her mother's fears, her own comfort in food. They were hiking along a steep embankment. Quick glimpses through the trees showed a spectacular vista of mountains and the bluest sky Carson had ever seen. Bright pink wisps of clouds speckled the deep horizon. Their vivid color against the clear indigo blue was way pinker than fresh spun cotton candy or the sugar heart candy that said pithy things like "Be mine." She glanced at Seth and blushed.

Later back at the camp, Torey sought out Seth and sat next to him while Dana talked about their upcoming solo hike. Carson found a log away from the group and sat. Relief ebbed through her sore muscles, but she became self-conscious of her rolls of belly fat.

"Is tonight's camp ready yet?" Dana waved her hand around the area. "Come on, don't get comfortable. Let's get the fire started. I'm hungry." She moved gracefully, as if she hadn't taken one step all day.

"Aren't you sore?" Carson groaned as she stood.

"You get used to it." Dana handed her kindling. "Here, start the fire."

"Me?" Carson nervously took the wood. "I'm not sure I can do this."

Dana put her hands on her hips. "You'll need to be able start a fire when you go on your solo hike. I thought you said you were ready."

Carson looked at the other campers. "I am." She lowered her voice. "Sometimes I get a little self conscious in front of others." She noticed miserably that Torey had begged a shoulder rub from Seth.

"Oh, that feels great. Torey rolled her head and managed to look like a Victoria's Secret model. "Those backpacks are so heavy." She looked directly at Carson.

Carson shrugged. "Yeah, they are." She felt the keen throb of soreness in her muscles where her backpack had hung.

"At least you have extra padding," Torey said to Carson under her breath.

Carson tossed the pile of kindling into the fire pit. Her chaffed shoulders hurt almost as much as Torey's remark.

Dana yelled to the group, "I need everybody to get the camp set. Then we can relax."

Later as they ate their beans and rice and fake chicken, the group sat silently. Carson was so tired it was an effort to use any energy to chew her food.

Dana stood. "It's been really dry here lately. Tomorrow, when you're out on your own, you must make sure any fire you start is completely out. No excuses. Okay?"

The rest of the group nodded. Carson was afraid of going into the woods by herself. She glanced at Seth, who sat staring at the fire. She wished he'd go with her.

Four days alone. It had sounded like a good idea when she had a soft bed to crawl into after entertaining a fantasy about discovering her inner self while in the peaceful solitude of the Rocky Mountains. Of course, in that fantasy, she could sing like a rock star, and she had a figure like an Olympic gymnast. Mostly, she wanted to prove to her mother that she could do something like this on her own, without being micro-managed and reminded of how dangerous everything was.

Darkness melted into the forest and the air chilled. She moved closer to the fire and was surprised when Seth sat next to her.

"You ready for tomorrow?" His smile was so perfect.

"No. Yeah. I think." Carson cringed. *I sound so stupid.* "Are you?"

He nodded. "I'm looking forward to it. But then I've done a lot of camping with my dad."

"My dad was killed in a car accident." *Carson! Just shut your mouth if you can't say something smart.*

"Oh, man. That's rough." Seth's sympathy seemed genuine. "I'd be a real juvenile delinquent if I lost my dad."

"No you wouldn't," Carson said. Shyness grabbed her tongue. She took a deep breath. "Umm, Seth? What made you decide to lose the weight?"

He looked right at her, his smile dazzled like diamonds.

Carson's heart fluttered, and her blistered toes tingled.

"It was weird," he said. "My parents fought all the time, and my dad was always pushing me in school and sports. Especially football." He laughed quietly. "It seemed like all the fights they had were about me and that no matter what I did, I was a screw up. So I ate all the time."

"You are so not a screw up." Carson blushed. *Did I just say that?*

Seth smiled. "My parents finally got a divorce, and I got more one-on-one face time with my dad. He told me that he just wanted the best for me. That's why he was riding me so hard. He didn't want me to make the same mistakes he did." Seth tossed a twig on the fire.

"How much weight did you lose?" Carson figured about ten pounds since he looked so hot now.

"Forty-two big ones."

"What! How?"

Seth shrugged. "I started doing more active stuff. I don't know how to explain it. Honestly, the more I realized my parents weren't mad at me, the less I ate." He shrugged again. "I guess I was just ready to lose the LBs."

"LBs?"

"Pounds." He patted his tummy.

"That's amazing." Carson said, sneaking a quick glance at his buff chest outlined in his "life is good" T-shirt. Carson's doctor had said she needed to lose about twenty pounds. Forty-two was a chunk.

"It's funny, my parents get along better now that they're divorced. Weird, huh?" He put his arms behind his head and grinned.

"Parents are so weird." Carson laughed. "Can't live with 'em, can't live without 'em." A pulse of homesickness hit her. Even though she was here to prove something to her mother, she still missed her like crazy.

CHAPTER 18

Bet thought she'd die of boredom in the tiny jail cell. She tentatively touched her cheek where it still stung from the parking lot slamdown. She lay on the small cot pushed against the wall and overheard snippets of conversation about her. *Space disaster. Daughter. Freaked out. Lost it.*

Earlier they'd sent a social worker in to talk to her. The woman was let in to Bet's cell by a uniformed policeman. She had tattoos and a blonde spiked haircut. Bet thought she lacked a certain sensitivity for the job, especially with the barbed wire tattoo that encircled her upper arm.

The woman suggested that Bet consider admitting herself to a psychiatric hospital to "relax and regroup after your loss."

That's all I need, Bet thought. To sit all day staring at cinder block walls, lacing leather wallets, and thinking about never seeing Carson again.

Before the woman left, Bet asked if getting the tattoo hurt.

"Yeah. But that's why I did it." She held her arm up like World War II's Rosie the Riveter. "I needed to prove that I could do it."

"And you're here to advise me?" Bet said under her breath.

"I'm sorry, what?"

"Nothing." Bet pointed to the barbed wire. "Maybe I'll get one, too."

The woman nodded, scribbled on her clipboard and left.

Bet sighed. Finding a way to get herself killed was going to be harder than she thought.

A girl that looked a little older, but rougher, than Carson stepped up to the cell. "Whatcha in for?"

"Running a stop sign without a seatbelt," Bet answered.

"Hey, Officer Z." The girl yelled down the hall. "Don't put me in the same cell as this one."

"I didn't finish." Bet sat up. "I tried to steal a gun, and I caused a police chase, too." She said it as if she'd just won the grand prize at a cake-baking contest.

"Oh, yeah. I heard about you." The girl opened the door and stepped into the cell.

"Isn't that locked?" Bet asked, surprised.

"Not all the time. At least not this cell. Most of the others are." She strolled inside. "I guess they don't find you a high enough risk."

Bet extended her hand. "Bet Harper."

"Yeah, I know." The girl sat down on another wall-mounted cot.

"I'm sorry, I didn't get your name," Bet asked politely.

"Roxie. Or Rox Star." She pushed her black-and-red tips razor-cut hair away from her face. "You can call me Rox."

"It's nice to meet you." Bet leaned back against the wall. "Is Star your real last name?"

"Not yet. I haven't had it legally changed."

"I see. It's a nice name." Bet really wanted to be left alone.

"You're awfully polite, considering you're behind bars." Rox chomped on a wad of purple gum.

"Should I be rude? I'm sort of new to this." Bet crossed her arms, not sure how to handle this girl. She could smell the over sweet grape gum.

"What happened to your cheek? It looks like you got a bad microdermabrasion."

Bet pushed a clump of hair off of the sticky cut. "Road rash. I...I fell on the parking lot."

"Fell. Yeah, right. I heard you gave the popo's a chase." She barked a laugh. "Pretty cool for someone, you know, your age."

"Popos?" Bet asked.

"Po-lice. They've been talking about you."

"I know." Bet turned away. Seeing this teenager reminded her of her loss. She wanted her to leave.

"I knew your daughter."

Bet gasped. "You did?" Her lip trembled. "How?"

"School." Rox blew a big bubble. It popped over a smatter of freckles on her milky complexion. "We had a class together. I got held back twice. I think it was last year."

"I miss her so much. Tell me everything you remember about her." Bet began to cry.

"Hey, don't get all emotional on me. I can't deal with that." Rox started for the door.

"Sorry," Bet whispered. "It's hard. Real hard."

"I'm cool with that." Rox sat again and fiddled with one of the many pieces of jewelry that either dangled from or was pierced into her. Her nails, painted with black polish, were chipped and dirty. "Let's see. I remember she was smart. I tried to get her to help me cheat in, um, I think it was English. She wouldn't do it." Rox looked at Bet and blew another bubblewad of gum. It popped, and she sucked the remains into her mouth. "She always wore a ponytail, and I remember she had real pretty eyes."

"Yes, she does...did." Bet cried harder. "I loved the way they lit up when she was happy." Bet thought sadly that she hadn't seen them light up for a long while.

"We had lunch at the same period. I sat at the freak table." Rox paused. "I don't remember who she sat with, if anybody."

"Mrs. Harper?" A large muscled police officer, his head shaved like a billiard ball, stood at the door.

"Officer Z, my man!" Rox stood and opened the door for him.

"Rox, are you bothering our...guest?" He smiled and high-fived her.

"No, Z, we were just talking."

Officer Z turned to Bet. "She hangs out and helps us here."

Rox flashed him a smile. "It keeps me out of trouble. Most afternoons I can't go home until my mom"—she looked down and ran her toe on the floor—"you know, sleeps it off or something."

"Oh, Rox, I'm sorry," Bet said. "Doesn't she worry about you?"

Rox snorted. "Yeah, she worries that I might come home and bother her."

Bet was floored. "How horribly sad." She thought of Carson, unable to even take the trash out by herself, and this girl ran the streets alone, unwelcome in her own home.

"Go help out front." Officer Z held the door for Rox. "I need to speak with Mrs. Harper."

"Okay, Z man." She turned to Bet. "We'll talk later."

"Yes, that would be nice."

Rox laughed. "She's so Mrs. Cleaver, it's funny." Rox turned to Bet and said, "Z man let's me watch old TV shows here. I love "Leave It To Beaver.""

"You could learn some manners, young lady," Officer Z said as she walked out.

As soon as Rox left, the officer turned to Bet. "I'm Xavier Hart.

"Xavier with a Z?" Bet asked.

"No." He glanced toward the door. "Kid can't spell. She started calling me Z, and it stuck. Now everybody calls me that."

"It's nice you help her out," Bet said and sat straighter. "May I please leave now?"

Z shook his head. "Not yet. A judge needs to review your file first. Hopefully, she'll do that tomorrow morning."

"What? I'm spending the night here?"

"I'm sorry." Officer Z looked apologetic.

"Z man. Dude!" Rox was back in the doorway. "You guys let drug dealers and bad guys outta here all the time. Give Mrs. Cleaver a break."

"Rox, go on. We're busy here." He gave her a stern face. Probably like the father she needed, Bet thought. Rox walked out and winked at Bet.

"Mrs. Harper, it's already after four. She'll never get to it today. We'll take good care of you here."

"I've never been in jail before." Bet was frightened. "I have to stay overnight? What about bail? How does that work?"

"You are certainly entitled to call an attorney." Z crossed his arms. "But the issue with trying to take a gun from a police officer is going to be tough to fight."

"Well, I wasn't planning on hurting him," Bet said, indignant. How would she explain that she was only out to hurt herself?

"You'll be fine. The food's not too bad here." He took time to jot down a few notes and explain the rules. "I want you to be comfortable here."

"I'd be more comfortable anywhere but here." Bet folded her arms across her chest.

Rox was back. "I just caught Judge Katherine in her office. She'll see you today."

Bet sank to the bunk. "Oh, thank goodness."

Officer Z laughed. "Rox, you better not start living a life of crime. We'd never catch you—you know too many angles." He slugged her arm affectionately.

"Dang tootin', Z man." She looked at Bet. "If you get out tonight, can you give me a ride somewhere?"

"Don't get Mrs. Harper in trouble, Rox," Z warned.

"Me?" She smiled sweetly and said to Bet, "I'll tell you more about your kid."

Even though Bet craved any crumb of information about Carson, she wasn't sure she could be with this obnoxious girl. "Rox, I really have something to take care of. Alone." But, Bet thought, God knew she had nowhere else to go.

CHAPTER 19

Carson had to pee. It was pitch black and cold outside, and she thought she heard something moving in the bushes near her.

It was probably a bear. A really big bear.

Last night she set her sleeping bag on the periphery of the girl's group. She didn't feel welcome to join them, but was too afraid to sleep alone—or near Seth.

She thought about last night around the campfire, how Seth had talked to her like a real person and encouraged her to make the hike.

"You'll be fine," he'd said, by the light of the fire. "It's so amazingly cool out there alone. You know that feeling you get in your brain when you have your iPod on just right? It's like the music is playing in the middle of your head." He looked at the stars and smiled. "And it'll give you time to think about tons of stuff."

"Like why I weigh a ton?" Carson couldn't help the sarcasm.

He turned and looked at her. His eyes bored into hers, but they twinkled in time with the fire. "Like why food is your best friend."

Carson tried to hold his gaze, his beautiful gaze. She blinked and looked away, shyness and shame about her weight, plus a big hit of homesickness grabbed her. "Sorry, I didn't mean..." she whispered.

"It's cool. I've been there. I know how it is." He continued to watch her. Then he did something that took Carson's breath away. He touched her. A light touch, his finger gently pushed some hair from her face. "It's too bad you don't see how pretty you really are," he said and then smiled warmly.

54

Carson's flush went from head to toe. It was like he could see her the way she wanted to be seen.

But now, in the wee hours of the morning, she tried to ignore her nearly bursting bladder and tried to remember the feel of Seth's finger on her face. The sleeping bag was so warm, and it was too early and dark to make a potty run. She hadn't gone before bed because she was mortified that Seth might see her. She was paying for it now.

Heat lightning slashed in the sky, and a slow rumble of thunder followed. She could see stars overhead and hoped it wasn't going to rain on the day she was supposed to go into the woods alone.

Carson had considered asking Dana if she could stay at base camp with her instead of doing the three days of solitary hiking. Maybe, she thought wickedly, Seth would ask her to join him. She shivered, not sure if it was because of Seth, the cold, or because she had to pee like crazy.

Unable to hold it any longer, she unzipped her sleeping bag. Bedwetting would be more embarrassing than taking the humiliating walk to the potty area. *At least everybody's asleep,* she thought as she rolled out of her toasty sleeping bag. She did a combo pee-pee-and-cold-outside dance while she grabbed a few toiletries from her backpack. She didn't want morning breath and a wigged-out ponytail when Seth woke up. She also grabbed a couple of hidden candy bars. *I'll just have a few bites, since the hike today will be so hard.* It was pathetic, she thought, that she remembered to pack candy bars but forgot her cell phone. She trotted away from the sleeping camp.

She wanted to get as far away from the group as possible so no one would know she had to use the bathroom, but she also wanted to stay close in case that noise she'd heard really was a bear.

She easily found the area that was designated for the potty because it stunk so badly. Carson decided to go a little farther, even though she could barely hold it. There were no paths, so she pushed through low hanging branches, jumping at every noise in the dark forest. She could practically hear her mother's voice. *Don't go out alone; there might be a wild animal with rabies or deadly venom; or a mountain lion could eat you. You could get Lyme disease from a tick or West Nile from a mosquito. If*

Carson's bladder weren't at the point it was, she'd have happily heeded her mother's advice.

She finally found a place to take care of business and prayed there were no poison ivy patches near. She tied her jacket's sleeves around her shoulders so she wouldn't get it dirty. Another flash of lightning along the horizon made her jump. Thunder quickly sounded.

Afterward, feeling blessedly relieved, Carson brushed her hair and teeth. She went a bit farther to the nearby creek and splashed water on her face.

Wiping off the frigid water with her sleeve, she was startled to see a pair of reflective eyes peering at her from the brush. She jumped back as the eyes retreated. *I don't care if Seth sees me gross and stinky, I'm getting outta here.* She backed away from the brush and turned to run just as a huge flash of lightning pierced the sky.

Carson screamed and hardly noticed that all her hair stood straight up. She suddenly felt a weird charge inside her. She would have a hard time remembering what happened next because the thunder and bolt of lightning seemed to happen at the same time. The lightning struck so close to where she stood, she was violently thrown back by the scaring electricity and barely had time to roll away from a big tree that toppled nearby.

Shaking and crying hard, Carson wasn't sure which way the camp was. She only hoped it was behind her, because the wall of fire the lightning had started was directly in front of her.

CHAPTER 20

Officer Z escorted Bet to Judge Katherine's chambers. Bet wasn't handcuffed, but she felt dirty and seedy all the same. Her new clothes were stained and torn from the parking lot, and her cheek burned where it was skinned.

"You're lucky the judge is getting you in this afternoon." Officer Z stayed close to Bet. "That Roxie is resourceful." He shook his head. "I only wish she'd finish high school. We try to keep her safe here."

"What about her mother?" Bet asked.

"A real piece of work. That's how Rox came to spend so much time here. No one was home to watch her while her mother sat in jail." He glanced at Bet. "I'm sorry for your loss."

Bet nodded. She couldn't talk with the huge lump in her throat.

"Here we are." Officer Z held a door open for Bet.

They walked into a small courtroom. A few people milled about. Two attorneys conferred with the judge at the front of the courtroom. An orange-jumpsuit-clad man sat at counsel's table, watching the hushed conversation with interest.

"Have a seat here," Z said, indicating a front row bench.

"Thank you." Bet sat, surprised when he sat next to her.

"Are you staying?" Bet asked.

Z laughed quietly. "Yes, ma'am. You are *still* incarcerated."

"Oh, yeah," Bet whispered. "I'm a prisoner."

They waited almost fifteen minutes while the judge called the orange-suited man to the front. She quietly spoke to him. He nodded and was escorted out. Bet tried to imagine what he was in for.

"Mrs. Harper?" Judge Katherine addressed Bet. "Why don't we meet in my chambers?"

"Special treatment," Z said quietly and smiled. "Hopefully, you'll get off easy."

As Bet stood, her knees felt weak. She was a prisoner. She couldn't just walk out of here. It seemed so foreign to her.

They settled in a comfortable office. Bet sat in a chair in front of the judge's desk. Officer Z stood near the door.

"Mrs. Harper." Judge Katherine took off her legal robe and hung it on an oak coat rack. "You've certainly been through a lot. I'm sorry."

Again, Bet nodded, afraid to speak.

The judge took a seat at her desk and opened a file.

My criminal record, Bet thought.

"Given your clean record, and considering what's happened to your daughter and home, I'm not going to put you in jail. That would be cruel."

Crueler than what I've already been through? "Thank you," Bet said, feeling a sense of relief. At least she'd get out of here.

"I am, however, going to recommend that you spend time at Green Hollow Psychiatric Hospital."

Officer Z let out a low breath.

Bet gasped. "As an outpatient, I hope?"

The judge looked over the file at her. "Mrs. Harper, you said you wanted the officer to shoot you. You created a dangerous car chase. That sounds unstable. I don't want you alone."

"I'll go crazy there! Please, let me go on my own. I'll make an appointment."

"The social worker thought you might need more than that. Really, it's for the best."

"And that would be the lady with the barbed wire tattoo and hair that looked like a landmine?"

The judge continued to look at Bet. "She's really quite good."

"Don't I get an attorney?" Bet snapped.

"Of course, Mrs. Harper. But I assure you that this is a reasonable recommendation." The judge stood and nodded to Z. "You may take her back to her cell." She said to Bet, "Get an attorney if you wish. I'll see you back in court, then. Thank you." She closed the file, indicating their conversation was over.

CHAPTER 21

Carson lay on the ground, shocked, scared, and sore. Two deer jumped from the fiery bushes and raced into the forest. They were so close Carson could see the panic in their eyes. Thick smoke made it hard to breathe. *Fire!* Her brain finally sent the signal to her body. She got up and ran the same way as the deer.

Flames sprouted from trees like magic. Carson ran hard, trying to stay in front of the quickly spreading fire. *Go to the water.* But, disoriented, she couldn't remember which way that was.

It was getting harder to catch a breath. The smoke was thick, and she was out of shape. *Run and don't stop.* Small animals darted in front of her, and she hoped the big ones were more worried about escape than hunger. She didn't want to be served crispy fried to a grizzly bear.

The air seemed thinner, and she became dizzy. She managed to climb a small mound of boulders. The smoke wasn't so dense here. She kept moving forward, climbing higher, tripping and skinning her knees and arms. Brambles caught her clothes and face, but she was afraid to stop. *Help!* she thought but couldn't scream. She did stop when exhaustion and pain overcame her, and she collapsed amid some rocks at the base of a mountain.

Carson wasn't sure how long she'd been asleep or unconscious. She thought the sun was out, but the eerie orange light could've been from the still burning flames or else the morning sun filtering through dense smoke.

Moving was painful, both from the last few days of hiking and now running like a madwoman through the smoke-choked forest. Her knees were bloody and scraped through torn jeans. Scratches crisscrossed her arms like a tic-tac-toe board. Cuts on her face burned her cheeks. Carson looked through the smoke to the top of the rocks. If she could climb them, someone might see her. A thick line of smoke kept her from seeing the very top, but she struggled to get on her feet and go up.

Ouch, ouch, ouch. Her muscles, however, thought it would be better to stay in one place. They'd done enough for a few days. Her singed tennis shoe squished against something as she stood. She looked down and saw the baggie she'd put her toothbrush and candy bar in. *Oh, good. At least I'll have nice breath as a corpse.* But she was grateful that she'd have something to eat until help came or she found her way out. She stuffed the bag in her jacket pocket.

The effort to climb even a few of the boulders was too much for Carson. Flames still burned in the forest where she'd run from. She looked up again, unsure of making the steep climb, and decided to try her luck in the other direction, on terra firma.

Carefully, Carson started down the rocks. Being so uncoordinated and out of shape, she felt like a turtle on its back, arms and legs flaying every which way, trying to find purchase with something solid. She coughed and hacked from the smoke and pulled her shirt over her nose and mouth to help her breathe.

She put her weight on a big rock and tested it. The rock held, but her foot slipped, and she tumbled a few painful feet. Her forehead smacked across a sharp jagged rock. *Dong!* A loud resonate church bell sounded in her brain, and a warm trickle gushed down her face.

Blood. Oh no, it'll attract sharks. No, wait, I'm not in the ocean. It'll attract animals. She put her hand to her throbbing head. *I'm probably brain damaged.* She started crying, sobbing in the thick air. Don't give up hope, she told herself, but hope was draining like sand in an hourglass.

Carson gave a final push and managed to clear the rocks. But the closer she got to dirt, the thicker the smoke was. When she felt grass under her feet she started running again, gasping for air, her body fighting to keep moving, blood and sweat streaming into her eyes.

She ran as long and as far as she could.

I'm sorry, Mom. You were right—it is a dangerous world. I

should've stayed home. What am I doing here? Fatigue and pain overtook her body first and then her feet. She couldn't go any farther.

She tripped over a large stone and landed face-first in a pile of dry leaves. *Tinder,* she thought. *I'm toast.*

She crawled until she found more rocks big enough for her to hide in. She nestled into a corner of two large boulders. Carson sat in a pile of dry leaves and waited. For what? Rescue? Death? Tears mingled with blood from her flowing head wound. She was almost too tired to wipe the mess from her eyes. *Am I ready for heaven? If I don't get burned or eaten, maybe someone will find my fat mummified body a hundred years from now.*

She sobbed, a big heaving sob, like a baby. *I didn't get to do everything on my life's list,* Carson thought angrily. *When I get to heaven I'll ask God why he let this happen to me. I just wanted to show my mom I could do something.* She scooted farther back between the boulders. She thought of her dad and wondered if he'd give her a big hug in heaven. But she didn't want him to see her overweight and boring. *I wasn't done living.* Carson wiped the tears and blood from her eyes.

Why, God? Why me?

CHAPTER 22

Officer Z took Bet to her small cell. Had it shrunk since she last left it? Claustrophobia clutched her lungs. *Why is this happening to me? Am I crazy? No, I'm not,* she told herself. *But how am I going to get out of here to kill myself?*

"I'm sorry, Mrs. Harper," Z said. "Green Hollow really isn't such a bad place. I'm sure you won't be in for long, considering everything."

The door closed behind her, and this time she heard the click of the lock.

She flopped on the cot and stared at the dingy ceiling. She started to cry. For Carson. For their lost future. For not living life when they had each other. For all those years wasted on fear.

Maybe, Bet thought, this was how Carson felt being confined to the house. Anguish overcame her, and she sobbed herself to sleep.

"Mrs. Cleaver."

Bet started awake. How long had she slept? It must have been dark outside, since the light was different than it had been earlier, a bright unnatural light. She was in jail, she remembered with a sour feeling.

"Psst, Mrs. Cleaver. You asleep?" Rox stage-whispered through the bars.

Bet sat up. "I'm sorry, who?"

"You know, June Cleaver. That's my new name for you." Rox

passed a water bottle and plastic-wrapped sandwich through the bars. "Here. I figured you were hungry since you missed dinner."

"Thank you, Rox." Bet stood and took the food. "Why don't you just call me by my name?"

Rox laughed. "You're so polite, it's funny."

Bet unwrapped the sandwich. Was it tuna? She wasn't sure and took a cautious bite. She chewed on the unidentified meat and swallowed before speaking. "Is politeness that foreign to you?"

Rox shrugged and grinned. "I like to be unique."

"Manners are always appreciated." Bet twisted the top off the water bottle and drank almost half the bottle. "Rox, can you do me a huge favor?"

"Sure. Ya need more water?"

"No, thank you." She recapped the top. "Can you open that?" Bet nodded toward the cell's formidable door. "Please?"

Rox tried the door. "Well, yeah. I know how, but Z'll kill me."

"If you can get my keys and purse, I'll pay you anything you want." Bet set her food aside and walked to the door. "I need to take care of something."

"I don't know, Mrs. Cleaver. That's aiding and abetting a criminal, isn't it?"

"I'm not a criminal, Rox." Bet looked down at the girl through the bars.

"Well, whatever you are. You're the one locked up." She studied Bet. "How much?"

"How much do you want?"

"A hundred dollars."

"One hundred? For heaven's sake child, raise your standards."

"What?" Rox got defensive. "Hey, if you can't pay, then you're stuck, lady."

"I'll give you five hundred."

Rox looked confused. "Five hundred?" She smiled and shook her head. "I really don't understand you, Mrs. Cleaver."

CHAPTER 23

Cupcakes floated in and out of Carson's dream. Lasagna oozing with cheese and juicy meat stayed just beyond her grasp. A Coke, crisply bubbling over ice, the glass sweating with cold, would quench Carson's dry, scorched throat. Carson tried to reach out to the food but could never touch it. She was so hungry, and the food was so close.

But never close enough.

Carson turned and almost fell off the rocks she'd collapsed on. *Oh, yeah,* she remembered, *I'm lost in the forest. The burning forest.* She woke from the uncomfortable position she'd been curled in. *Bring the dream back, please.* Better yet, make this part the dream. She opened her eyes and confirmed her nightmare.

Her head throbbed from the gash, and her muscles ached. Every inch of her body, inside and out, hurt. She tentatively touched her cut forehead. It was sticky with congealed blood and caked with dried leaves and dirt from her face-planting fall. The rest of her mug felt icky. It was caked with something. Probably either dried crusty blood, or all the skin had been burned off in the fire and her insides were showing.

Carson tried to stand but felt like someone had nailed all her joints together. She pushed up, and pain shot through her arms. She couldn't get them over her head or find the strength to press off the rocks.

It reminded her of how much her arms hurt the time in seventh grade when she tried out for volleyball. She'd begged her mother to let her play. "Everybody gets picked for the team," Carson pleaded. Her mother thought that of all the sports, volleyball was probably the safest, and let her try out.

For three days, Carson tried to get the ball over the net. When the team was picked and the names posted on the gym door, Carson was afraid to go look.

"I thought everybody makes the team," her mom said as she made Carson get in the car so they could drive to school to check the list.

"But I was terrible," Carson wailed, massaging her sore pudgy arms.

"I'm sure you did fine," Bet said reassuringly, and patted her leg.

As they drove into the parking lot, Carson saw a group of girls jumping and screaming in excitement as they read the list.

"I'll go with you." Bet seemed excited, like she was the one being picked for the team.

"No, I'll go." Carson slid out of the car seat.

Slowly, she walked to the gym door. The names were typed in a large font on the paper pasted on the inside of the window.

The cluster of girls, most still giggling or talking, made room for Carson to look. The crowd got quiet, and Carson could hear a few of them whispering.

She scanned the list twice.

Her name was not on it.

Carson turned and looked hard at the sidewalk as she walked to the car. She managed not to cry until after she got in and closed the car door.

That night she got a three-scoop ice cream sundae from Baskin Robbins.

Turned out only two girls didn't make it: Carson and a girl who was so freaky weird that on most weekend nights she'd take her out-of-tune guitar and sing for money in the parking lot at the local mall.

And even she was picked to be the team manager.

Angrily, Carson pushed off against the rocks. *I will not be a loser again.* She forced through the excruciating pins and needles to stand. A rush of wooziness overtook her and she bent over. *Maybe I am brain damaged.* Slowly, she stood and looked at the forest. Smoke still spiraled around the trees like ghosts, and the air was thick and charred. Embers danced in the air like after a firework blast. She fought to breathe and was relieved that she didn't see any flames coming her way.

She took a few steps. Everything hurt, but she forced herself to keep moving. Which way? She wiped her face with her hand, feeling the crusty matted blood. *I probably look like Carrie from that old horror movie where she's in a prom dress walking down the street drenched from head to foot in blood.*

Her mom used to encourage Carson to watch the stupid show, *Survivorman*. A series about a guy who went alone, with no food or water, into the wilderness and survived for seven days.

"You never know when you might need to use some of his ideas." Carson could hear her mother's voice in her head.

"Yeah, like if I'm in the backyard and the lights go off," Carson had shot back.

Now, looking out at the vast smoldering landscape, Carson tried to recall something about the show other than the episode when he ate grasshoppers and naturally distilled his own urine to drink.

Through all the physical agony and hunger, thirst gnawed at her hardest. Carson smacked her cracked, dry lips. *Water.* Where was the stream she'd washed in? She noticed an area of trees a few hundred yards away that held their green color better than the blackened stubs she passed. Okay, maybe Mr. Survivorman knew what he was talking about.

She limped toward the trees.

CHAPTER 24

Bet craned her neck to see through the bars of her cell. Where did Rox go? The girl was supposed to be tracking down her purse and car keys. Where was her car? Bet hoped the police hadn't impounded it downtown. Lot of good it would do to be a middle-aged escaped convict hoofing it to freedom.

She heard footsteps coming toward her cell and saw Rox rounding the corner. "Got 'em," Rox whispered.

"Do you know what they did with my car?" Bet asked.

"Yeah, it's in the parking lot. I'll bet they thought you'd walk outta here." Rox went to a desk in a central area. Bet could barely see her as the girl tapped on a keyboard.

Rox looked around before hitting a final key. "The security officer on duty is in the kitchen. We gotta hurry."

Bet heard a click from the cell lock after Rox punched the button. She tried the door but it wouldn't budge.

"You are such a weakling." Rox threw Bet's purse over her shoulder and ran to the cell. She heaved the heavy sliding door and it opened. "Shhhh," she warned. "C'mon, hurry." She grabbed Bet's shirtsleeve and gave her a tug.

"Carson, honey, maybe we shouldn't. I'm not sure—" Bet put her hand over her mouth, shocked she'd called Rox Carson.

Rox turned on her, fuming, and shook a finger at Bet. "Don't call me 'honey' or your kid's name. It creeps me out."

Bet pushed her back to the wall and swallowed her daughter's name as she nodded to Rox. She wiped at a tear that stung her skinned cheek.

Rox grabbed Bet's arm and quickly pulled her along. "C'mon, if we're going."

They crept through a dimly lit hall to an exterior door with a keypad. Rox punched numbers in and the door opened. "I'm so going to big jail for this. Juvey will be over for me."

Bet hesitated, backed away from the door, and put her hands up. "Rox, maybe this isn't such a good idea. I don't want you to get into trouble because of me. Please go back. Tell them I forced you."

"Yeah, like that'll work. They'll figure it out." She took Bet's shirtsleeve again, pulled her in front, and gave Bet a light shove out the door.

Bet breathed in the air. *Freedom.* She was tempted to run but turned around. "No, Rox, I'll go back. It's not worth having you go to jail on my account." Bet reached for the handle, but the door had closed and locked.

"Officer Z won't let me see my boyfriend, Crank." Rox still had Bet's purse and jogged through the parking lot, pulling Bet along. "I gotta get something from him. It's real important." She quickly ducked between some cars as a police cruiser passed.

Bet hid in the shadows and followed. *Serpentine,* she thought wryly as she crouched and ran through the cars. She couldn't believe she was executing a jailbreak. *I'm a felon!*

"You need to take me to Crank," Rox said as she pointed to the corner of the lot. Bet's car sat under a tree. "If not, I'll steal your purse and car anyway."

"Well, in that case," Bet took the keys from Rox. "Let's get going."

Nervous, Bet hit a button on the key fob, and her car alarm shrieked. Both she and Rox hit the ground. Her headlights flashed and the horn blared. Bet was sure every police officer within ten miles could hear it. She kept hitting buttons until the alarm shut off and the car gave a final whup-whup.

Bet put her head in her hands. "Are they coming? I'm not a good criminal."

"Shush." Rox put a finger to her lips and listened. "I think we're okay. It was only a car alarm. No one pays attention to them anyway." She stood bent over and opened the driver's door. "Get in." She crawled to the passenger side.

Bet stood and scrambled in. The car door slammed too loudly. Her hand shook so hard she couldn't get the key in. Rox grabbed the keys and shoved them in place. Bet started the engine.

"Don't turn on the headlights until we pull out," Rox advised.

Bet slowly rolled through the parking lot filled with empty police cruisers, her leg trembling so much she could hardly control the foot pedals. "I'm glad this isn't Alcatraz. My swimming is worse than my driving." Bet felt both terrified and electrified. *Carson wouldn't believe this!* "Put your seatbelt on, dear," she said to Rox as she clicked hers on, pulled into traffic, and turned on the headlights.

CHAPTER 25

Carson coughed. Her throat felt like she'd swallowed a ball of fire. The smoke, still so thick, obscured the horizon. In the far distance, she thought she heard a helicopter. Were they looking for her? Or putting the fire out? She wanted to run in that direction, to be rescued, but if she didn't get something to drink soon she'd go crazy.

She continued to the line of green trees. Every limping step was agony. *Why did I pick a three-week hike in the mountains to prove to mom that I could be independent? Why not a trip to the mall by myself instead? At least they have a food court and clean restrooms.*

The dense air smelled like an extreme campfire. She couldn't take a deep breath without coughing. Sweat mingled with the grit and blood on her face. She kept walking. *This is so hard. I want to go home.* Tears trickled down her burning cheeks. *My face probably looks like a roadmap.* She touched her cut forehead. A big sticky scab formed from the gunk. *Do I need stitches? Am I going to bleed to death? If I do survive, maybe I'll have a cool scar like Harry Potter.*

She figured Outward Bound had called her cell phone by now trying to get hold of her mom. For the first time since she'd left, she was glad she'd forgotten it. Her mother was probably on an airplane or had already rustled up a search party to look for her.

Oh, man. After this adventure, she'll never let me out of her sight.

Carson stopped. A horrified thought crossed her mind. What about the others in camp? Did they survive? Seth?

She took as deep a breath as the air would allow and trudged forward. She hiked her jeans up and tied her jacket around her waist, being careful not to lose the baggie with her toothbrush and candy.

The fire had burned patches of trees, but a few tall green pines still stood near blackened stubs. It was like walking in outer space on some weird planet the way part of the landscape was charred to the ground in places, yet still green in others.

Approaching the trees, Carson happily found that *Survivorman* was right. A wide stream ran through the greener tree line. *Yes!* She lurched forward as fast as she could and fell face first into the cold water.

She sucked in bits of hard floatie stuff and who knew what else. She didn't care; she needed to quench her thirst and soothe her burned throat. The relief was immediate.

Gasping between gulps, she looked upstream and remembered a story her mom had told her about a group of boy scouts that drank water from a flowing creek. They didn't know that a dead cow had fallen in the water upstream. All the boys but one, who didn't drink, died from dead-cow germs.

Carson spit out a large chunk of wood. *Don't freak yourself out. This is good water. Try to be normal.* Yeah, she thought, *I'm lost in the wilderness, and I need to play normal. Maybe I can hike to Barbie Dream Mountain.*

Her thirst sated, she scrubbed her face with the freezing water and brushed her teeth. She was afraid to touch the gash on her forehead so she cleaned it out as carefully as she could. Refreshed, but a little woozy because she'd drunk so much so fast, she began to feel nauseous. At least she hoped it was because she'd gorged and not because the water was poisoned. *I need food. Real food, like a cheeseburger and fries with extra ketchup and lots of pickles.*

She began imagining every combination of delectable edibles. Her mom's Thanksgiving dinner, the potatoes and dressing smushed together and swimming in gravy. The Easter buffet at the Doubletree Hotel with every kind of food ever invented. Her stomach rumbled.

I need to find my way back. I'm not cut out for camping, much less being lost, alone, and hurt. I want my couch and remote control.

Carson rested her muscles for a few hours before trying to find her way back. She could barely move, but feared if she didn't, she'd be stuck in the same position forever. She thought it best to hike along the edge of the stream. Carson looked at the sun, still partially obscured by smoke, and tried to figure out what time it was. Four? Five? She didn't have a clue. She wasn't even sure which way was north or south, she'd gotten so turned around running away from the fire. East and west she'd figure out when the sun dropped a little more, but even then it would be hard to tell with the heavy layer of smoke. She only knew that she didn't want to spend another night out here alone and cold. Camp must be close. How far could a fat kid run?

She figured she was bound to see somebody if she started walking along the water. Preferably a rescue worker with Band-Aids and food. She'd been gone seven days in all. A pang of homesickness hit her. Oh, how she wished she'd never done this stupid trip. Before heading out, she drank a few more sips and splashed water on her face. She heard her stomach growl fiercely. *Get back to camp.*

But the growl was deeper and farther away. Slowly, she looked across to the other bank. Not twenty feet from her, a large wolf, fangs bared, was crouched and ready to pounce. He cast his cold beady eyes on her. No doubt the smell of blood from her cut was like bacon. Carson heard another long snarly growl as two more wolves joined him.

CHAPTER 26

Bet was careful to drive within the speed limit. "We should go to a few ATMs now before they track my accounts. I need to pay you your money."

Rox nodded. "Five hundred bucks, right? Did you really mean that?"

"Yes, of course." Bet glanced at the girl. "I am a person of my word."

"Boy, Z's gonna be mad." Rox looked out the window. A small shadow of regret passed over her face.

"Rox. You're young. Don't screw up your future on my account." Bet stared ahead. "I'll get you your money and drop you wherever you want to go. In fact, I'll even tie you up and leave you at the police station. You can tell them I held you hostage and made you do it." She thought of Carson. "I want to take care of something. By myself."

"That's cool. But you said you'd take me to Crank's."

"Crank? What kind of name is that?" Bet asked.

"His." Rox shrugged. "What kind of a name is Bet?"

"It's short for Betula. You can imagine why I've shortened it." Bet checked her rearview mirror.

"Betula? Now *that's* a weird name." Rox laughed.

"I didn't have much say in it." She stared ahead. *Carson.* When she was born, Bet and Carson's daddy wanted her to have a good strong name. Carson Harper. Her husband teased that they'd have a child with two last names. But it was a name they both agreed on. Now Bet would never see Carson grow. Would never see how that strong name would make a difference in her life. Bet's lip trembled as she considered Carson Harper the actress, Carson Harper, Esq. the successful attorney. Paging Dr. Carson Harper. She smiled through the tears.

"I said, don't you want to know where to go?" Rox's voice pierced Bet's thoughts.

"Yes, I'm sorry." Bet swiped at a tear.

"First, let's stop and get the money." Rox leaned against the door looking at Bet, her shoulder belt looped under her arm. "Are you going to cry all the time?"

"Yes, probably." Bet bit her lip. "Carson was my life." She felt like her soul had been skewered.

"You need to meet my mom. She'll show you how to have a life without kids." She twirled at a piece of nose jewelry. "I'm gettin' hungry."

"I should probably eat something as well. There are a number of restaurants up the street. We'll stop after the bank."

"Did you major in English in high school? Who says 'as well' like that?"

"One doesn't major in anything in high school. That would be college. Didn't you graduate?"

"No. Who needs school? I'll never use algebra in real life. 'Sides I got too much livin' to waste any time in class." Rox sat straighter. "There's a big world out there waitin' for me. I want to see it all."

Bet clamped down on her lip again, trying not to cry. This vagabond child had probably done more than Carson ever had being confined to her home.

Bet managed to get fifteen hundred dollars from three ATM machines. She handed Rox five one-hundred-dollar bills. "Use this wisely. Maybe," she paused, "buy a plane ticket to somewhere exciting." She considered the rest of her money, prudently sitting in savings and 401k accounts. She wished she and Carson had taken a cruise or hiked the Grand Canyon. Then she remembered the tickets to New York and started to tear up again.

"Geez, lady. Get a grip!" Rox said as she stuffed the bills in her jeans pocket. "Let's eat."

They pulled into a Wendy's drive-thru. Bet ate more for nutrition than hunger but did finish a whole Biggie order of

French fries. Considering where she was "going," Bet no longer needed to worry about fat, salt, or what the double meat burger would do to her arteries or waistline.

But first, she had to drop the girl off at Crank's.

CHAPTER 27

Carson froze.

The wolves drooled, their tongues worked through the growls. The only thing separating Carson from becoming dinner was the fast moving stream. But considering the full coat on each wolf, she didn't think the cold water would be much of a deterrent.

No time to think! She moved faster than she ever had in her life, jumping and taking two huge steps to a tree with low hanging branches. She grabbed a limb and pulled herself up, her feet dangling as she tried to find something to push off on.

As soon as she moved, the wolves jumped into the water and raced after her. She managed to get a foothold on a small limb and reached to a higher branch just as the bottom limb cracked under her feet. Like a monkey, she held onto the branch with both hands, her feet swinging helplessly above the wolves' snapping teeth.

This was so much worse than the Presidential Fitness test she had to do in school. Not only could she not do the sit-ups, she didn't even *try* the pull-ups. Her sore arms began shaking and her grip loosened. She remembered the kids snickering at her meager attempts to do the exercises, the shame hurt worse than her weak muscles. Tightening her grip, and her resolve, she swung her legs out of reach of the yellow fangs. With sheer will, and a little luck, Carson managed to wrap her legs around the trunk and get a better hold with her hands. She hung upside down like a sloth, as three wolves jumped and snarled at her, way too close for comfort. *Can wolves climb trees?*

She gasped for air, unable to get a good deep breath. Aren't these fur balls afraid of fire? Sweat beaded on her face, and her hands started to slip. She held her legs tight and inched her hands closer to the trunk.

The wolves circled the tree, jumping every few seconds. *One good running start and they'll reach me.* Carson grunted and gasped and scooted closer to the middle of the tree, wiggling her way to an upright position. *I can do this.* Suddenly, Carson both heard and felt the branch crack. Her hands slipped a notch.

A miracle. That's what I need. The branch gave a little more. She looked down. *I will not be the main course tonight.* In a split second, she gauged the distance to a sturdy middle limb, screamed and let go. She reached, clawed, and tore through the branches and found herself hugging the center of the tree. *A miracle!* It happened.

Carson shimmied higher to a point where she could look down. Still clutching tight, she tried to catch her trembling breath. *Tree, please hold,* she willed. A few of the branches had been singed from the fire, but most of it was still green and strong.

The wolves stopped jumping but kept their cold marble eyes on her. Snarling, they circled the base of the tree. Every now and then they'd give a loud yip and lunge.

This was supposed to be a controlled adventure. *I was only going to hike a few days, say I accomplished something, and then go home. This wasn't the plan.* Carson scooted closer to the trunk and squeezed tighter.

"Beat it! Scram! Help!! Each time Carson screamed, the wolves became excited and started jumping again. The sun was going down, and the smoky air became chilly. Carson couldn't untie her jacket from around her waist and put it on. She sat shivering and crying, chilled, tired, and hungry. Maybe I should give up. Who am I kidding?

Just as the sun dipped behind the mountains and dusk shrouded the smoke, the wolves' yips became higher. They crouched lower, snapping at each other, their attention diverted, for the moment, away from Carson. Another animal rustled in the bramble of a shrub. *This must be the alpha bitch.* Carson remembered a Discovery Channel show about the animals. Even though she'd heard the word for a girl dog a million times at school, it still sounded funny hearing a TV announcer say it. The show said one wolf controlled the pack. The others each had a job to do, but all bowed down to the boss.

I'm dead. I'm sure she'll order them all to get me down from here and serve her Royal Highness Carson a la mode. Carson shivered, fear creeping down her spine with the cold air. She gave another feeble, hoarse, "Help," into the air.

Crawling on their bellies, the wolves made way for their leader. Each ran back to the tree and gave a shrill bark as if to say, "Look what we got for you."

A growl emitted from the bush. The wolves backed away, and boss dog pranced out as if the world was hers.

Carson shrieked and then laughed. "You have got to be kidding me," she said to the animal that was making her way to the tree. "You're a pinhead!"

A brown, mangy-haired Chihuahua strutted to the tree. She shivered, glared at Carson with her big round eyes and bared her tiny teeth.

CHAPTER 28

Mark thought the pale yellow walls were getting smaller in his military-issued room. Being the new recruit, none of the others housed in the complex paid much attention to him. Being in a heap of trouble didn't help his popularity, either.

He hadn't seen Steve or Officer Coffey for a few days. Mark waited for Officer Coffey's "dealing-with-you later" punishment, figuring that Steve was probably already scrubbing every toilet on base with a toothbrush. Hopefully, Officer Coffey's.

Restless, Mark flopped on the bed and turned on CNN. He'd already seen most of the stories they were teasing, but a new one caught his attention. A fire raged in the Rocky Mountains, and a teenage girl was missing from an Outward Bound camp. "Stay tuned for this story and more."

Mark turned the volume up and went to the window. Sure enough, he could see a line of black smoke that looked like low storm clouds hovering over the mountain range. He sat on the bed and waited through a series of stupid commercials until the story came on.

Finally, after a number of inane political stories, the news anchor segued to the fire. She introduced a local field reporter who said: *"Firefighters believe the blaze started from lightning or a campfire. There'd been no rain for weeks, and the mountain range is like a tinderbox. A seventeen-year-old girl is missing from an Outward Bound camp. The other campers have been accounted for and, except for a few minor burns and injuries, are okay. There is a search and rescue operation under way for the teen."* The camera cut to a view of the flaming vista. *"There are still patches of burning timber, so the going is slow and dangerous. The identity of the camper is being withheld until the family can be notified."*

Mark jumped from the bed and went back to the window. Dusky light turned the smoke and clouds a deep pink and red color. Purple darkness cloaked the eastern edges of the range. Since he was going stir-crazy in this tiny room, maybe he could get permission to help with the rescue mission.

It would at least get him out doing something, and if he could help save this girl, perhaps it would help him deal with the guilt of having had a hand in the death of the other teenager.

Carson.

Carson Harper.

CHAPTER 29

"Where does Crank live?" Bet asked, navigating a part of town she'd never been to before—and one that she'd forbidden Carson to enter.

"Keep going. We're almost there," Rox said, counting the hundred-dollar bills for the hundredth time.

"Put the money in a safe place," Bet warned. "You'll lose it if you keep playing with it."

"I've never seen this much money in one place before." Rox shuffled the bills again. "And it's really mine!"

Bet was becoming impatient with this child but was concerned about her, nonetheless. "How long have you, um, dated Crank?"

Rox folded the money. "I've known him about six months. We sorta started dating a while back."

"Sorta started?" Bet glanced at her. "I don't feel right about leaving you in this neighborhood. It doesn't seem safe."

"Chill out. I'm fine here. This is my 'hood."

"You're a young girl holding a lot of money. What if someone tries to, you know, hurt you?"

"Crank'll take care of 'em." She stuffed the money in her jeans pocket. "It's up there." She raised her right hand. "Turn right."

Bet did, feeling conspicuous in this neighborhood. Her shiny new Honda generated more attention than she was comfortable with, and she wanted to put something on her still painful cheek scrape. She'd drop off Rox, then... then what? Isn't this where she wanted to be? Wasn't she ready for someone to pull out a gun or knife and get the job done? She relaxed a little.

Tonight would be the night.

"Hey, Mrs. Cleaver, just go up there and turn that way." Rox pointed left into an apartment complex parking lot.

Bet was surprised how busy the place was. Young children ran around unsupervised. Groups of adults clustered together as if they were at a tailgate party. Everybody stopped what they were doing and watched them drive by.

Bet smiled and waved. She wanted to get somebody's attention, preferably someone with a weapon. But the people just smiled and waved back.

"What's with the waving? Do ya think you're in some kind of a parade?" Rox crossed her arms. "Are ya lookin' to get yourself killed?"

"Which way?" Bet rolled down her window and didn't answer her.

"Straight."

"What if Crank isn't home?"

"He'll be there." Rox sat straighter. "There's his car."

"What do you need to get from him?" Bet slowed.

"Nothing important. Well, it's important to me but no one else." She pointed to an old Trans-am. "That's his."

Bet noticed Rox had become nervous. "Are you sure I should drop you off? Do you want me to wait for you?" she asked, reluctantly. She needed to drop Rox somewhere so she could take care of business. After all, the police would be looking for her, and the thought of spending any more time in jail or in a mental hospital scared her more than finding someone to kill her. She didn't want Rox to witness anything that would traumatize her.

A handsome, muscled, swarthy man in a tight ribbed tank top walked to the car. "Well, well, if it isn't Foxy Roxy." His white teeth flashed, and Bet could smell heavy cheap cologne.

"Crank." A young woman, whose face glittered with sparkly blue eye shadow, thick gold-flecked eyeliner, and so much blush she looked like Raggedy Ann, stepped in behind Crank. "I thought you said she was history." She gave Rox a killer glare.

"The more the merrier." Crank laughed. "I'm one lucky dude."

"Who's the Bratz Doll?" Rox got out of the car and faced off with the woman.

Bet leaned over the passenger seat and said out the window, "Rox, do you want to get what you came for, and I'll take you home? I'm in a hurry."

Rox waved her off, never taking her eyes off the woman.

"I'm leaving now." Bet started to drive away. "Thank you for your help."

Rox didn't turn around.

Through the rearview mirror, Bet saw the Bratz lady shove Rox. Bet stopped the car and got out. *This is going to take forever.* She watched Rox push Bratz, and the woman lost her balance. For a second, her gold stiletto heels held the brunt of her weight. Then she fell flat on her bottom and screamed, "Crank, help me!"

"No way." Crank laughed with three other men who stood behind him. "Two chicks fighting? This is a dream come true." They all cracked up.

Rox stormed over to Crank. "Give me back my stuff. If you're going out with this trash, we're history." She ran a hand through her short hair, looking as if she was going to cry. "Now!"

"Get serious, baby." Crank sidled up to her. "I can handle more'n one at a time."

By this time, Bratz stood and tried to hitch her halter-tank top back in line. "You're dead meat," she said to Rox and then turned to Crank. "If you don't cut her, I will." She pulled a switchblade, or maybe it was a nail file, from her purse. The blade swished out of a gold-jeweled case.

Bet stood straighter. *Now we're talking.* She wished Rox would run for it.

Rox stuck her chin out. "Let me know when I'm supposed to be scared of you."

Bet stepped between them. "Fight me instead." She looked Bratz in the eye.

The woman laughed. "Are you kidding? You're old."

"This keeps getting better!" Crank and his buddies were doubled over in hilarity.

Bet shot Crank a look. "You're next." *Whoa, did she really challenge this young man?*

That comment almost caused Crank to fall over laughing. "Pinch me, man! I think I'm dreaming." His friends high-fived and slapped each other.

Bet walked straight toward Bratz. She got right into her space, but the woman backed away, flailing the knife at her. "Beat it, lady.

Don't make me use this."

"Use it." Bet kept walking. Out of the corner of her eye, she saw Rox jog toward an apartment.

Bet and Bratz circled each other. Bet wondered how she could impale herself on the blade. "I dare you," Bet said.

"You are one crazy..."

Bet jumped at her, and Bratz swung the blade, slicing through Bet's shirt. Bet felt a sharp pain and warm blood dripping from her upper arm.

"Hey, moron, don't hurt her." Rox ran out of the apartment, shoving a small box in the front of her pants.

Crank grabbed Rox by the arm, stopping her mid-stride. "Just a sec, Fox. Give it back." He held his hand out.

"No, this is mine." Rox bent over, her hand protecting her stash.

Crank shoved her to the ground and fell on top of her. "It ain't nobody's but mine." He tried to grab her hand. When she wouldn't release the box, he smacked her face. "It's my good luck charm."

Bet turned at the crack of the slap. "Let her go!" She turned back to Bratz, knocked the bejeweled knife from her hand and pushed her hard. The woman fell flat on her bottom again and screamed, *"Crank!"*

Rox tried to roll on her stomach. "It's not yours. It's mine," she wailed.

Crank managed to grab the box and toss it to his friends. "Hey, what's this?" He held Rox down with one hand and stuck his hand in her pocket with the other. "Where'd you get this?" He held up the hundred dollar bills, smiled, and stuffed the bills into his pocket. "Another gift for the Crankster. Thanks."

Rox kicked and struggled but was no match for Crank.

Bet ran toward Rox, surprised how the parking lot had emptied of people. She wanted someone to call the police, but no, they'd take her back to jail. She didn't want Rox to get hurt because of her, but she couldn't go back to that cell.

Blood stained her shirt and streamed down her arm. Bet was surprised that it didn't hurt, and disappointed the woman hadn't inflicted a more serious wound. *Carson, I'm trying to get to you.*

She reached Crank and Rox. He held both of the girl's arms together with one of his hands. Rox still tried to fight him off, to no avail.

Bet put her foot on Crank's side and kicked him off of Rox. She was so out of her comfort zone.

"Hey, ol' lady." He rolled on his side in the grass, releasing the girl. "You did *not* just kick Crank." He got to his knees. "I don't like hurting old people, but I'm going to have to make an exception in this case." He stood to his full height, brushed off his pants and turned to his friends. "C'mon. We're gonna have fun with this one."

CHAPTER 30

Carson sat hugging the tree limb, shivering in the cold mountain air. Night had fallen, and with the darkness, Carson became more frightened. It was bad enough that she was being held hostage by a pack of hungry wolves being bossed around by a dog the size of her big toe, but she was also afraid of what lived beyond the dark.

The little dog paced under the tree. Every now and then, she'd look at Carson and growl, causing the others to go into a frenzy of jumping and snapping.

Carson's gashed head throbbed, she was starving, and, again, she had to pee. Considering that's what got her into trouble in the first place, she tried not to think about it. Exhaustion weighed heavily on her sore muscles, and she couldn't sleep for fear she'd fall out of the tree. Especially since the animals were waiting on dinner, and she was slated to be the main course.

Her stomach grumbled.

The Chihuahua bared its teeth, its round unblinking eyes glaring at Carson.

"Go find a nice bunny to scare. Leave me alone."

The spit of a dog growled.

"Nacho. That's what I'm going to call you." She closed her eyes. *Nachos. Crispy chips with hot melted cheese—real cheddar, not the fake microwave stuff. Ummm.* Her mouth watered as she let the fantasy take over.

She snapped out of her dream, hunger gnawing at her gut. "Hey, Nacho, why don't you and your Alpo Gang beat it and leave me alone."

The dog stopped pacing, looked at her and peed on the tree. The little hairball semi-squatted and even held her back leg up!

"You are one weird dog." Carson leaned over a smidge. Even in the weak moonlight, she could see the Chihuahua had a beat-up collar clasped tight around her neck. The leather was worn and ripped. A rusty bell stuck out the side, its ringer gone.

"You were someone's pet?" She peered closer. "I'll bet you were such a bad dog, they dropped you out here and drove away."

Nacho's short brown hair stood rigid along her back as she gave another snarl.

Carson could see that the collar dug so deep into the dog's neck it choked her. Not enough to kill her, but it looked uncomfortable.

"Look, dog chow, I'll get that thing off you if you let me go."

Nacho strutted among the wolves, but kept her big bug-eyes on Carson.

This is crazy. I'm hungry, tired, sore and, I think, still bleeding. Why don't I just hurry the inevitable and throw myself into the middle of the pack? Okay, maybe not. It would be a terrible and painful way to die. She hugged the tree tighter.

Carson snapped a branch off the tree and lobbed it at the wolves. "Beat it! Fetch!" she screamed. This caused another frenzy of excitement. She untied her jacket from around her waist and looped as tight a knot as she could around a branch. That way, if she fell asleep, she wouldn't fall off her precarious perch.

Stupid dog, she thought as she rested her cut face on the rough bark of the tree.

Carson's body jerked reflexively. She felt something crawling in her ear. She shrieked and swiped crazily at her head. She slipped and nearly fell off the branch. *Oh, yeah. I'm not having a bad dream. This is reality, and it sucks!*

She held still for a moment, making sure she got whatever critter had taken a hike down her eustachian tube. On the tree limb, under her nose, trails of ants marched single file. Carson's first reaction at home would be to grab bug spray, but she was sort of confined to this spot. *I hate nature.*

There was no sign of Nacho and her gang, but Carson was afraid to move in case they were waiting to ambush her if she crawled down. She looked around warily. It was early; the sun was just rising. She'd spent another night in the woods. Red-and-gold light mingled with dingy smoky air. Wasn't the fire out yet? Carson couldn't see flames but could still smell the forest smoldering.

Her bladder was bursting, and her stomach churned with hunger. She was feeling too weak to generate much energy. She remembered Survivorman talking about eating bugs. He said that ants are good protein and delicious. *Yuck!* But he warned not to eat the aggressive ones. She wished he would have been more specific. How do you know which ones are aggressive? Then she figured they were probably the ones that bite back.

She considered her hunger against the live ants as she watched them journey along the tree.

Then she remembered her candy bar. She grabbed her jacket and rustled through the pockets until she found her toothbrush baggie. To her enormous relief, the Snickers bar was still there, squashed, melted and oozing caramel and chocolate. *Hallelujah!* It was food. Sustenance. A slice of heaven.

She tore open the baggie and grabbed the candy. She slipped and almost lost the Snickers and toothbrush. *No!* She scrambled back into place. Ripping the shredded wrap away from the sticky bar, Carson sank her teeth into the gooey delight, taking almost half the bar. *Chew. Slow down. Think.* Carson tried to take her time savoring the chocolate and nuts. She took one more bite and then rewrapped the candy and put it back in the baggie. *This is so hard! I'm sure someone will find me today; it's probably okay to finish it.* She opened the package again, but stopped. *No, I'll save it just to be safe.*

Oh, it felt good to have something in her stomach. But she knew she'd have to have to deal with the bathroom thing. She couldn't hold it any longer, and wetting her pants was not an option.

Stiffly, she untied her jacket and put it on, making sure to secure the baggie in a pocket. She stretched her sore muscles and peered around. The coast looked clear. She climbed carefully down to the ground, amazed that she could move since her muscles felt like stone.

With great relief, she took care of business. Zipped and ready, she considered hiking along the water, downstream, right? Go down the mountain. She looked upstream and considered her path. *How do I know which way camp is? I think I came from that direction. No, that way,* she turned and took a few steps toward the water.

Before she got to the stream, a menacing low growl sounded from the brush.

CHAPTER 31

Bet stood over Rox, holding her painful stinging arm. She didn't know how deep the knife had cut, and hoped she'd be able to help Rox.

Crank approached, hate in is eyes. "I've never beat up an old lady before, 'cept maybe my mother." He grinned, his friends followed, smiling. The Bratz girl had gotten up, brushed off her tight capris and stood pouting behind the gang.

"You seem the type that would hurt your mother." Bet straightened and waited for him. She stepped in front of Rox, blocking him from the girl. "I had you figured for a discipline problem the moment I saw you."

Crank burst out laughing. "Discipline problem? That's the understatement of the year. Let me show you discipline." He snapped open a switchblade and held it in the air.

"Crank, don't!" Rox had gotten to her feet and stood behind Bet. "You'll go to prison if you do anything else."

"You shut up, Fox. This is between me and her." He pointed the shiny blade at Bet. "No one pushes Crank. I just need to teach her a lesson is all." He glared at Rox. "We'll play cat and mouse."

Bet stood her ground and looked Crank full in the eyes. "Come on. Use it or lose it."

"Are you for real, lady?" He laughed and waved his knife. "You'd be my fantasy girl—if I was fifty!" Crank doubled over. His friends held back but circled Bet.

Rox ran in front of Bet. "Stop!" The girl rushed to Crank's side and grabbed his arm. "C'mon, we'll leave; just give me my stuff," Rox pleaded.

"I don't have your stuff, I have *my* stuff." Crank shoved her to the side, still watching Bet.

"Rox, take the car and go. I'll be okay." Bet held out her keys to the girl.

Crank jumped first and grabbed the keys. He tossed them to one of his friends. "Here, we got some new wheels, too. This has been a real productive night." He nodded at Bet's purse. "Why don't you hand that over, too." He smirked. "It must be Christmas in June, and Crank's been a good boy."

Bet slung it higher on her shoulder; the leather was sticky with blood. "No. You'll have to come and get it." The money. There was almost a thousand dollars in her purse. She stole a quick glance at Rox. The girl stood and tried to get between her and Crank again.

"Rox, here." Bet tossed her the purse. "Run!"

Rox missed the catch, and the purse landed in the grass next to one of Crank's friends. He grabbed it and looked ready to run until Crank menaced, "Don't even think about it. Hand it over."

The guy tossed Crank the purse. "No sweat, dude." He nodded to Bet. "She looks pretty tough is all," he sniveled.

Crank put the purse over his shoulder like a girl.

"Nice look." Bet crossed her arms. Now the cut in her arm started to throb. And her scraped cheek itched. "It doesn't go with your outfit, though."

"I need both hands to carve turkey." He held both hands up, pointing the blade at Bet.

She didn't move.

Crank stopped and let the purse drop from his shoulder. He snatched the wallet and opened it. His eyes lit up when he saw the money. "Oh, yeah. Pay day." He wadded the money and shoved it in his pocket.

Bet felt sick.

He tossed the purse in the grass.

"Hey, are you crazy?" Bratz ran to it. "This is a Coach." She picked up the blood-soaked bag and held it in the air. "It's real, right?"

"Give it to me." Bet held out her hand and took a few steps toward the girl. The only pictures she had of Carson were in her wallet.

Crank jumped between them and pushed Bratz toward the car.

"Get in and wait for me." He nodded to his friends. "You take care of jailbait."

Rox shot Bet a panicked look. "How did they know you're jailbait?"

"Rox." Bet shook her head. "That's not what he meant." Bet watched two of Crank's friends get behind the girl.

"I think you're looking forward to getting Cranked." He threatened Bet with the knife.

Rox stood to the side wringing her hands. "Crank, stop!" Then screamed, "Somebody help!"

One of Crank's friends grabbed Rox from behind and put a hand over her mouth.

Crank was almost on top of Bet when Rox must have bitten the guy's hand. He jumped back, and Rox flew forward, landing on Crank, yelling, "I said stop!"

"No, Rox." Bet tried to pull the girl away. "It's okay."

Crank's attention turned to Rox. "That's the last time you talk to me. Or anybody." He smacked Rox again and pointed the knife near her throat.

Why couldn't Rox mind her own business? Bet felt obligated to take care of her, but this was the last time. After tonight, Bet would take her someplace safe.

Crank had Rox in a choke hold, and with his knife, pressed it hard against Rox's neck. "Do you want me to brand you, Foxy girl?" Bet could see the girl's carotid artery pulse behind the sharp blade.

She sobbed and tried to look at the knife.

Bet stormed over to Crank and yanked him by the hair. "Go pick on someone your own size." He lost his grip on Rox.

He speared the blade toward Bet, but she dodged it because she was winding up for a punch. Who knew where she got the strength or ability to land such a hard hit smack into Crank's nose? She heard and felt a crunch. He sank to his knees.

Bet felt her arms pulled behind her. The knife slice in her arm split open more. She tried to kick backward, but never landed a flesh and bone hit.

"Kill her," Crank snuffled through his broken schnoz.

"Dude, I ain't no killer," his friend said, trying to hold onto Bet, who squirmed hard. "Let's get outta here, man. Someone's gonna call the cops."

Crank waved off Bratz, who'd gotten out of the car and was trying to help him up.

Bet and Rox were hauled into a wooded area behind the apartments. Bet looked around and saw no one. *Where had everybody gone?* She could feel eyes on her, but not one person came to their aid.

Duct tape was violently pressed over her mouth, and her hands and feet were bound by tape. She and Rox were tied together and shoved into a shallow, dry creek bed.

CHAPTER 32

Which bush growled?

Prickly goose bumps rose on Carson's arm. She'd gotten too far away from the tree to make a fast run for safety. Slowly, she took a few steps backward to see how far her tree was and figure out where the wolves were.

The dry leaves and twigs that crunched under her shoes sounded like shotgun blasts. She thought she saw movement in a leafy bush across from her. *Five feet away? Two feet? Did it matter?*

She yelped and ran back to the tree. Hairy snarling fangs seemed to come out of nowhere and snap at her legs. Searing pain jolted through her ankle and lower leg and her foot was pulled back. She grabbed a low hanging branch and lost her balance. She pulled up on the branch, begging it to hold, and kicked the wolf's mouth with her other foot.

The wolf growled through gritted teeth but didn't let go. Two more wolves bounded toward the tree, a blur of fur and yellow teeth.

Panic, adrenaline and sheer desperate need overwhelmed Carson. *Fight or flight.* She kicked the wolf's teeth again and heard her jeans rip. The two other wolves tore into the bloody piece of fabric then turned to Carson, fangs bared.

Did he get my whole foot? It hurts so much, so deep. No time to look at my bloody stump now. She grabbed a branch and clamored to a safe spot in the tree.

Shaking, Carson's heart pounded in her chest like the thunder of racehorses at the finish line. Dripping blood from her leg sent the wolves in a hysterical frenzy. They jumped so high Carson knew it was a matter of time until one got close enough for a chomp.

Shock paralyzed Carson. She couldn't move, could barely breathe as she stared dumbly at the crazed wild animals. Her leg throbbed and dripped blood. A sob broke from deep inside. "Somebody please help me," she whimpered through hot tears.

The denim chunk from her jeans had been shredded to fluff. *That could be me. Is this really happening?*

Carson sobbed as she pulled her injured leg up, remembering advice from her mother. *Keep the injured extremity elevated above the chest so the blood drains back toward the heart. Don't run. Your heart rate will increase, and blood will pump out faster.*

Why could she remember something like that silly tidbit, but not how to get out of the woods?

Hope drained faster than the blood from her ankle. *There are how many billions of people in this world, and not one could, by chance, be taking a nice hike in the mountains? Won't somebody rescue me?*

She readjusted on the branch and raised her bleeding leg higher. The wolves gnashed at each other and the mutilated piece of denim.

Mom was right. The world is too dangerous. Carson would have given just about anything to be home, snuggled on the couch and doing nothing.

I got myself into this mess, she thought. *I've totally gotten what I deserved.*

She leaned against a sturdy limb, wondering how long it would take for one of the mongrels to figure out how to climb a tree. Her heart rate slowed a little, and the shock of almost being eaten had ebbed into throbbing pain. Carson reached into her jacket pocket and pulled out the Snickers bar. If she was going to die, she wanted to die happy. She unwrapped the candy and finished the whole thing, licking the wrapper clean.

Although she was still sore and bleeding and thirsty, she felt better. It was amazing what chocolate could do for her mood.

It didn't take long for the sun to start blazing on her skin. *It's freezing at night and roasting during the day. Make up your mind!* She re-situated her seat and kept close tabs on the wolves.

They'd calmed down and had crawled back to hide in the brush, watching her closely. The Chihuahua was the only feral beast in the clearing near the tree.

"Hey, Nacho, I'm tired and hungry and my leg hurts. Please let me go."

Nacho stretched, ignoring her.

"You are such a kibble-for-brains." Carson's hurt leg prickled as if asleep, and the rest of her was just numb.

Nacho walked closer to the tree. The wolves stayed in the brush.

"Nacho, remember that story about the mouse helping the lion?" Nacho shot her buggy eyes at Carson then sat and scratched at a flea. "I'll take that awful collar off, if you let me go."

For a fraction of a second, Nacho sat still and looked like a pet.

Carson remembered her pet retriever, Roady, short for Roadkill. It had been her dad's dog before he and her mom were married. Her dad had saved him from running across a busy street. After that they became best buddies.

As a toddler, Carson would crawl, tug and annoy that poor dog. Roady would take any abuse she'd hand out. He even suffered the indignity, more times than Carson could count, of having his hair tied up in tiny ponytails or curled and cut. Roady always sat proud and happy for the attention, no matter how stupid he looked. Carson looked at the wild Chihuahua and wiped away a tear as she recalled Roadkill. Mostly, Roady had been security, someone to curl up with who made her feel safe and warm.

Two years after her father died, Roady became too old to stand anymore. Carson came home from school one day, and he was gone. Empty air hung heavy where the old dog's bed had been. Dust motes glittered like a speckled memory in the sun's rays, falling to the floor among wisps of Roady's long blonde hair. The hole where her heart beat filled with hurt and emptiness.

Carson didn't know if it hurt so much because she'd lost a great friend, or because it was a last link to her father.

Her mom only said "it was his time." A few months later, Carson's mom asked if she wanted to go look at puppies. Carson didn't answer, just went to her room to cry. Again.

Her mother never brought up Roady again.

"Hey, Nacho, let me tell you about the best pet ever." Carson sat on the limb and talked to her tiny captor. "Roady was nice and always protected me. He would've eaten you in one chomp. You would've been like a piece of spinach stuck in his teeth. He especially liked Mexican food." The dog sat in a patch of grass under the tree, watching Carson. "You were probably the kind of dog that bit your people. Did they dump you, or did you run away?" Carson glared at the rat-dog. "I'll bet they tossed you out while the car was still moving."

Nacho shifted and quivered.

Carson again saw how tight the collar was around her neck. "Look, burrito breath, I don't like you, but I hate to see an animal in pain, even a stupid one like you." She slowly scooted down the limb.

Nacho didn't move.

Carson held her hand out.

Nacho stood, and the others began growling. The tiny Chihuahua chased the wolves farther back into the brush and then turned and walked confidently toward Carson.

She either just gave the warning for her pack to surprise attack me, or she's going soft. Should I take the chance?

Carson kept her hand out.

Nacho approached, turned her back to Carson, looked over her shoulder, and stood still.

The dog was just out of reach, so Carson shifted down another branch and cautiously reached Nacho's collar.

The dog growled but didn't turn and bite. Her back leg jerked a little. Carson must've found her tickle spot.

Quickly, Carson unclasped the collar. The fabric was so embedded in Nacho's neck, Carson had to tug hard to peel it off.

Nacho bared her teeth, watching Carson's every move.

Carson yanked, and the collar released, pulling clumps of skin and hair along with it.

In a flash, the dog jumped, still growling, and quickly distanced herself from Carson. Carson scrambled back to safety, wiping her hand where the dog had quickly licked her.

"I won't tell anybody you were nice, even if only for a second." Carson still held the dirty, hair-encrusted collar. "But you have to take your friends on a long hike away from me. Deal?" She put the collar in her pocket.

Nacho peed again, swiped her feet and kicked up dust, then trotted off. She hoisted her curled tail high like a victory flag.

Carson watched as Nacho strutted to the brush with the others. The dog stopped and rolled happily, running her indented neck into the scratchy dirt.

About thirty minutes passed before Nacho stood, gave a short yelp and waded into the water. The others followed, glaring at Carson until they hit the freezing stream.

All the wolves except Nacho could walk across the chest high water. Nacho's legs kicked in a confident dog paddle, and she bobbed like bait across the deeper part, but never lost her rhythm. She made it to the other side, shook the water off and trotted into the thick trees with nary a backward glance.

Carson waited a good hour before she untangled herself from the tree. Pain shot through her foot and ankle when she put weight on it. She looked at the wound, thankful that the fang puncture had scabbed over. *I'll probably get rabies now.*

With great caution, listening intently, Carson went to the water's edge, drank her fill and rinsed her cuts. She packed the bite with mud because she thought she'd read somewhere that mud was good for cuts. Then she stood and began running in the opposite direction the wolves had gone.

CHAPTER 33

Bet lay in the creek bed. A long weed tickled her face whenever the breeze caught it. Rox, bound behind her, squirmed and cried around the muzzle of duct tape.

Twilight's meager glow shadowed the wooded area. Bet's arm throbbed, and her cheek felt tight. She wasn't sure how deep the knife wound in her arm was but figured it had stopped bleeding by now.

She grunted and pushed against Rox. The girl stilled and tried to talk through her taped mouth but only made muffled sobbing noises. Bet gave a hard shove trying to get Rox to leverage herself against Bet so they could stand.

The girl seemed to get the message and leaned her back into Bet. Together, they stood but couldn't walk because of their bound ankles.

This is not the way I want to die, Bet thought. *Bound, starving and itching.* She and Rox teetered and almost fell a few times. Bet kicked her feet, and the binds loosened a little. Then she tried her hands. They were tied tighter, and the more she worked against the tape the more chaffed her wrists became.

Duct tape held her and Rox together at their waists. With enough stretching and pulling, the tape loosened a smidge, but they couldn't peel it off without their hands.

Bet grunted an indication for Rox to shuffle with her to some nearby trees. With great effort, they made it to one with a few low limbs. They sawed the duct tape against the rough bark. Finally, the waist binding tore, and they fell forward. Rox screamed through the tape and flounced around on the ground like a fish out of water. She rubbed her face in the dirt until she managed to rip the tape halfway off her mouth.

"That jerk!" She spat dirt and venom. The dirty tape flapped against her face. "He took my money! And my...argh! He's gonna get it." She looked up at a steep rocky embankment to the apartment buildings. "Crank! Get down here and untie me. You're a stupid idiot!" She spit again. "And you have horrible taste in women."

Bet worked her gag, loosened it enough to move her lips. "Rox, forget him," Bet croaked. "They're gone." Bet sank to her knees. *They've gone with my car, my purse, my money, and worst of all—my last picture of Carson.* Anger shook her as she furiously kicked at the tape around her ankles until it loosened enough to cut through with a branch. Maybe Rox was right to chase him.

Revenge. Oh, yeah, this felt good. She wanted to get that picture of Carson back if it was the last thing she did. Bet tried to run up the steep embankment but couldn't keep her balance without her hands.

"Hey, don't leave me!" Rox cried.

"Let's get him." Bet yelled back. She couldn't stand the thought of Crank even *looking* at Carson's picture.

Bet got a few steps closer, close enough to see red flashing lights from a police car ricochet against the trees. Her first instinct was to scream for help, but no, she was wanted. She'd go back to jail or worse, the mental motel.

Bet slid the short distance she'd climbed and went to Rox. "The police are up there. Give me a head start and then scream for help. Tell them I tied you up and left you here."

"No way. They're gonna know I let you out. I don't want to go back to juvey."

"Please, Rox. There's something I need to do...by myself."

"Like what?" Rox's lips trembled. "I need your help. Crank did me wrong. He needs to pay. I can't get him if Officer Z's watching my every move." The duct tape flopped like a ribbon on her cheek.

Bet looked at the flashing lights. "Yeah, Crank has something of mine as well."

"Ya think? He has your car and money. 'Sides, by the looks of you the popo's will think *you* murdered somebody."

Bet looked down at her blood-soaked shirt and stained jeans.

"Forget about me. This is your chance to escape. I don't care what you tell them about me. I just don't want to get caught."

"No. We're in this together." The girl looked defiant. "And if you don't say yes, I'll scream now and get us both busted."

Bet sighed. "Fine. I'll get you home, then we'll part ways."

"Part ways?" Rox smiled. "We'll see. I still like the funny way you talk."

"Can you get the tape off your ankles?" Bet asked. She went to a tree and began sawing at the tape that bound her wrists. "We need to hide in the trees so they don't find us." Bet felt the binds loosen. "Hurry!"

Rox rolled and kicked until the tape tore. They ran to the cover of the woods just as a searchlight swept near where they had been.

Bet cut the tape enough to free her hands. She untied Rox, and together they followed the creek. The darkness made each step an adventure. Bet could hear city noises echo in the treetops, but no others ventured along the greenbelt of urban nature after the sun went down.

Oh, Carson, if you could see me now. I'm sorry I kept you like a caged animal. Although the world is a crazy place, you had so much living yet to do. Bet wished beyond the full orange moon that she and Carson were together now.

She and Rox walked for almost twenty minutes. Bet's arm pulsed, and her sleeve was drenched with blood.

Rox kicked at some leaves. "I can't believe Crank's with that snarky piece of work."

"Snarky is not a real word." Bet ducked under some low-hanging limbs.

"So?"

Bet smiled. "It might be onomatopoeia."

Rox looked at her like she was an alien from another planet.

"You know, a word that sounds like it what it is."

"How do you even know that? And why is it important?"

"Knowledge is power," Bet said.

"Then think us out of this mess oh powerful-smarty-pants," Rox griped, as she trudged ahead.

Bet noticed that the girl had twigs and some leaves in her hair. She reached out to pluck them from Rox's hair, but a sharp stab of pain in her arm stopped her. She was sure they both looked like they'd had a mud bath. Bet glanced at her shirt—or a blood bath.

Bet was hungry, tired, and craved a hot shower. "Rox, we need to eat, and I need to find a change of clothes."

"We don't have any money. How're we gonna eat?" Rox carefully picked her way around broken bottles and rocks.

"I have a little over forty dollars in my pocket."

"Really! Where'd you get that?"

"After we broke a fifty at Wendy's, I didn't put the change in my purse. Now I'm glad." She wondered if she'd resort to stealing if she got hungry enough.

Rox suddenly gasped and stopped. They'd reached the opening to a bridge. The road above was silent; no cars passed by.

Bet rushed to Rox's side. "What?"

Rox pointed and began backing away.

Shadows moved under the bridge. Moving silhouettes of four grizzled men, whose tattered, loose clothing draped their frames so they looked like walking zombies. They approached them, and one spat and cackled, "Lookie what we have here, boys. Are you ladies lost in the woods?"

CHAPTER 34

A search-and-rescue team had been called to help find the girl lost from the Outward Bound camp. Mark suited up in heavy gear for a rough ride in a helicopter.

He was happy to be doing something, anything, other than sitting in that hotel room awaiting punishment.

When Mark went to Officer Coffey to offer to help with the rescue, the senior officer said, "Don't even think about it."

It was hard, but Mark had to throw his father's name around and confide in Officer Coffey before the senior officer waved his hand and said, "Yeah, you can go, but I'm not done with you yet." Mark hated that the reason he'd left home, the thing he'd run away from, was what got him in the rescue copter.

One of the rescue workers handed him the assignment when he boarded the roaring helicopter. He clutched the pages of the detail as he ducked under the blades sluicing the air. The belted harness of his jumpsuit clinked with each step.

He climbed into the copter with three others from the rescue team. The pilot and co-pilot studied a map, and the guy in the back handed him a headset. After he fastened the heavy earphones on, he heard flight instructions amid a lot of static. His backseat partner waved to get his attention.

"Look over the detail," he yelled into the microphone as he pointed to the papers in Mark's hand. "We're going to start where the campers were and head out from there. We'll fly until it gets dark, okay?"

Mark gave a thumbs up and opened the papers. As he read, his heart skipped and a cold chill slid down his spine when he saw the name of the missing girl.

Casey.

Casey Harper.

CHAPTER 35

Carson ran like never before. She wanted to put as much space as she could between her and the wolf gang.

Wolfgang, she thought wryly. *Wolfgang Puck. Who cooks food that would fill my empty stomach.* Carson had never been this hungry before. So hungry it hurt. But more than an empty stomach, she wanted to fill her empty heart. She missed home. She missed her mom.

Her pace became a rhythm, and she began to enjoy the scenery. The air was clearer, but a layer of haze still lingered. Beyond the smoky wisps, the sky was an unreal dome of blue. For the first time in years she could run *and* breathe. It felt good! Was this a runner's high? Then her wolf-bitten ankle started throbbing painfully, slowing her down more than the fact that she'd actually run for the first time in forever.

So that was what—thirty seconds of my first runner's high? Her steps slowed, and she looked back, surprised how far away the tree line was now. She'd gone a pretty good distance.

Ahead, the rocks at the base of a mountain loomed. *If I could climb those, maybe I could see camp and scream for help.* She pushed harder, but jolts of pain from her injuries and muscles slowed her down. Eventually, she reached the line of rocks at the foot of a steep grade.

Big, gray boulders stair-stepped the mountain. She stopped to catch her breath and check her ankle. So far, the scabs held under the mud, but her foot was swollen and tingly. Hopefully from the run and not because she had a fatal infection. *Maybe, like a vampire, I'll have wolf DNA in me, and I'll start snapping at people. Carson Harper, Wolf-Girl.* She smiled at the thought. Salty sweat trickled into her gashed forehead and stung. She used her shirt to wipe her face clean, wishing she could take a big drink of cold water. Maybe there'd be another stream along the rocks.

She took a few minutes to regroup and then climbed. Her arms ached from hanging on the tree limb, and the rest of her muscles clunked along behind her brain's signal to move. Hunger gnawed deep in her gut, and she felt her energy sap with each step.

The higher she got, the harder it was to get a good foothold. Fear crept into every push to get higher. *Don't look down.* She looked down. *Why does it always seem so much higher than what you really are?* But she knew one wrong move and she'd be a pancake if she fell, mostly because she'd land on a bunch of sharp, really big rocks. She pictured her head as a cantaloupe bouncing then smashed on a boulder. *People climb mountains every day and they survive. Of course, it helps to have equipment, ropes, and energy to make it.*

She shimmied along sideways, thinking she heard a trickle of water. *Water good, slippery rocks bad.* But her thirst burned more than the fear of falling. She was sure that she heard water flowing somewhere near. Less than thirty yards up, Carson spotted a plateau with dense trees. *Maybe there's a flat space for me to rest.* There was no way she'd be able to sleep here, hanging on a rock.

Like an inchworm, she scrapped her way closer to trees. *Now watch there be a road or path that I could've easily walked up. Maybe there's a ski lodge with buttery drinks and hot turkey-and-cheddar sandwiches up there.* Carson grunted up a few more rocks.

She got to a rocky ledge and collapsed in exhaustion. Above her, a big rock jutted out, almost perpendicular. To get to the top, she'd have to pull herself up and over the edge, leaving herself dangling over nothing but a huge drop to the bottom.

Water. I have to have water. She got to her knees, the raw scrapes stinging as she crawled to an edge. She reached her hand around and felt wet rock. *Yes!* She cupped her hand and caught a few drops. She hungrily slurped the tiny drink. She stood and reached farther and was able to catch a little more. There were mushy clumps of green that she grabbed with the water, and she sucked them dry. After twenty minutes of catch-and-drink, she looked at the green clumps she'd dropped and thought they looked like something that Survivorman had eaten when he was in Alaska. *Fiddleheads? Did they grow in Colorado?* She sure hoped so, because she took one and stuffed it in her mouth. It was bitter but juicy, and she ate the others she'd dropped. They quenched her thirst and took an edge off her hunger. She reached around and grabbed as many as she could and feasted on them. *These would go nice with a crispy fresh soda and a steak. Let's just hope they're not poisonous. I don't want to die a painful, gassy death.* She burped.

The hot sun scorched her sunburned skin, and Carson crawled under the rock for shade. She decided to rest a while and then try to climb over that cliffhanger. She curled against a shaded corner and fell asleep.

Thwap-thwap-thwap.

Carson turned her head, her food dreams morphed to a school day morning. Her mother clanking around in the kitchen, the stupid traffic helicopters that always woke her up when they flew over. Why did they have to start so early every morning? Her mom hated them flying so close, afraid one would crash into the house.

She registered the *thwap* noise again. *That noise. What's that noise?*

Carson jolted awake. She heard a helicopter approaching. She couldn't see it because of the trees, but she could hear it. *Go, go, go!*

She jumped up and got as close to the edge of the rock as possible. She waved her arms, watching her step and waited for the copter to appear. *Come on, I'm over here!* If she could get over that rock, she'd be more visible. *Okay, here goes.* She grabbed hold and started to climb. *This time don't look down.* With great caution, but as fast as she could, Carson pulled and squirmed around, trying to keep at least one foot on something solid.

"Help! Here I am! Help!" she screamed. The helicopter flew closer.

Almost there, she could barely see over the edge to a flat grassy area. But before the last push to get over, Carson heard a great roar. Not from an engine, but from a huge grizzly bear calling her cubs. Carson saw the momma bear stand then turn toward her, sniffing the air as her cubs ran scared to their mother.

Their eyes locked, and the bear roared again. The huge beast dropped to all fours and charged toward Carson.

No! Carson swung, dropped back to her perch and scrambled back under the overhang. The bear was just above her, grunting and barking. The bear snuffed and sniffed at the rock. Carson could smell her fetid breath and pushed herself harder against the rock. A huge paw with long nails swiped the edge of the cliff.

Just then the helicopter flew over, so loud the air vibrated around her. "Help me." Carson whispered through sobs. "Please, please, come back."

The engine noise sounded farther and farther away.

Despair filled her insides. *This trip sucks. What if I never get saved? I'll never sleep in my own warm, cozy bed again. I'll never see my mom. I want to go home!*

They'll be back; they have to come back. She got mad and stood up. *I'm going to be saved. Please let me be saved.*

Had the helicopter scared the bear? Carson was afraid but needed to find out. She didn't want to stay hidden in case the helicopter flew back this way. She tried to peek over the ledge and fought a great temptation to jump screaming from her hiding place, like a panicked quail flying into a hunter's bullet.

CHAPTER 36

Bet pushed Rox behind her. The men advanced from beneath the darkened bridge. "Stay close to me. When you get the chance run, you're probably faster than them." The lone streetlight cast a weak spotlight on the filthy bunch of vagabonds.

"We can fight 'em. I know some karate." Rox swiped the air with a flat hand.

"There's four against two. Let's be smart." Bet hoped the girl would run to safety, letting her take care of what she set out to do. Although these tattered men didn't look like killers, maybe they were just crazy enough to do something stupid, and Bet could be with Carson tonight.

"Just don't give them your money. We need it." Rox peered around Bet's shoulder.

The men stopped less than ten feet from them. One thin, toothless man waved them closer. "Come on in, ya'll got any food?" They all cackled.

"No food. We're trying to get home," Bet called back.

"Ya'll lost?"

"Duh!" Rox spat. "D'ya really think we'd be takin' a nature hike through this place?" She stepped beside Bet.

"Rox," Bet whispered. "Get behind me."

"Are you makin' fun of our nice home?" the dentally challenged man asked. "We don't like anybody makin' fun of us." He stepped closer, and Bet noticed he had a long piece of pipe in his hand. The other men circled Bet and Rox.

Another guy with buggy eyes said, "We don't want no trouble. Just give us your money."

"We don't have any money," Bet lied. "I just had my purse and car stolen. They took everything."

"Yeah, some jerk named Crank. He lives up in those apartments." Rox pointed. "Go find him; he has like more than a thousand dollars."

"Sounds like you ladies had a bad night." Toothless wheezed. "And we're gonna make it worse." He raised the pipe like a knife.

"Stop." Bet grabbed Rox. "Let the girl go. I'll stay."

"Lemme think about it." He smacked the pipe in his hand. "No, don't think so."

"Whaddya mean?" Rox shook Bet's hand off. "I'm not leaving you here alone with these geezers."

"I'll be okay." Bet turned to Rox. "Run! Go!"

Instead of running, Rox bent and grabbed a big stick and started swinging. The men backed away, laughing.

Bet sighed. Was this girl ever going to leave? Bet felt responsible to her, after all Rox had saved her from jail. But for crying out loud, why did she continue to hang around like a boa constrictor on her neck?

Bet pushed a pile of leaves away with her foot until she uncovered a large stick, too. "Okay, Rox, you take those two, and I'll take Smiley and his friend." She raised the stick and quoted Shakespeare, " 'Cowards die many times before their deaths, the valiant never taste of death but once.' "

"What?" Rox asked. "You come up with the weirdest things."

They both advanced on the men, wielding their big sticks. Bet's left arm throbbed, and her shirt was stiff with dried blood. She kept her eyes on the men in front of her but could hear Rox behind her.

"I'm gonna knock that last tooth outta your ugly mouth!" Rox screamed.

Bet heard the whoosh of Rox's stick. Then she focused on her prey. How much fight should she give? Would that pipe be enough take her out? She thought again of Rox and knew she couldn't leave her here alone.

In college, Bet had been a pretty good tennis player. She held the stick like her old Wilson racquet and swished a backhand at Smiley. He raised the pipe and started swinging. The other guy took off running.

One good forehand swing and Bet caught his hand with her stick. He lost his grip on the pipe and backed away, holding his injured hand.

"Lady, you're crazy."

Bet hit him again, this time on his shoulder.

"Owww!" he yelped and turned, running after his friend as fast as his rickety gait would allow.

Bet looked for Rox. She saw the girl chasing the other two guys through the woods still swinging her weapon, "Come back here and fight, you creeps." Rox stopped, grabbed a handful of rocks and threw them at the retreating men and then took off after them again.

"Rox!" Bet called. "Let's go."

Rox slowed, but not before she wound up and fast-pitched a big rock. It hit one of the men smack in his back. He grunted and lost his balance but kept running. "A little higher, and I would've brained him." Rox leaned on her stick and wiped her hands. "This is better than WWE. I'm pumped, man!" Rox jogged to Bet.

"You're not scared of anything, are you?" Bet asked.

"Yeah, I'm probably scared of some things." She shrugged and twirled her stick like a martial arts weapon or drill team's baton. "But I think it's better not to worry about them. Then I'd be jumping at my shadow all the time." Rox stopped and waved her stick-sword at her shadow cast by a streetlight.

Bet let her words sink in slowly as they headed under the bridge. It was how she'd raised Carson: to fear everything. Bet watched her own shadow elongate then disappear as they walked into the darkened tunnel.

CHAPTER 37

Miserable, Carson sat on the edge of the rock and looked down. *I should get a T-shirt that says "don't look down." It could be my new mantra.* As the sun set, a big orange moon rose on the horizon. It lit the jagged mountains with a soft glow. Below her stony ledge, a chasm yawned into a deep hole, the bottom so dark she couldn't see below the rim. Cold air whipped around the mountain. Carson shivered and put her jacket on. *What next? Will the bluebird of happiness fly over and take a big dump on my head?*

She'd hoped to use her jacket as a flag when the helicopter flew back over, but it never returned. *At least they're looking for me. Or maybe they're putting out fires. Or sightseeing. They have to know I'm out here.* She didn't relish the thought of spending another freezing night out here alone. A thin ribbon of hope threaded through her. *They'll come back tomorrow.* But she thought for sure that by today she'd be clean, fed and in a warm bed somewhere.

Her stomach grumbled and growled. The fiddleheads helped, but also gave her a case of stinky gas. She wished she'd brought more Snickers bars with her, but who could've imagined this mess? She'd only ventured out to use the bathroom, not get lost in the wilderness.

A fire, I need warmth. How many ways had Survivorman shown how to start a flame? I guess I could go find a tree still burning and toast my buns with that. Ummm, toasted buns. Carson licked her cold, chapped lips.

Survivorman had been successful rubbing sticks together and

by using a rock on an axe head. He'd also used some kind of potassium and nitrate stuff when he was in Africa. *Lot of good that'll do me. I don't have any tools.* She felt in her pocket for her toothpaste and wondered if Crest was flammable.

Thank goodness for the few hours of sleep she'd gotten that afternoon, since tonight would be too cold to get comfortable. Carson stood on weak shaky legs, felt dizzy, and quickly stepped away from the edge of the cliff. She took a deep breath. *Dang, one false move and I'm a goner.* The base of the mountains, so far down, came together in a small canyon like a serrated cereal bowl.

Stop! Focus. I need food. She wondered if grass was okay to eat. Roady used to eat it. But afterward, he'd usually throw up green mush.

Okay, forget grass. She reached over the ledge and pulled herself up as far as her frozen, shivering body would allow. No bears in sight, no ski lodge either. She grabbed a handful of dry grass and set herself back on the cliff. Carson wadded the grass together and put it in the corner of her shelter, away from the wind gusts. *Maybe I can use this for tinder.* There wasn't much in the way of sticks that she could reach. She patted her hand over the ledge, hoping a hungry animal didn't mistake it for a small jumping critter and try to eat it. Quickly grabbing what she could, she made a small pile for her pyre.

She took a stone in each hand and settled back in the rocky sanctuary near the pile of dry grass. She bundled her jacket around her and tried to close the ripped holes in her jeans. Her knees, skinned and scabbed over, hurt. She took her shoes off and looked at her ankle. It was red around the bite and still swollen. Blood and mud had stained her sock and made it stiff and gross. *First a bath. No, food first. Better, I'll eat while soaking in the hot steamy bubble bath. Yeah, that'd be nice.* She rubbed her foot.

She huddled under the ledge and set about chipping the rocks together, trying to get a spark. Her body needed warmth, but what if she actually did get a fire started? She might be responsible for burning down the rest of the Rocky Mountains. Carson shuddered as she remembered the lightning and the powerful electric jolt.

For the next twenty minutes, she chipped the rocks together, at least generating body heat by the exercise. Carson never got one stinking spark, though. Her toes were frozen, so she tried to wiggle them. She finally put her shoes back on, stood, and did jumping jacks, then ran in place on the small ledge. She didn't want to sweat, a big no-no according to Survivorman, because the sweat would freeze. But she needed inner warmth.

She thought of Seth and lit up inside.

Maybe he was out looking for her. Maybe he'd be the one to rescue her. *On a fiery white stallion, wearing long warm robes to wrap me in.*

A shooting star soared across the sky, so close and bright, Carson could almost reach it.

CHAPTER 38

Z's commanding officer's office was one of the few with a real window.

"What do you mean, she escaped?" His boss sat at his desk glaring at Z, who stood contrite. He found it difficult to look the man in the eye.

"Sir, she was low risk, really no risk. She'd been through a lot losing her daughter and her home. That's why we only had her in the holding cell. May I sit?"

"No."

Z sighed. "And Rox had come around. She wasn't getting in any trouble and was a real help to us at the station."

"Yeah, I see how much she helped." He tapped the desk, his voice heavy with sarcasm. "You taught her well, it seems."

"We're looking for them, sir. We traced withdrawals from three ATM machines."

"How hard can it be to find these two women?"

"We found Bet Harper's purse and wallet." He shook his head sadly. "But it doesn't look good. Her blood is all over the purse."

"What about the girl? What's her name?" He grabbed a sheet of paper and looked it over. "Roxanne Mayhill?"

"No sign of her." Z turned and paced in front of the desk. "She...she probably had something to do with hurting Bet Harper. The video from the jail escape shows Rox pushing Bet out the door." He whistled through his teeth. "It's not like Rox; her boyfriend was the one with the goods." He stopped. "I'll take full responsibility, sir." Z shook his head. "I still can't believe she'd get involved with something like this. She's never been violent."

"Have you talked to the boyfriend?"

Z ran a hand over his bald head. "Umm, no sir. He got away, too."

"What?" The officer stood up so fast his chair almost fell. He leaned over his desk. "How did he get away? Are all your officers as incompetent as you?"

Z didn't answer the questions. "We got a few of his friends, and we're talking with them."

"Are you teaching them how to beat the system, too?"

"No, sir."

The commanding officer smacked the desk with the flat palm of his hand and yelled, "You better find Bet Harper soon. I just got a weird phone call from some military guy named Coffey. He wants to talk to her about a missing girl in the Colorado wild fires."

Z looked at him. "Why?"

"The girl's name is Casey Harper."

Chapter 39

Bet hiked in the dark next to Rox, weariness mixed with pain. Concentrating on each step helped take her mind off the ache of losing Carson. Move, she thought. If she stopped she feared she'd sink into a hurt so deep it would swallow her like quicksand.

"I'm starving," Rox whined. "Let's go eat."

"I'll hardly be able to go anyplace wearing these bloody clothes." Bet looked down at her shirt. "I need to take a shower and get into something clean. There are no stores open at this hour, though."

"Hello, this is Wal-Mart country," Rox said. "There's one not too far from here."

"How do you know your way around here in the woods?" Bet picked her way through the littered creek bed.

"I can smell a Wal-Mart from miles away." She laughed and jogged up a short hill to look at the street. "Yeah, it's still a good hike, but we can make it. It's almost spittin' distance from here." Rox sighed. "You remember the story about the girl that lived in a Wal-Mart for months? That would be like a dream come true for me."

About an hour later, they stood in a copse of trees near the blazing-lit Wal-Mart parking lot.

Bet took out a handful of money and gave it to Rox. "I can't be seen like this, someone will surely call the police."

"Shirley will call the police?" Rox giggled. "I heard that in a movie." She took the bills from Bet. "What do you want to eat?"

"I don't really care. Just be prudent with the money, it's all we have."

"Prudent? What's that?" Rox put the money in her jeans pocket.

"Don't spend the wad. We don't have much." Bet thought she sounded a little like Carson.

"Well, duh!"

"Please, buy me a new shirt as well. And maybe some personal hygiene products, you know, toothpaste, soap."

"Personal hygiene." Rox snorted and rolled her eyes. "You sound like a Kotex commercial."

Bet felt her stomach growl. "And for some reason I'm really craving a Snickers bar."

"Will that be to go, or do you want to eat here?" Rox joked as she cut through a broken chain-link fence and walked into the bright lights of the parking lot.

While Rox shopped, Bet sat in the dark shadow of the trees, fatigue and pain consuming her. *I'm too tired to be tired.* She leaned against a big tree but then sat up. Now would be the time to run from Rox. Get out while the girl was safe in the store. Bet sighed and sat back down. *No, she'd come looking for me in the dark woods and would probably get hurt. I need to get her home. Then I can take care of what I need to do.*

Before long, Rox walked out of the store holding bags in each hand. The girl stepped up her pace and glanced back before squeezing through the fence, meeting Bet under the shadows.

"Here. I got each of us a double cheeseburger at McDonalds. They're only ninety-nine cents." She handed Bet the food bag, along with the change.

The smell enticed Bet's taste buds. "Let's get away from here before we eat," Bet said. "I'm sure they have cameras all over the place." They headed back to the creek. "Did you remember my Snickers?"

"Yeah, I even got you the giant size. It cost about the same as a small one."

They didn't go far before hunger took hold. They sat in the shadows and dug into their burgers and fries. Bet thought of all the lectures about nutrition she'd given Carson. Well, if the burger had enough fat to give her a heart attack tonight, so be it. She grabbed a handful of fries and stuffed them in her mouth. After finishing the meal, she ate every bit of the Snickers.

Sated, Bet leaned against a tree and rubbed her cut arm. "I should've had you get something for pain. If my arm's this sore now, I'll bet I won't be able to move it tomorrow."

"Well, don't go getting all paralyzed on me." Rox shoved a plastic bag at Bet. "Here's a new shirt and *toiletries*." She giggled. "I don't live too far from here, we can go there and take care of our *personal hygiene*." Rox laughed as she stood, then quickly ducked back in the shadows.

"What?" Bet asked just as she heard the whine of a golf cart motor. She backed behind the tree and watched a uniformed guard sweep a flashlight beam across the wooded area.

Rox waved for her to be silent. "Security," she whispered. "Let's go."

They ran into the woods and followed the creek for about thirty minutes until Rox stopped at the outskirts of a dilapidated apartment complex. The dingy white brick of the buildings had graffiti painted over most of it, and garbage was strewn around a dusty area that should have been grass. Rox held her hand up to Bet. "We've got to be real quiet. I don't wanna wake everybody." She glanced at the apartments and hesitated before saying, "If my mama's with someone, we can't go inside. 'Kay?"

Bet nodded. Her heart went out to this neglected, but independent, child.

"Change your shirt in case someone does see us. I don't want 'em to call the police."

Bet quickly tore off her bloody, button-down denim blouse and pulled out a black T-shirt with—Bet could barely make out the design in the dim light—a print of a smiling skull. "Umm, Rox?" She held up the shirt.

"It was on sale, and you'll look cool." Rox parted a tangle of branches to look through.

"Well, in that case." Bet pulled it on, careful of her sore arm. "I would like to take a shower before I put on anything clean."

"Soon," Rox crouched and crab-walked into an open courtyard and headed toward the back window of an apartment where the screen had been torn from the window frame and lay bent and broken on the ground.

Bet stuffed her bloodied shirt in one of the Wal-Mart bags and chucked it in a dumpster near the window where Rox peered in.

All of a sudden, Rox stiffened and put a hand over her mouth, her eyes wide with fear.

Bet rushed toward her. "What?"

Rox grabbed Bet and pushed her against the brick building and whispered, "Shhh, Officer Z's in there talking to my mother!"

CHAPTER 40

Carson jerked awake then shimmied away from the cliff's edge. The bottom of the canyon was pitch black, like what she'd always imagined a black hole in the universe would look like. She shivered so hard she figured that was what woke her up surprised she'd slept at all. She huddled against the rocks and tried to recall how miserable the hot Texas sun could be.

She had no idea what time it was. The bright stars twinkled happily at her. She wished she knew how to navigate the stars, like which one was the North Star. They all looked big and brilliant and amazingly beautiful. The moonlight reflected off of the snowcapped mountains making them look like giant ice cream sundaes.

Her injured foot was asleep and tingled painfully. She took her shoes off, wiggled her toes, and did leg stretches. When she tried standing, pins shot through her foot, and she couldn't put any weight on it. She hoped it wasn't mortally infected and needed to be cut off. She carefully moved it in circles and walked in place until the tingle stopped.

She drank her fill of water and brushed her teeth, savoring the minty freshness in her mouth, even though the rest of her was a crusty mess. The gash on her head throbbed a little, but it didn't hurt as much as yesterday. Checking the horizon, Carson noticed a small pink band of light holding the promise of the sun and warmth.

Carson leaned against the rock and peeled off her dirty, stiff socks. She shook the dirt out and tried to ignore the freezing rocks underfoot. She sat and massaged her feet, trying to see how bad the bite was on her ankle. Too dark to get a real good look, she could tell it was still caked with dirt, but it didn't look like it had bled through the mud pack.

She put her socks and shoes back on, stood up and got a good stretch, determined to be rescued today. *No more wilderness adventure for me. I'm going home.* She noticed that when she stretched, her jeans bagged around her hips. She hiked them up and turned to scale the ledge again. She had to get over the top of that rock.

Don't look down.

Carson took a deep breath and grabbed the edge. Like a kid trying to climb a kitchen counter, she pulled herself up and dangled for a split second of panic. Then she screamed and threw her right leg over the top. She startled a small varmint—rabbit she hoped—and heard it dash into a nearby shrub.

Another push, and she rolled on to the top of the cliff. She scurried on all fours until she felt she was a safe enough distance to look back. *Whoa, I can't believe I just did that!* She stood and began walking briskly along the dome of the mountaintop.

It felt good to move. She began to get warm as her muscles loosened. Her ankle still hurt, but she was able to put more weight on it. *Okay, helicopter, I'm ready to be rescued.* She looked to the pink-and-orange tinged sky, willing the chopper to fly over about now.

Wary of running into mamma bear and her babies, Carson skirted a line of trees and followed the foliage to a small icy blue mountain lake fed by a stream that ran over the mountain's edge. *That's the water I was drinking,* she thought as she went to the lake and dipped her hand in it. The water was freezing, and she scooped up and drank as much as she could before her fingers stiffened from cold.

Refreshed, she shoved her hands in her pockets to warm them and walked around the lake. Fish darted under the water, and Carson decided that she would have seafood—or *lake*food—for breakfast.

But first she needed a fire. Otherwise she'd be eating sushi.

Survivorman had rubbed sticks together to start a fire. Carson took a wad of dried mossy stuff and a bunch of dry twigs and piled them on a rock, away from the trees. For the next hour, she worked the sticks together and chipped at stones with no luck. Frustrated, she tossed the tools into the pile. *This stinks.* She rooted through her pockets looking for something, anything, to ignite the pile.

She found a gum wrapper.

And Nacho's collar.

She took the dirty, hair-encrusted collar, scrubbed it in the water, and then dried it as best as she could. She unfolded the gum wrapper and placed it, foil up, on the moss. She tried to aim a reflected beam of sun off a silver tag from the collar onto the foil. As she waited, and waited, and *waited*, she read the engraving on the tag. "Chiquita" and a phone number with an area code Carson didn't recognize. *I guess Nacho-Chiquita had a home after all— probably until she bit the owners and they tossed her out here. Maybe, later today, after I'm rescued, I'll call the owners and tell them she's living the good life.*

It took a long while, but the sun's rays heated up considerably and poof, a small spiral of smoke rose from the moss. *Oh my gosh, I did it! I made fire!* Carson bent and blew on the tiny embers. The little pile smoldered, and she ran to get more tinder. Easy, considering the mountain was so dry.

After getting a respectable blaze, Carson took off her jacket and basked on the rock. The sun was fully up and warmed her more than the fire. For the first time in days, Carson enjoyed the moment. She smelled the air, it was sweet, not sugar sweet, more like cut grass, flowers and blue sky mixed together. She was still hungry and sore, but there was also a feeling of well being baked in by the sun.

I started a fire! All by myself. Now, I can't let it go out. She got up and walked to the water's edge. There were enough fish to practically reach in and scoop one out. Like one would really let her. She remembered the Tom Hanks movie where, after his plane crashed, he survived on a desert island. He killed fish by spearing them with a stick. Carson found a big enough stick and tried to sharpen one end by chipping rocks at it.

Close enough. She looked at the blunted end. It wasn't sharp enough to slice a ham, but hopefully she'd get something to eat using it.

She lay on her stomach and wiggled to the edge of the water.

"Here fishy, fishy," she said as she waited for a fish to swim near enough for her to jab the weapon into the water. After a few desperate attempts, she'd only managed to scare away anything below the surface and didn't get even close to a fish.

Jab, jab, jab. Nothing. Now she was getting hot. *I'll probably die of pneumonia or a cold between being freezing and boiling.* She grabbed Nacho's collar from her pocket and held it in the water, just below the surface. Before long, a few fish swam near, seeming to be mesmerized by the shiny flash. "You're getting sleepy," Carson whispered hypnotically.

Still holding the collar in the cold water, Carson lifted the weapon, aimed, and shot the spear into the water. She managed to pin a fish against a rock. She levered the fish up and out of the water, tossing it as far away as possible so it wouldn't flop back into the lake.

Eat your heart out, Mr. Survivorman! Carson Harper, mountain girl, spears big fish!

Ecstatic, Carson put the collar back in her pocket and rolled away from the edge of the lake to claim her catch. She stopped cold when she saw mamma bear standing less than fifteen feet away, eyeing her and her fresh catch.

CHAPTER 41

Fear paralyzed Bet and Rox as they hid behind the apartment, listening to Officer Z argue with Rox's mom.

"She ain't here. But if you see her, send her back. I need some stuff." Rox's mother's voice was hoarse and deep. Her shoulder-length red hair looked like a bird had nested in it, and the pilled yellow bathrobe that hung from her thin body made her sallow skin look jaundiced.

Officer Z stood in the doorway, trying to peek around the tiny woman. "Rox, are you here?" he yelled past her.

Mrs. Mayhill put her hands on her hips. "I said for the hunreth time, I ain't seen her. Now git on."

"Let me come in and have a look around."

"You got a warrant?"

"No. But I can get one."

"She ain't here. You should know that. You keep her hangin' 'round the *police* station, tellin' her lies about her mamma." Her thick Texas accent dripped like cream gravy over biscuits.

"I don't tell her anything. I'm trying to give her an opportunity to help herself." He stepped sideways and shouted, "Rox?" Then he said in a lower voice to her mother, "Rox is in a lot of trouble. She needs to turn herself in."

Rox still clasped her hands over her mouth. She jumped when he'd called her name. Her eyes, wide, darted back and forth. Bet could tell she was looking for an escape, but Z was too close.

"She wouldn't be in no trouble 'cept you keep her at the jail 'round all those criminals. They're a bad influence. Now send my girl on home, or I'll report you."

"I'll get a warrant." Bet could see Z cross his arms.

"You get what'evr you want, you still ain't comin' in here."

"Mrs. Mayhill, please."

The woman slammed the door and Bet lost sight of Z. She was tempted to turn herself in, and face whatever punishment was in store. Too bad it wouldn't be the death penalty. But then, she'd probably languish in appeals while on death row. "Rox, turn yourself in. I'm sorry to have gotten you in this much trouble," Bet whispered.

Rox shook her head fiercely and mouthed, "No."

A car door shut and an engine started. Bet peeked around the corner and saw Officer Z drive out of the parking lot.

"I can't go in there now. She'll whup up on me for having the popos after me." Rox peered in the window. "C'mon, I have a friend nearby."

Bet followed her, and they ran back to the cover of trees. Two buildings over, they stopped, and Rox looked around. "See that patio? That's Shauna's house. We were in cosmetology school together." Rox took a few tentative steps toward the building. "She'll help us. Hurry!" Rox bolted from the trees and ran to the patio. Bet followed, ducking while she ran.

"Shauna. Sha-*nana*," Rox said as she jumped on the fence. "Let me in, it's Rox."

A young woman, not much older than Rox, came to the sliding glass door with a baseball bat ready to swing. Her hair was in a towel, and she wore dingy sweats over her slim frame. "Dang, you scared me half to death."

Rox rolled over the wobbly fence and landed on the other side. "I got someone with me. Can you cover for us for a while?"

"The police are looking for you, girl. I saw you on the news. What're you getting into?"

Bet popped her head over the fence. "Any chance you can open this? I'm not sure I can jump that."

Shauna shook her towel wrapped head. "Nah, we dead bolted it, and I can't find the key." Shauna looked at both Bet and Rox. "Looks like you two are in a mess of trouble. I'm not sure I want to get involved."

"Please!" Rox pleaded. "Just for the night."

Shauna hesitated, then said, "Okay, but just for tonight. My mom's gone till tomorrow and I hate stayin' alone here—but if the police come lookin' for you, you gotta go." Shauna smiled. "But you got to tell me what you did. You're practically famous, girl!"

"Thank you, you're a true blue friend." Rox headed inside the apartment. "Where's your mom?" Rox asked, looking around.

"At her stupid boyfriend's. Mom wants me to spend the night with Cat, but she's got plans. I'm here alone."

"Um, excuse me." Bet waved. "Can I get some help?"

"Oh yeah, just jump. It's easy," Rox said.

Bet gave a few hops and tried swinging her leg over. She scraped her sore arm and fell backward on the wrong side. "I'm sorry."

"You're hopeless." Rox grabbed a chipped plastic chair and handed it over the fence to Bet. "Here, but we need to get it back over on this side so no one else uses it to get in. A bunch of weirdos live around here."

Bet set the chair on the grass and hoped it wouldn't crack under her weight. She stepped up and straddled the fence, then lifted the chair with a foot to try to flip it over the fence. "Catch me if I..." She lost her footing and fell to the other side, dropping the chair. Rox did her best to catch her, but Bet still landed hard on her good shoulder and on top of Rox. Ouch. More pain.

"Whoa." Rox landed on her butt with Bet in her lap. Then she started laughing. "Remind me not to rob a bank with you."

In spite of everything, Bet couldn't help but giggle, too. "I think we're already in enough trouble."

Shauna shook the towel off her head and tossed it on the stained carpet inside. "Shush, I don't want to go to jail because you're a couple of loud klutzs." She looked both ways over the fence. "Let's go inside. I'll go out later and get my chair."

Inside, Rox couldn't take her eyes off of Shauna's hair. "That looks so cool! Did you just do that?"

As Shauna pulled curtains over the door, she ran a hand through her hair. "Yeah, I haven't even seen it yet. Does it look good? She opened the curtains a little and stared at her reflection in the glass door. She finger-spiked her short white-blonde hair with a Mohawk band of bright almost fluorescent orange through the middle. "It does look cool." She closed the curtains.

"Maybe you could do our hair like that," Rox said. "You can

help us with a disguise."

"Okay. I need to practice color anyway. So far I'm failing that."

Bet winced at the thought of this girl coloring her hair.

"You're almost graduated." Rox flopped on a ratty brown and plaid couch.

Shauna held up a mirror, admiring her work. "Maybe I'll get extra credit for mixing colors so good. You shoulda' stayed in school, Rox Star. You'd almost be done, too."

Rox shrugged and pulled her black, red-tipped hair through her fingers. "They were lookin' to flunk me anyway."

Bet stood holding the Wal-Mart bag with the stuff Rox bought. "Would you mind terribly if I showered here?"

Rox snickered. "She talks funny. You'll get used to it."

"Yeah, just use that towel." Shauna pointed to the wet towel she'd dropped in a heap on the floor. "I need to do laundry, that one's still pretty clean."

Bet stared at the towel. "Thank you." She bent, picked it up with two fingers and hoped she wouldn't turn orange after using it.

"Bathroom's down the hall." Shauna pointed.

The tiny bathroom was as Bet would have imagined. Hair and face products were strewn across every inch of counter space. A roll of half-wet toilet paper sat on the top of the potty. The floor was sticky with what she hoped was hairspray. She sighed, tempted to scrub the place clean, but then she'd probably have to use the cleaning rag to wash her face.

She undressed and, for the first time, saw the knife wound. An ugly slice of red went from her shoulder to mid-arm. The cut looked deep, probably needed stitches, but wasn't bleeding anymore. It wouldn't take much to split the tenuous scab. Bet needed strong Band-Aids or butterfly adhesive to hold it together. She took a second look at a giant can of AquaNet hair spray. That might do the trick.

Bruises, some new, some shades of yellow and green, ran along her torso, arms, and her wrists where they'd been bound. The scrape on her cheek was almost healed, although still red. She turned on the shower and stepped in, savoring the warm, clean water. She reached for a dingy cracked white bar of soap that sat congealing in a puddle of water, a few hairs stuck to it. *Oh, well. Maybe I'll die of dysentery.*

She missed Carson. Her insides ached for her child. Life was not worth living without her in it. All Bet wanted to do was lay down and let the Lord take her to Carson. Or at least take her out of this misery.

After the shower, Bet dressed in her new skull-and-crossbones T-shirt. The sleeve didn't completely cover the oozing slice on her arm. She went out to the living room and sat with Rox and Shauna while they flipped channels on TV.

" 'Bout time. Hope there's some water left in the world." Rox stood. "My turn." She headed to the bath. "Were you cryin' again?"

Bet nodded.

Rox turned away. "Is the towel in the bathroom?"

Bet didn't answer. Rox had already closed the door.

Shauna stood. "I'm going to go get that chair before some creep uses it to get in here." She went out the front door.

Bet picked up the remote control and changed the nerve-clanging rock-TV channel to CNN. She leaned back on the couch and closed her eyes. Exhausted, she'd almost fallen asleep, when Shauna ran back inside. "Hide! There's a bunch of police cars in the parking lot!"

CHAPTER 42

The helicopter landed as darkness set in. "That's all we can do tonight," the pilot said into his microphone.

Mark struggled to hear the rest of the instructions as the engine and rotors wound down.

"We're going to the camp where this girl was last seen. Because of the fire and the missing girl, the other Outward Bound campers want to help us with a modified search and rescue," the pilot's static-laced voice announced.

"Modified?" the co-pilot asked.

The pilot nodded. "Yeah, they're only a bunch of teenagers, but they really want to help. We'll take as many sets of eyes as possible. They'll be closely supervised, though." He flipped switches as he spoke. "I don't want another kid to get lost."

For the second day, they'd flown over the mountains without luck. Mark had seen deer, elk, even a grizzly bear with her cubs on top of a beautiful mountain canyon that had a small, clear lake near it. The bear looked like it was on the attack. Mark lost the view as the helicopter passed over. After the girl was safe, he might try to find the area again and hike it. What a perfect place to find oneself.

The forest fire, almost completely contained, now only burned in a small area, but there'd been no sign of the girl anywhere.

Mark tagged along with the pilot and rescue crew. "This is like looking for a needle in a haystack," one of the workers said as he took his headgear off.

"Yeah, but how far could one girl go on foot?" Mark asked.

The pilot shrugged. "The fire was pretty big..." his voice trailed off. "She may not have been able to outrun it."

"We wouldn't be out here if we didn't have hope," Mark said. "Don't give up."

They got to the Outward Bound camp and found the teenagers sitting around a small fire. The campers had moved to a safe area away from the burned forest and closer to the rescue team. Most of the teens were unpacking or organizing their bags.

Dana stood when they approached. Her eyes asked: *anything?* The pilot shook his head.

"Please, sit down." Dana pointed to a log near the fire. "We're getting ready to start dinner." She looked at the young group. "I'm glad they all want to help find Casey. But with the fire as close as it was, I'm scared someone may get hurt."

The pilot set his medic kit down. "Just make it clear they're not to go out without one of the rescue team."

Dana agreed. "They're all pretty upset that one of the group is missing. They feel like they need to stay and help."

Mark walked away and turned on his satellite phone as he sat on a log near the campfire. Officer Coffey had called numerous times. Mark was tempted to shut the phone off so he wouldn't have to listen to Coffey scream at him again.

A young man, muscular and lean, with shaggy long hair sat next to Mark and extended his hand. "Hi, I'm Seth."

Mark shook Seth's hand.

"You didn't find her?"

"No, not yet." Mark put the phone in his lap. "Did you know her?"

Seth shrugged. "We'd only talked a few times. She had pretty eyes." He shifted on the log and smiled at Mark. "I liked her sense of humor, too, but I was worried about how she'd make it on the solo hike." Seth glanced down. "She wasn't in the best shape."

"How could she do a hike like this without being fit?"

"I don't know. Outward Bound has pretty strict rules about that kind of stuff." Seth leaned back. "I used to be overweight, too, and thought it was cool that she got in and was going to hike. Training for this was the best exercise I ever got."

"She was overweight? Did she seem strong enough to survive out there?"

"I didn't really know her. But she had spunk, I'll give her that."

Seth kept nodding like he had a song playing in his head.

The satellite phone shrilled. Mark looked at caller ID. Coffey. He silenced the tone. "Do you have a picture of her?"

Seth shook his bobbing head. "No, we're only allowed to take a few things. I'd rather pack food than a camera."

"I understand." The phone rang again. "Excuse me, I'd better take this."

"Seth held his hands over the fire to warm them.

Mark stood and waked away from the camp. "Officer Coffey, sir. I was just about to call you."

"Yeah, I'm sure you were."

"We just landed."

"Did you find the girl?"

"No, sir." Mark sighed. "Not yet."

"I expect you to find her soon."

"We're trying."

"Try harder. There's been a new development."

"What development?"

"Just find the girl."

CHAPTER 43

Carson crouched on a rock near the bank of the lake, watching the big brown bear grunt at her. The bear was still about fifteen feet away, between her and the still flopping fish. If she jumped into the water, she'd freeze instantly and probably go over the waterfall. But heading toward the bear didn't look like a good route, either.

Mamma bear sniffed at the fish. *Oh no, you don't, you big fur ball. I caught that.* Carson looked around for something to throw. *Who would've thought I'd be fighting for my dinner with a huge grizzly bear? But then, who would've thought I'd ever have to hunt for food?*

The bear grabbed the fish in her mouth and stood on all fours keeping watch on Carson. "No!" Carson screamed, as she jumped up, waving the stick. She found a rock to throw at the bear, who turned and ran into the woods. "That was mine! I caught it."

Carson collapsed on the rocks in tears. *It's so not fair. I spent the whole freaking day catching that, and I don't even get a taste.* She angrily tossed another rock into the water, scaring the fish away again. Then she realized how stupid it was that she just yelled at a grizzly bear that could easily take her out in one swipe.

She got up and dusted off her torn, dirty jeans, then added tinder on the smoldering flame. *At least I'll be warm tonight. Let's just hope that mamma bear doesn't come looking for another tasty morsel. I don't feel like being served a la dead. And where is that stupid helicopter? It should've been here by now.* She looked at the late afternoon sky.

Still angry, Carson kicked over a big stone and then jumped

back when a lot of squiggly bugs ran from under it. She turned over another rock and looked under it. More disgusting bugs scampered away, while a few slugs clung to the rock. Carson swallowed hard. She was starving, but *that* hungry? She remembered another episode of Survivorman when he ate slugs and roasted insects. She'd gagged when he pulled the long bug legs out of his mouth.

She grabbed a juicy brown slug, held it between two fingers, and walked to the water's edge. I can't believe I'm doing this. She plunged her hand into the frigid water and tried to clean the nasty slime ball off. Then she went back to the fire, speared the live glob with a twig and held it over the flame. She turned her head, and scrunched her eyes shut when the poor thing tried to wiggle off the stick. *I'm sorry slug-o, but that big mean bear ate my dinner.*

After a minute, she took the slug off the stick and refused to look at it. Her eyes cast to the sky, she dropped it in her mouth and swallowed. *Gag. Swallow. Ewwww.* It tasted like, no not chicken, but dirt with a wad of snot around it. She raced to the water and gulped as much water as she could swallow.

Burp. *Yuck, it tastes like earth.* Carson wiped her mouth and tried to shake off the grossness of what she'd eaten. She looked to the horizon, where the water cascaded over the edge of a cliff, and wondered if she should take a chance going fiddlehead hunting. But she was afraid of slipping over the edge. Between the bear, the wolves, the frigid cold and blazing sun, Carson knew this wasn't a "lost kid in aisle fourteen" kind of lost, this was "survival-of-the-fittest" lost. Carson thought she felt the slug do a back flip in her stomach.

Why couldn't she be like Snow White, where the happy woodland creatures draped wreaths of flowers around her as she danced and flitted in the forest? The fair maiden cooked and cleaned while the squirrels, birds, and cute little bunny rabbits made her feel at home. And not one of them tried to eat her or steal her food.

But then there were those creepy guys she stayed with. And right now Carson felt pretty grumpy. Where was that helicopter?

The air chilled as the sun began to set. Carson rekindled the blaze and set a few large rocks near the flame. Another Survivorman trick, she'd use them to stay warm tonight. She glanced around warily. *I'm hungry and afraid. If the bear comes back, I'm a goner.* Too late to hike down the mountain, but she knew, in the dark, she'd get little sleep.

Carson heard a hushed swoosh overhead. She ducked and looked upward. A bald eagle soared above, a silhouette in the waning dusk. The sight was striking, and gave her a tingle of awe as she watched the giant bird circle in the purple-tinged sky. In a quick graceful move the eagle plummeted toward earth, talons extended, and plunged into the water. Carson jumped back as the eagle rose into the air—holding a large fish.

Oh, man. Drop it, please, let it go. Carson ran near where the eagle had taken off, trying to distract it. The eagle must have noticed Carson's movements because it turned enough to look at her just as the fish twisted in the bird's grip. *Come on, Baldy, give me a break.*

The eagle spread its wings and headed for the heavens with the fish firmly grasped in its talons. *It's easy for you, birdbrain. You have wings and really sharp claws.* Carson tossed another rock in the water and watched the ripples track then become tranquil. She stared until the dark violet sky reflected stillness in the water. She began to cry as she walked back to her fire.

Carson sat near the fire and felt the air temperature drop. She took her shoes off and warmed her toes, careful not to catch her stinky socks on fire. *These things will probably spontaneously combust, they're so dirty.* Carson wiped away her tears, feeling the sting of sunburn on her cheeks. *I miss Mom. I miss home.* She sniffled and remembered a time when she and her dad went on an Indian Princess Campout. There were cabins, bonfires, blankets, friends, and the security of her father's arms.

Darkness settled deep along the mountain. The chill Carson felt along her spine was both from cold and fear. What if the bear came back? Were there really such things as ghosts? She closed her eyes, smelled the burning campfire, and tried to bring back the memory of her dad. His smile, his goofiness, his hugs. She tried but could barely picture him. She remembered his big brown eyes, always full of laughter. People always said she had her dad's eyes. With her own eyes closed, she recalled the tiny lines on his face: they were connect-the-dot perfect, especially when he smiled.

Carson opened her eyes and looked into the impenetrable

darkness of the forest. She felt a sense of peace. She wasn't afraid any longer, as if her dad were near to protect her. She smiled and wiped her face.

Tomorrow. I'm getting rescued tomorrow.

CHAPTER 44

Shauna ran into the apartment and slammed the door. "What are we gonna do? The police are swarming the place."

Rox ran to the window.

"Get away from there," Bet said. "They'll see you."

"We've got to get out of here." Rox ran from the window and leaned her back against the closed door.

Shauna closed the drapes. "I don't want to go to jail for having you here."

"Well, think about us!" Rox was hysterical.

"Calm down," Bet whispered. "If you're running around acting guilty, they'll pick up on it. Try to relax and act normal."

"Normal? *Normal?* We're getting ready to go to jail, and you want us to act like everything's hunky dory?" Rox jumped up and down.

Bet turned off one of the lights. "Shauna, go out and see why they're here."

"Are you plain dumb? I think we *all* know why they're here." Shauna crossed her arms.

"No, you don't understand." Bet stood. "Go ask *them* questions. They don't want to be bothered by a nosy neighbor and will probably tell you to go home and leave them alone."

"Is this before or after they ask if you're in my living room?"

"Shauna, they might ask if you've seen us." Bet walked to the window and peeked out a crack in the curtains. "But you could find out what they know and deflect any suspicion off you."

"Deflect? Say what? I don't get what you're saying."

"Go ask them where Rox is."

"But I know where she is. What if they ask me?"

Rox said, "I get it! If she asks them a bunch of questions, then they'll think she doesn't know where we are." Rox smiled. "Shanana, this is your chance to try out your acting."

"I kinda sorta see what you're saying. But I don't know if I can pull it off." She wrung her hands together. "What if I crack under pressure?"

Rox ran to her and grabbed her tangled hands. "You're the best actress ever. Pretend you're in a movie. Tell 'em that you're lookin' for me, ask *them* where I am. Get it? That way, they'll think you haven't seen me."

Shauna nodded but had a confused, worried look on her face. "Okay. Let me get dressed." She raced to the bedroom.

The TV droned on in the background. Bet stayed by the window and continued to peek outside. A news anchor on CNN spoke about some new development in the case of the missing Outward Bound hiker in Colorado, followed by "more after these commercials."

Bet waved to Rox. "Turn that off, please. I can't hear what's happening outside."

Rox shut off the TV.

Shauna ran out of the room, fully made up, wearing shorts and red high heels.

"You look great!" Rox said.

Bet closed the curtain. "Don't bring extra attention to yourself. You only need to act curious." She looked Shauna up and down. "It may be counterproductive to play drama queen."

"What? A counter-culture drama queen?" Shauna looked at Rox and rolled her eyes. "You're right, she does talk funny."

Bet crossed her arms. "At least put some tennis shoes or thongs on."

Shauna grinned and smacked her own bottom. "I already got the thong on." She and Rox broke into giggles. "But I'll change shoes." She went to the bedroom and came out wearing flats. "In today's world, ma'am, these are called flip-flops, not thongs."

Carson had told her the same thing to her a few months ago. "I know. I forgot." Sadness took hold again, and Bet was tempted to run screaming into the throng of police outside. *Stop the pain.*

"Okay, you two hide. I'm going in for my 'close-up.' " Shauna headed to the front door. "Ya sure I look okay?" She ran a hand through her two-toned fluorescent hair.

Bet and Rox nodded as they ran to hide in the dark kitchen.

"Do us proud, Shanana," Rox whispered, as Shauna opened the door.

After the door clicked shut, Bet and Rox ran back to the window. A flashlight beam swept the area, and the two of them ducked. From the back patio at the sliding glass door, they heard voices and crouched lower in case they could be seen.

"Looks like someone used this chair to hop this fence," a male voice said as a beam of light shone bright through the drapes.

Rox looked at Bet with panic in her eyes.

Bet thought this might be it. Tonight they'd be caught. She regretted bringing Rox into her crime-ridden spree and felt personally responsible to make sure the girl didn't get hurt in all this mess.

They heard Shauna at the back patio. "Hey, that's mine! I use it to get in when I forget my keys."

"You live here?" a male voice asked.

"Yeah," Shauna said.

"Have you seen these two women?"

He must've shown her a picture, because she answered, "That's Rox! Where's she been? I've been trying to call her."

"So you haven't seen her lately?"

"No. What's going on with her? I saw her on the news. Is she in real trouble?" Shauna fired off questions. "She was my best friend until she quit cosmetology school. Is she going to go to jail?"

"If you see her, will you let us know?" the male voice asked. "And don't leave this chair outside. Someone could use it to get inside."

"Okay."

"Have a nice day."

"Hey, wait. You didn't answer my questions..." Shauna's voice faded as she walked away from the porch.

Ten seconds later, Shauna's questions continued at the front of the building. Bet and Rox crawled from the kitchen and crammed close to the slit in the curtain to watch.

"Miss, I can't talk about the case. Please go inside. We're conducting an investigation here."

"Just like on *CSI*? Cool! What's in that bag that everybody's looking at? Eww, is that blood?"

Bet froze.

"Miss, please. Go inside."

"It's a free country, and I live here. Are those body parts in that bag?"

"What are they looking at?" Rox whispered.

"My shirt," Bet said. "I threw it in the dumpster."

CHAPTER 45

Mark hung up the satellite phone and sat, stunned, on a fallen tree away from the campers. Officer Coffey had told him that there was a reasonable likelihood that Casey Harper and Carson Harper were one and the same.

Mark was afraid to believe it. What were the chances?

When Officer Coffey received videotape footage of the airport's security check-in they'd know for sure.

Mark hoped beyond all hope that it was Carson they were looking for. The guilt of being partly responsible for that piece of debris getting though had been eating him from inside out.

What if?

He went to find Dana. Hopefully, she'd have Carson, or Casey's, application here so they could match the handwriting. Then Mark would talk to Seth. Seth and the other campers could identify the girl as soon as Coffey got the pictures to him.

He couldn't wait.

He couldn't wait for the pictures, or the videotape, or tomorrow morning when they would fly out again to search for the girl. He looked at the star-filled heavens and said a prayer. *Please let it be Carson, and let her be okay.*

But Officer Coffey also had news about Carson's mother.

Bad news.

CHAPTER 46

Z recognized the shirt. Bet Harper had been wearing it while in custody. Considering the blood and shredded fabric, Z figured their next find would be a dead body.

"Bag this and compare the blood to what we found on Bet Harper's purse," Z told the forensic tech who had preserved the crime scene. The shirt was in the dumpster right next to Rox's apartment. Z was angry that Rox's mother said she hadn't seen them. He pulled the warrant from his pocket and strode to Mrs. Mayhill's door, hoping to God he'd find them here, and they were okay.

He pounded on the door. "Mrs. Mayhill, it's Z, I have a warrant." He paused, waiting for her to answer the door. The next building over, he saw one of his officers talking to a young lady with, he took a closer look, orange and blonde hair. *What are kids these days thinking?*

He turned back to the door and knocked again. "Mrs. Mayhill, I'll bust open this door if you don't let me in." Then he yelled at the officer talking to the orange-haired woman. "Go around back and make sure no one escapes out a window."

"Yes, sir." The officer ran behind the building, leaving Shauna still asking questions.

Shauna headed toward Z. "Excuse me, but what's going on here?"

Mrs. Mayhill opened the door. "I told you, you ain't comin' in here." She saw Shauna. "You can come in, Shauna. Look at your hair! Have you talked to Rox?"

Shauna shook her head and cast a quick, and what she hoped

wasn't a guilty, look at Z. "No, ma'am. I was wonderin' if you seen her. I think that's why the police are here."

"Mrs. Mayhill." Z handed her the paper. "This is a search warrant. Either you let me in, or we handcuff you and take you to jail." He smiled. "And we still go in."

Shauna asked, "What was in the bag that you found? It looked like blood."

Z didn't answer.

"What bag? What blood?" Mrs. Mayhill looked concerned. "Is my baby all right?"

Z looked at Shauna. "Do you know Rox?"

Shauna nodded. "Yeah, we went to cosmetology school together."

Z glanced at her hair. "I see. Have you seen her recently?"

Shauna didn't look him in the eye, said, "No."

"What blood are you talkin' about?" Mrs. Mayhill began to sound worried.

"Do you know whose shirt that is?" Z continued to stare at Shauna.

"What shirt?" Shauna's voice cracked.

Rox's mother hit Z on the chest.

"Ouch! What did you do that for?" He clutched his upper body.

"You ain't tellin' me nuthin'. Where's my baby? What'd you do to her?" She looked between Z and Shauna. "Is she okay?"

"I was hoping you could answer that." Z turned his attention to Mrs. Mayhill.

"Come on in, then. Have a look." She held open the door. "I ain't seen her. Shauna, you seen her?" Rox's mother asked. Worry laced her voice.

"If I talk to her, ma'am, I'll tell her to call you," Shauna said.

Z paused before entering the apartment. "And you'll let me know if you hear from her, okay?" His eyes bore into hers.

"Y-y-yes." Shauna ducked out. "Mrs. Mayhill, tell Rox to call me." She ran toward her building.

Z watched her go, his gut telling him that she knew something.

CHAPTER 47

Carson got as close to her homemade fire as possible. It amazed her how cold the air got once the sun went down. She was afraid to go to sleep in case she froze into a human icicle; plus, there were wild animals. Hungry wild animals.

She placed the heated stones around her and leaned against a large boulder that blocked the bitter wind.

Leaves rustled nearby, causing Carson to jump. The fire had died to a mere smolder, and her feet were so cold she could barely wiggle her toes. She must have fallen asleep.

More rustling. There was something out there. Close. Very close. Carson held her breath, as if that would keep whatever was cracking twigs from seeing her. Slowly, she reached for the sharp stick. Yeah, she'd poke her way to victory—especially if it was big mamma bear. The stick, at least, offered a small measure of comfort.

I can't run because I have no feeling in my feet. Crawling would just humiliate me. So I'll stand my ground and hope whatever it is gets a whiff of my stinky socks.

Crack. Rustle. Snap.

Carson exhaled and pushed back into the rock.

And there it was. In the light of a bright moon, a buck with antlers big enough to climb, stepped into view.

Carson smiled, relief filling her insides as she began to breathe again.

The buck stopped, raised its head, and sniffed the air.

"Hi, deer. No reason to be afraid. I'm just a girl lost in the woods."

At her voice, the buck froze, muscles tightened, and looked at Carson. He blew a few snorts, tossed his antlers, turned and trotted into the darkness.

At least I know the bear isn't around. Carson blew on the fire. She rubbed her feet, trying to get feeling back in her tootsies. The fire made an anemic attempt to ignite but needed more fuel. She put her shoes on, pain shot through her cold muscles. The wolf bite on her ankle itched like crazy, but she didn't want to scratch it, or look at it, in case it was getting infected. *I need a bath. But it's so danged cold!*

She stood and tried to stomp out the pins and needles in her joints. Quickly, she threw tinder on the fire and watched a small blaze take hold. In the darkness of the forest, Carson marveled at the beauty of the stars, the quiet solitude, the place inside her that filled with a feeling of pleasure. *Why? I'm cold, hungry, dirty...but there's something about this place that puts me at peace. It kinda gets under the skin. Or maybe it's the chiggers.* She breathed deeply, letting the crisp smell of evergreens and early dawn seep into her senses.

By the time the sun was fully up, Carson decided to take a bath and wash her clothes. She needed to let them dry in the sun before the cold set in again. *Maybe I should forget about laundry and start walking so the helicopter can see me.*

She stripped to her undies and went to a shallow area of the water. Self-conscious, even though there was no one around, she started with her feet. The frigid water shot tingles up her legs, and she gasped for air. She scrubbed the mud off of the bite wound. There were two puncture marks, scabbed over, and a fair amount of swelling and bruising around her anklebone. It was ugly, but it didn't look infected. She washed as best as she could, never having the nerve to fully submerge. The cut on her head hurt, but she was able to clean it.

Carson glanced around nervously then stripped off all her clothes. *Now watch a bunch of boy scouts come hiking over the hill. That would be an interesting badge for their vests.*

As much as she wanted to get rescued, she didn't want to get caught like this!

She rinsed her underwear first, wanting to put them back on even if they were wet. As she dressed in the cold, wet, semi-clean garments, she was surprised how much they'd stretched out from being wet.

Or had they?

The cold forgotten for the moment, Carson slid her hand over her tummy and looked down. *My toes. My frozen, chafed toes—I can see them!*

Why hadn't she noticed the weight loss before? *I guess I've been a little preoccupied with survival.* She laughed and twirled, her wet sopping underwear spraying the rock she danced on.

I did it. I lost weight. This is so cool! She bent and touched her toes, the cuts, bruises, and hunger forgotten for a second.

Okay, now the hair. She pulled at the elastic band that held her long, oily hair in a mass of tangle. She lay stomach-down, no, *flat* stomach-down, on a rock and let her hair tumble into the cold water. *I feel like a shampoo commercial except my hair is one big knot.*

The hot sun on her back contrasted with the freezing water her head was in as she worked the tangles out with her fingers. She scrubbed and finger combed, then let her blonde hair sway in the water. A few fish came close. Carson held still, waiting. One fish took a nibble on her locks then darted away. Another fish swam close, and Carson grabbed it with both hands. It fought and flopped, but Carson held on to its slimy body, squeezing it hard. She scooted back, her cut knees scraping on the rock. But she had it. Food. She rolled and threw the fish on dry ground.

"This one's mine, mamma bear," Carson shouted to no one. She stood and made sure the fish was far enough away from the water so it couldn't flop back in. *Well, if this isn't a pretty picture: an almost nekkid girl fishing with her hair.* She laughed and shook out her dirty jeans and shirt and got dressed without washing them.

She was too hungry to worry about that now.

CHAPTER 48

"You threw your shirt in the dumpster? Are you nuts?" Rox looked like she was going to hit Bet.

"I'm sorry. I'm new at this criminal lifestyle." Bet begged forgiveness with her eyes. "I didn't even think about it."

"It's okay. I probably wouldn't have, either." Rox kept staring out the window and biting her fingernails. "Look, here comes Shauna."

Shauna opened the door calmly, waved to someone, then shut and locked it. She sank to the floor and whined, "He knows. I know Z knows that I know where you are."

"Do you think you could say 'know' one more time?" Rox crawled next to Shauna on her hands and knees. "I was watching you. You did perfect." Rox scooted next to her, and they both leaned against the door."

"I did?" Shauna pouted.

"Yeah. You should get an award." Rox turned to her. "What did he say? Tell me everything. What did my mom say?"

"He told your mom that he was going to break the door down if she didn't open it. She wasn't gonna let him in, but then she looked kinda worried, especially after they found a bloody shirt in the dumpster. Was that y'alls?"

Rox looked hard at Bet. "Yeah, it was Mrs. C's. She didn't think about anybody findin' it when she tossed it in the trash."

"How'd it get all bloody?" Shauna gave Bet a questioning look. "I thought your last name was Harper."

"I call her Mrs. Cleaver. Like the *Leave It to Beaver* mom. And Crank had a knife and ...

Bet interrupted and changed the topic back to Z. "Shauna, what did Rox's mom say about us?"

Shauna shrugged. "Nuthin' really." She looked at Rox. "Is she still taking those pain pills for her back?"

Rox turned away and nodded.

"She sorta acted like it," Shauna went on. "Z said you were in a bunch of trouble." She giggled with excitement and said, "Then that other officer said they were conducting an investigation—just like on TV!" She nodded at the back door. "He also got on me about the chair ya'll left outside."

"Sorry," Rox said. "Did Z act like he knew where we were?"

"Nah, not really. He just wanted to talk to your mom. But then he kept staring at me, so I left."

Bet looked at the cluster of police in the parking lot. "You know, Rox, maybe I should turn myself in. I'll tell them I made you bust me out of jail. I'll pay for a good attorney for your defense."

"No. Just help me get my stuff from Crank. Then we'll be even."

Bet felt a deepening affection for this girl. Losing Carson, Bet wanted no more ties to this world, but she wasn't going to leave this child alone and with nothing. Bet sighed. Even though she wanted to jump off of a bridge and end her pain, she said, "I won't go until you're taken care of."

"Where ya gonna go, anyway?"

Bet waved her hand and ignored the question.

"Hey, I gotta idea!" Shauna brightened. "Ya'll need a disguise. Lemme do your hair."

"Perfect!" Rox jumped up. "Can you do mine like yours?"

Shauna ran her hand through her colorful spikes. "I don't think so, since your hair's so black. The yellow might turn it green." Shauna stood and checked Rox's head. I'll bet I could getcha more red and maybe even a cool purple."

"Would ya do it?" Rox seemed excited. "I wish I'd finished color before I quit school."

"Me, too. You'd be so good at it," Shauna squealed.

"I don't know." Bet smiled. "I'm not sure I'd look good in any color. Especially one from the primary palette."

"The what?" Shauna scrunched her face. "Come on, you look like you haven't had anything done to your hair for a real, *real* long time. Whaddya got to lose?"

"My dignity?" Bet pulled her shoulder-length, graying hair back.

"Your dignity can grow back," Shauna said.

This wasn't the curl-up-and-die job Bet was going for, but oh well.

"C'mon, Mrs. C, it'll be fun. Me first."

By the time it was done, and all of Shauna's damp smelly towels had been used on their heads, Bet and Rox had been transformed.

Especially Bet.

"I look like the Bride of Frankenstein with a crew cut." Bet tried to look at the back of her head in the bathroom mirror with a hand-held one. Her hair was spiky short, except a few long locks in front that dangled in her face. Shauna had bleached the long hair white-blonde and scorched the back a dark, dark brown. Now Bet was almost as two toned as Shauna.

"You don't like it?" Shauna looked pouty again.

"It's not that." Bet smiled at her. "I just need to get used to it. You did a good job."

"I love mine." Rox fingered her short-cropped hair. A large half-moon slash of red at each temple accented the purple-tipped black-dyed hair.

Bet thought she looked like an Oompa Loompa from Charlie's chocolate factory.

Throughout the coloring, Bet and Rox kept watch on the police. Crime scene tape went up around what they could see of the dumpster. Then, one by one, each police car left the parking lot. They couldn't be sure if a lookout had been posted nearby.

"I wonder if we should try to sneak out the back," Bet said, peeking through the curtains.

"I'm too tired and hungry." Rox stretched and rubbed her hair. She turned to Shauna. "When's your mom coming home?"

Shauna shrugged. "Not tonight. She's out with her boyfriend, and she thinks I'm stayin' with Cat."

"Can we stay for a little shut-eye?"

"Yeah, 'cause I can't sleep here alone. I'm too scared."

Bet was so tired, she didn't want to argue, or worse, sleep outside. "Maybe we can sleep for a few hours and leave in the morning."

"Good idea," Rox said. "Ya got any food?"

While Shauna and Rox went into the kitchen, Bet sat on the couch. She was almost asleep when the girls came back in with a huge plate of pasta.

"Here Mrs. C. We put extra butter on it." Rox handed Bet a plate.

Bet took a small bite and then dug in. It was delicious. Butter and Parmesan cheese dripped down her chin. "This is wonderful. Thank you."

Shanua sat cross-legged on the floor. "We're having a slumber party!"

With a mouth full of pasta, Bet asked, "Do you need to check in with your mother?"

Shauna shook her head and wiped her mouth with her hand. "Nah, she won't call until the morning. We're cool."

After they finished, Bet rinsed off the plates in the messy kitchen. *How do they live like this? What mother leaves her child alone and doesn't check on her?* She stacked the clean plates on the counter and went back to the living room.

Shauna stood. "Rox Star and I are sleeping in my room. You can sleep here." She didn't offer a pillow or blanket, but Bet was so tired she could've slept standing up.

"We'll get up and out early. Thank you for taking care of us and for"—Bet touched her long bleached bangs—"doing our hair."

"Anytime." Shauna smiled. "You both look pretty hot."

Bet curled up on the couch and didn't wake up until the sun was fully up and shining through the crack in the curtains.

CHAPTER 49

"I'm not sure we're going up today. There's a storm coming in." The helicopter pilot blew on a steaming cup of coffee as he stood at the small helipad.

"We have to." Mark was already suited up and ready.

"We can't risk four people for one girl who might not even be alive." The pilot patted Mark's arm.

Mark looked up at the crystal blue sky. "What storm? It's perfect out."

The other man pointed to the mountain range, where a band of black clouds pushed against the peaks. "It's heading directly toward us."

"Can we at least fly until it comes in?" Mark pleaded. "There's a girl out there that needs to be rescued."

The pilot shook his head. "If she's still alive, she can take cover on the ground. I'm sorry."

Mark's phone shrilled. He looked at caller ID: Officer Coffey. "Yes, sir," Mark answered.

"Have you found her?"

"No, sir." Mark eyed the pilot. "Apparently, there's a storm nearby, and the pilot doesn't want to risk taking the helicopter up. Do you think, sir, you have the authority to dispatch another pilot?" Mark tried not to smile.

"Where's the pilot now?" Coffey's voice held the familiar anger Mark knew well.

"Right here, sir."

"Put him on!" Coffey barked.

Mark handed the phone to the pilot, who gave him a dirty look.

All Mark could hear was muffled yelling. The pilot turned his back to Mark, but Mark still noticed the top of the pilot's ears turn an interesting shade of crimson.

"Yes, sir. I'll get the crew." The pilot snapped the phone shut and gave it to Mark, then shook a finger at him. "If anything happens to my crew, I'm holding you personally responsible. Got it?"

Mark nodded. "Thank you, sir."

CHAPTER 50

Carson was thrilled to have caught a fish. She was so hungry, it was a struggle not to rip into it with her teeth while it still flopped and gasped for air.

"I'm sorry, fishy, really I am." She thought of the wolves almost tearing her to shreds. How was it any different for the poor fish?

She took the fish downstream, near the cliff, and laid it on a flat rock. That way, the scent and the guts would run over the edge after she cleaned it. Carson didn't want to entice mamma bear again.

Picking up a large stone, she raised it above her head. Carson hesitated and lowered her hand. She said a prayer, asking forgiveness for taking a life. She squeezed her eyes shut as tears threatened. *I need to be a vegan.*

It took her a few more minutes to gather the courage to raise the stone again. She was hungry and needed food, but it was so hard to kill something. Before she had the nerve to bring down the rock, she looked at her mark and noticed the fish had stopped gasping. It was dead. "Thank you," she whispered.

She'd only been fishing once in her life with her dad when she was four or five. He'd shown her how to scale and gut a fish, but she'd been too busy playing with the live bait and hardly paid attention. Now she cleaned and sliced the fish as best as she could, using her sharpened stick and a couple of sharp edged rocks.

Carson found a flat stone, laid the fish out and put it on the fire. By now, hunger had overtaken her guilt and she couldn't wait to dig in. But it was a different kind of hunger than she was used to, she realized. This food was to fill her belly, not to fill aches or needs or just boredom. The fire crackled, and the mossy stuff she'd rekindled the flames with was smoky and smelled like burnt sugar. While the fish cooked, she kept a close watch for the bears and on a big black cloud along the horizon.

I need to get moving. It was almost noon, and she didn't want to spend another night freezing on a mountaintop. She needed that helicopter to fly back, especially if those clouds turned into a storm. *Besides, I just washed my hair and I don't want to get it all dirty again.*

She flipped the fish over and waited a few more minutes before taking it off the fire. The wind caught her hair, and she enjoyed the free feeling of not having a ponytail. When was the last time she'd worn it loose? Second grade, maybe?

The fish was the best meal she had ever eaten. Was it the mountain air, the ambiance of nature, or maybe because it was the first meal she'd had in days? Probably all of the above.

She cleaned up the remains of the fish bones, taking it back to the edge of the cliff, and let the waterfall wash it over. She brushed her teeth and wrapped her jacket around her waist. The fire had gone to a smolder. She hesitated before putting it out completely. *I have to get going.*

She stopped at the water for a last long drink. Before she headed out, she took another look around. Maybe she'd try to come back here and camp with the right equipment and, she smiled, maybe even Seth.

Carson grabbed her stick and started walking, not sure which was the best way to go. She regretted not paying better attention to Dana when the instructor talked about directions and using a compass. While the group had hiked, Carson's only real point of reference had been the back of Seth's head.

She didn't want to go down the rocky side she'd climbed from and risk falling into the canyon, so she turned and headed into the forest. As she walked, she tried to count how many days had gone by since she'd left home. She'd left on a Friday and stayed with the group in an indoor facility the first two nights. Then, Sunday through Thursday, they'd hiked and trained together. How many nights had she been on her own? She counted with her fingers. Had it really been two weeks?

Her mother must be worried sick.

CHAPTER 51

Bet jumped off the couch and looked at a clock. It was already nine-thirty. What if Shauna's mother came in and found them there?

Her long, bleached bangs fell in her eyes, and her shaved neck felt exposed. She ran her fingers through her short cut, remembering salon night with the color-blind kid. *What have I done?* She headed to the bedroom to get the girls up, but stopped before waking Rox. *Maybe this is when I should escape. Leave the girl be. I've caused her nothing but trouble.*

She quietly stepped into the bathroom and cleaned up. Shauna's notebook on how to color sat opened and stained. She opened it, tore out a blank page, and began writing. She stuffed the paper in her pocket. After washing, Bet tiptoed down the hall and gathered her things. Before she ventured outside, she went to the window to check for police.

Good, the coast was clear.

The phone rang—no screamed. Shauna's phone had a bizarre ring-tone that laughed until it shrieked. So annoying.

She heard Shauna answer the phone, and Rox appeared in the living room all sleepy-eyed.

"Hey, Mrs. C." She stretched and scratched her tummy.

Bet noticed a long piece of jewelry pierced through her belly button. "Doesn't that hurt?"

Rox looked down. "Nah, it only hurt when they stuck it in." She patted her stomach. "I'm starving hungry."

"That's redundant," Bet said. All hope of escape gone.

Rox looked at her quizzically and looked at her belly again.

"No, it's a pendent not a...whatever you said."

Shauna ran into the room. "That was your mom, Rox Star. She wants me to come over."

"Why?"

"I don't know. She said that she's worried, and that Z cop really scared her last night"

"Then why does she need to see you?" Bet asked, concerned. "Maybe she suspects something."

"She also asked me to bring her some of my mom's beer." Shauna went to the fridge and opened the door. She looked at Rox. "She said her back's hurting her again."

Bet noticed that Rox turned her head away, but didn't say anything. Bet also noticed that there was little else in the refrigerator but beer.

"Shauna, thank you for letting us stay here. When is your mother coming back?" Bet didn't want to hang out much longer.

"She's with her jerk of a boyfriend, so I probably won't see her until tomorrow."

"You stay here alone?" Bet asked.

Shauna shrugged. "Usually I invite a friend over. But I'm almost eighteen." She pulled out two long necks from the fridge. "I'll be right back. Then I got to get to school."

Rox stopped her. "Don't freak, okay? Keep acting like you're an actress in a movie or something." She stepped aside to let Shauna pass. "Make sure she drinks one of those before you start talking."

Shauna nodded and ran outside, still in her pajamas.

She had been gone for about thirty minutes, and Bet was beside herself. "We've got to get out of here, Rox. Maybe Shauna broke down and told your mom everything. The police are probably on the way now."

"No, she didn't. If my mom's drunk enough, she won't even care." Rox took a dripping bite of cereal. "This is good stuff, Lucky Charms, my favorite. Hey, how much money do we have?"

"Not much; maybe fifteen dollars."

"Where did all the cash go? Wal-Mart and Mickey-D's are not that expensive."

Bet smiled and pointed to her skull shirt. "This must have cost a fortune. And I can't cash a check or use an ATM now, thanks to the police looking for me and Crank for taking all my identification," Bet said, nervously pacing.

"We're gonna get Crank. You promised you'd help, right?"

Bet stopped and nodded. "Yes. I'll help you. Then I want you to go to the police."

"Are you nuts?" Rox set her empty bowl on the cluttered coffee table. "I don't want to go to jail."

"You're young. Use the time to get an education."

"You're off your rocker, Mrs. C. What would I study; how to shower in prison?"

Bet handed her the folded piece of paper that had been torn from Shauna's spiral notebook. "I wrote this for Officer Z. It explains that I made you do what you did."

"And where do you think you're going? What about Crank?"

"I will help you get Crank. He has more than my money and ID. He has my last picture of Carson. I hate to think he's even looked at it. Then, I have to go and take care of something."

"What?" Rox eyed her.

Just then the door burst open and Shauna ran in. "I'm late. I have to go to school!"

"On Saturday?" Bet asked.

"Yeah. It's our busiest day. We have real customers, and we get graded."

"What'd my mom say?" Rox followed her to her room.

"She kept asking me if I thought you were all right and if I thought you were with Crank." Shauna turned to Bet. "She also said that Z talked to some space guy about your daughter."

Bet gasped. "Carson?"

Shauna nodded. "They think they've found her."

"Oh, God!" Bet collapsed on the couch crying. "No!" She held her head in her hands sobbing.

"But I thought..." Shauna started.

Bet lifted her wet, tear-stained face. "What did they find? Was she whole"—another rack of wailing sobs—"or did they just find pieces? I don't want to identify a *part*."

"Oh... I guess I didn't understand." Shauna backed away.

Rox sat next to Bet and put an arm around her shoulders. "Sorry, man. That's rough."

Bet shook her head, crying. "At least... if they hadn't yet found her...there was a small ray of hope. You know? Like maybe she was still alive."

"Yeah, but..." Rox tripped on her words. "This is hurtin' me inside, too, Mrs. C."

Bed nodded and sat straighter, took a deep shaky breath. "Now I *must* finish what I need to do." She stood and wiped her face with a dirty towel that was on the floor. "Let's deal with Crank. Then promise you'll talk to Z."

"Yes to the Crank part. Not sure about Z."

Shauna said, "You guys can use my car, but you have to drop me off at school first."

Bet nodded, still crying, said, "Come on, let's go kick some Crank butt."

CHAPTER 52

It didn't take long for the crew to suit up and pile into the helicopter. Mark tried to ignore the others shooting dirty looks at him. His priority was rescuing Carson Harper.

He had to make amends, find the girl and help her deal with the news of her mother possibly being a murder victim. What a terrible twist of fate. Mark swallowed as the craft began to ascend.

As the helicopter took off, a gust of wind caused it to sway as they climbed. Mark's stomach did a flip, and Rick, one of the rescue workers gave him a snide smile. "I hope you barf your guts out for making us fly today."

Mark gave a wan smile and scooted closer to the window. He was surprised how quickly the storm had moved in. And the pilot was right, they were heading straight into it.

CHAPTER 53

Carson jogged through the dense trees. A fawn and her mother startled Carson as much as she scared them. She laughed and loved the lightness of running. Strength she never knew she owned pumped through her. She wanted to get into an open area in case her rescue helicopter came back. *I am not going to miss them again.* The wind picked up and the sky quickly darkened. It almost seemed like twilight.

She enjoyed being able to run, and loved that she had to hold her pants up because they were so loose on her. Her injuries still hurt, but she felt stronger, like she could tolerate the pain while moving, and for the first time in as long as she could remember, her body worked in sync. The extra baggage was gone.

Grasping her oversized jeans, she smiled. *Mom probably won't even recognize me.* Her hair flowed in the strong wind. The scent of rain blended with the pines. She pictured herself running in slow motion, like in a commercial. *And Seth. Maybe Seth will ask me out. Like a real date! Not a date I have to make up and daydream about.*

A sharp burst of thunder cracked in the sky. Carson shrieked and ducked instinctively. The lightning strike still haunted her. She didn't count the seconds, but lightning lashed the sky seconds later. The forest lit up with an eerie movie strobe effect. *All these trees. What if lightning strikes again? What if I take a direct hit this time?* Fear clutched her insides and she ran faster, not sure what to do or where to go.

She'd lost track of the stream and wanted to find it in case she needed to jump in the water if another fire started. She could tell she was at least descending the mountain. *I need shelter. I can't go through another fire.* The trees were too thick to see through, and she wanted to find the horizon line to check the storm.

Wait. Did she hear a helicopter? Or was it the wind?

A gust of wind almost knocked her over. The treetops swayed violently. She looked up at the blackened sky. The clouds churned and changed, but stayed a dark purple. Thunder rolled above her. She heard the sound again.

It *was* a helicopter. She was sure.

Carson sprinted back to where she'd come from. *Run, Carson, run.* She thought of *Forrest Gump*. Rain hammered down. She couldn't see the through the wall of water and hoped she was still on course.

Between the downpour, thunder, and wind, she couldn't tell which direction the helicopter was coming from. *Please, please don't fly away.* She pounded up the mountain, agile and strong, but blinded by the driving storm. The next boom of thunder sounded like she was smack in the middle of it. She broke through the clearing and turned 360 degrees looking to the swirling skies.

No helicopter.

I heard it; I know I heard it. It was hard to see more than thirty feet ahead because of the storm. *How will they ever see me?*

Just as a fresh rush of tears mixed with the rain on her wet cheeks, the helicopter roared close over her head. The rotors slashed through the rain, and the carriage swayed side to side. She screamed and waved her arms. "I'm here! Help! Come back!" She chased it to the edge of the cliff, but it kept going and going and going. It flew until it disappeared into the clouds.

"Noooooo!" She screamed so loud she could hear her voice over the thunder. How could they have missed me? She sank to the ground, crying and muddy.

Another burst of lightning and a clash of thunder. Carson didn't even flinch. *Not again,* she thought. Despair seeped into her with the rain, and hope puddled to anguish.

A minute later, she saw the helicopter coming back toward her. Directly to her. She jumped and waved her arms. "They see me! They're coming!" She danced and shouted. The copter flashed a light at her. She waved.

Carson hoped there was enough room to land, especially in

this storm. She backed toward the trees to give the craft space. Still more than fifty yards away, Carson could almost feel the power of the rotors. Yes. Today is the day!

As it flew over the canyon, a gust of wind caught the copter's blades, making the whole craft spiral around in a circle. It struggled gallantly to right itself properly but continued to buck like a rodeo bull in the driving rain.

Steady. Don't lose it. Fly away from the canyon. Carson bit her lip till it bled.

The helicopter twisted, turned, and spiraled like a corkscrew, until it fell behind her view, behind the mountain, and into the crack of the chasm.

Then she heard the crash.

CHAPTER 54

After they dropped Shauna off, Rox drove to a gas station. "We don't have enough gas for a fart."

Bet stayed in the back seat after Shauna got out, fighting the crushing sadness of the news of finding Carson. She pushed a pile of fast food bags and soda cans out of her way with her feet and moved a baseball bat to give her some legroom. *Shauna either plays ball or hits a lot of people.* She leaned toward the front seat. "I have five dollars left; we can use that."

"What happened to the fifteen? Are you holding out on me?" Rox pulled in to a mom and pop convenience store and parked at the gas pumps.

"Shauna needed some money." Bet fingered her hair. "For the hair color she used."

"She's gonna make tips today. We need it more." Rox shoved the clanky car door opened and grabbed the gas nozzle. "Five bucks ain't gonna get us any place in this gas guzzler."

Bet scooted the seat forward and climbed through the trash out of the two-door Camaro. "I'll go inside and pay."

"Do you have any change at all to get me a candy bar or something?"

Bet checked her pockets. "Thirty-six cents." Her empty stomach grumbled. Lucky Charms hadn't sounded too good this morning. All she'd wanted was to end the agony. But first, she needed to make sure Rox was taken care of. She had an idea and turned back to the car, eyed the baseball bat, but grabbed a velour jacket that lay wadded up in the backseat. "Put five in and wait for me with the engine running." Bet slipped the jacket on and strode into the store, pocketing the pen she'd written Rox's note with.

"All right, but hurry. I don't want to burn any more gas than we have to," Rox called.

Bet entered the store and nodded to the man behind the counter, who was working a crossword puzzle. She went to the back and got a V8 for herself and a soda for Rox. She grabbed a big bag of chips and a few packages of nuts and walked to the front. She was shaking so hard she could barely walk to the counter.

"Will that be all?" The cashier set his crossword puzzle to the side and peered at Bet over his reading glasses.

"And the gas." Bet took the money from her jeans pocket. She waited until he rang it up and bagged the groceries, then put her hand in the jacket and pointed the pocketed pen at him. "And give me your money."

"What?" The man looked quizzically at her, then his eyes got wide when he realized he was being held up. "You're kidding, right?"

"No." Bet trembled so hard she feared she'd wet her pants. "And put your hands up." She was getting the hang of this.

The man slowly put his hands over his head. "Lady, how do you expect me to get the money with my hands up here?" He had a light Mediterranean accent.

"Oh, yeah. Then okay, use them to open the register. Please." Bet pointed to the register with the hidden pen, which the cashier eyed suspiciously.

He opened the cash drawer and took out some bills.

"I only need about forty or sixty dollars. Please." Bet couldn't look him in the eye but kept the pen pointed at him.

He put two twenties on the counter then held his hands up again.

"Thank you." Bet grabbed the money with her left hand and shoved it in her pocket. She took the bag of groceries and backed up, still pointing the pen. "I'll pay you back. I'm sorry, sir. Really." Tears threatened. She turned to go out the door.

"Hey, lady."

"Yes?" Bet turned to see that the man had a pistol pointed at her. After the initial shock of having a gun leveled at her chest, Bet felt calm inside. *Today is the day. I'm sorry, Rox.* She faced the cashier, slowly extended both arms out, and closed her eyes. The plastic grocery bag dangled in one hand, and she still grasped the pen in the other.

Rox honked the horn outside, and Bet opened her eyes. The man still held the gun but looked at her like she was crazy.

"Are you looking to get yourself killed?" he asked.

Bet dropped her arms. "Yes. Just do it." She closed her eyes again and held out her arms.

"Why?"

Rox honked again.

"I've lost everything." She started crying. "Please, put me out of my misery."

"So, that's your gun?" The cashier nodded at Bet's hand. "A pen?"

Bet nodded.

He shook his head and put his gun away. Then he reached in the cash drawer and pulled out another twenty. "Here." He held out the money. "Looks like you need this more than I do."

"I *will* pay you back." Bet went to the counter and took the cash. "You are kind."

"And be careful with that pen." He raised a bushy eyebrow. "You could get hurt."

Bet nodded and couldn't resist saying, "So the pen *is* mightier than the sword?" She smiled through her tears.

"Don't push it, lady, I could still shoot you." He smiled at her and closed the register. "Get your head screwed on straight. Life is a good thing."

"It was, and I didn't even know how good. Thank you again." She rushed out the door, almost knocking over a newspaper kiosk. She didn't look back, just ran to the car, missing the front-page headline: *Girl From Space Accident Likely Found Alive. Mother Feared Dead.*

Rox stood with her hands on her hips by the pumps. "What were you doing? Sweeping the floor for food?"

"Something like that." Bet opened the car door and got in. She saw the cashier watching out the window and toasted him with her V8.

CHAPTER 55

The helicopter spun wildly. Mark's stomach couldn't sync up with his equilibrium. The world turned upside down. He closed his eyes and put his head between his legs.

Through the headphones, he heard the pilot screaming, "Mayday, Mayday, we're going down! I repeat, we're going down!"

Mark wondered how the pilot could even form a sentence. All this was his fault. He saw the girl on the mountain. They had all seen her. It wasn't a dream. They'd been so close to rescuing her. Now the crew was going to die and he was responsible. Everything had been his fault.

Suddenly, the engines stilled. Mark heard the pilot again.

"Engines shut down. Fuel dump. Mayday!"

Mark heard a crack of thunder then heard another sickening crack as the helicopter hit the rocks.

For a blessed split second, the spinning stopped. He sat up just as the copter began rolling down the side of the mountain.

Chapter 56

Carson's hopes fell with the helicopter. She stood in the lashing storm and wailed. She cursed the thunder and lightning and shook her fist at the heavens. "You want me that bad? Just take me!" She sank to her knees in the mud and waited for a bolt of lightening to take her out.

The sky churned and changed as the storm moved through. A line of bright white clouds now bisected the mountain range, making the purple clouds above them even more brilliant. The torrent had decreased and was now a steady shower. She could see the heavy thunderheads beyond her now, still angrily shooting bolts of lightning. She walked as close to the edge of the slippery cliff as she dared and peeked over. All she saw was that she was above the clouds.

She needed to get down there.

She'd get down there if she had to take a swan dive off the stupid mountain. They came to rescue her. Now, maybe Carson needed to rescue them.

CHAPTER 57

"What do you mean the helicopter crashed?" Officer Z paced in front of his commanding officer's desk. "Why would they go up in bad weather?"

"Apparently that Coffey guy gave the order." He shook his head. "Those guys in the space program think they can fly though anything."

"Did they find the girl?"

"No. But the last transmission before the emergency alert was they may have seen her."

"So she's okay?" Z asked, hopefully.

His boss shrugged. "If it was her, maybe." He leveled his gaze at Z. "Have you found that juvenile delinquent yet?"

"Rox? No, not yet, but we did find Bet Harper's bloody shirt." He stopped pacing and rubbed his chin. "I just can't believe that Rox would hurt anybody."

The officer clicked his computer keyboard and the video of Rox and Bet escaping from jail came on the screen. "So why is she forcing the woman out by her shirt sleeve and threatening her?" The video showed Rox with Bet's purse over her shoulder wagging a finger at Bet while Bet nodded and wiped away tears.

"Sure Rox has some problems, but she's always had a good heart."

"Yeah, I can see that. She kidnapped a prisoner and probably killed her. I'm sure Santa will stuff her stocking with lots of good toys this year."

"That's not like Rox." Z ran a hand over his bald head. "We need to get our hands on Crank. I'll bet he's the one with the answers." Z started pacing again. "Rox always knew how to find him so we could keep an eye on him. Now, we don't even have a blip on his whereabouts." Z's walkie-talkie cackled from his belt.

"Find him. Find her."

"We're trying sir. We're trying." Z excused himself and walked out.

He'd just sat at his desk when one of the rookie officers ran in.

"Sir, we just got a call about a burglary at Theo's convenience store. Seems two women took sixty dollars and some food."

"Sixty whole dollars?" Z smiled sardonically and leaned back in his chair. "Call the FBI," he joked. Then he became serious. "Don't bother me with stuff like this."

"No. I mean, sir, except for the hair, the girl in the getaway car fit the description of Rox Mayhill, and"—he paused and squirmed a little—"and the woman who held up the store looked like Bet Harper."

Chapter 58

Carson walked along the edge of the cliff searching for a way down. The small mountain stream where she'd caught the fish had turned into raging rapids, spilling violently over the side of the mountain, making the bowl of the canyon look more like a toilet. The rocks were slippery, and she couldn't see past a line of clouds below her. She wanted to get to the helicopter, but feared what she'd find.

I don't want to see a bunch of broken dead bodies. But what if they survived? She hadn't seen a burst of flame where the copter went down. But the awful metal clanking seemed to go on for a long time. Too long for much hope.

Water cascaded over the ledge she'd crawled up, so she couldn't get down that way. She picked a place beyond, though it looked wet and steep. She turned and lay on her belly. Facedown, she scooched her body over the cliff, kicking her legs out, and tried to find a solid step. The mud under her caused her to slide farther then she was ready for, and she found herself hanging off the cliff, dangling over a narrow ledge. With a leap of faith, she swung forward and let go, landing on the rocks. For a terrifying second, she lost her balance and almost fell backward over the cliff. She recovered enough to step forward, and paused to take a deep breath. *That was close. Too close.* Now she was stuck. With the mud and slippery rocks above her, she wouldn't be able to climb back up, so she decided to keep going down.

At least her body was stronger. She could feel the difference in how she moved. *If only I can keep my jeans on.* She tugged on the waist of her pants and buttoned her jacket so it wouldn't get hung on anything.

With agonizing slowness, she inched one step at a time, hugging each wet rock, and worked her way down. Mud caked her face and eyes. She wasn't sure if her head gash had reopened or the wet was from rain and dirt. Clouds engulfed her like a death shroud and blinded her view. *Not seeing anything may be a good thing: if I could see what I'm doing I'd probably be paralyzed with fear.*

Step by step. Slip, grab, pray. Breathe.

Hours passed. Her fingers were scraped raw, and her knees ached from constantly hitting them on the sharp rocks. She was exhausted, but afraid to rest, so she kept moving. A gust of wind that blew from the bottom of the mountain carried a strong scent of gas and oil. *I'm closer; I'm getting there.*

A few steps more and another blast of wind swirled the clouds enough that Carson could see below her. Less than a football field away, down a sheer cliff and inside the bowl of the canyon lay the smoldering wreckage of the helicopter.

CHAPTER 59

"You what? You robbed that store?" Rox grasped the steering wheel and sped away.

Bet ripped open the bag of nuts and stuffed a handful in her mouth. With her mouth full, she said, "Yeah, can you believe it? Don't go too fast, we don't want to get pulled over." She offered the bag to Rox.

"This adventure is starting to scare me." Rox glanced at Bet. "*You're* starting to scare me."

Bet sat back and took a sip of V8. "I never thought I'd be so desperate that I'd steal. Or worse, threaten someone for food and money."

"You threatened him?"

"With this." Bet held the pen up.

"Was he afraid you were going to write all over him?"

Actually, I do need to write down the name of the store. I promised I'd pay him back." Bet put the V8 between her knees as she wrote, since the old car didn't have cup holders.

"That makes no sense. So you didn't steal it, you borrowed it." Rox took the soda. "But by using excessive force—ink."

Bet uncapped her drink again. "Rox, in case something happens to me, I want you to please make sure he gets the sixty dollars back."

"What's going to happen to you that's not going to happen to me?"

Bet shrugged. "Do you know where Crank is?"

Rox nodded, and changed lanes. "I know where his hideouts are." She glanced at Bet. "But can we eat? I'm starving again."

Bet closed her eyes and thought of Carson. "Sure. Too bad I can't cook you a nice meal."

Rox laughed. "Really? Man, I can't even remember the last meal my mom made for me."

Bet stuffed another handful of nuts in her mouth. "I'm sorry. That's so sad."

"No biggie."

But it was. Bet took another piece of paper and wrote. "I am of sound mind and body..." She scrawled a revised will, sloppy because of Rox's driving. "What is it that Crank has of yours?"

"Nothing important. Well, except to me." Rox zoomed through a yellow light.

"It must be something special."

"Look, there's a McDonalds. Can we go?" Rox pointed, ignoring Bet's remark.

"Yes, but drive thru. Then we find Crank." Bet folded her hastily written last will and testament and put it in her pocket. She wanted to protect Rox financially. The poor girl needed guidance. She was smart, energetic and a good person. For all the trouble Bet had caused, it was the least she could do.

"I'll call Shauna and see what time she's going to get off. We may not have much time before we have to pick her up."

Bet tapped the pocket with the will folded inside. "Yes. Today is the day I want to finish this."

CHAPTER 60

Mark heard groaning. He lay on his side, still buckled in. The seatbelt had kept him from falling out of his chair. He couldn't turn his head because the crushed side of the helicopter left little room to move. Plus every muscle in his body hurt.

"Is everybody okay?" His voice was hoarse from the seatbelt choking his neck.

"No, Einstein, our helicopter...crashed. What do... you think?"

Mark recognized the pilot's voice, which sounded weak.

There'd been four in the helicopter including Mark. "Can you see the co-pilot? How is he?"

"We're both...alive. How's Rick?" the pilot gasped around the words.

Mark did an extremity check, wiggling his fingers and toes to make sure he wasn't paralyzed. "I can't see him. I'm all twisted in my seat. Give me a sec..." He grunted and reached for the buckle, surprised to see his right hand was a bloody mess. The window next to him had shattered and left tiny diamonds of glass all over him.

The groaning sounded again, right next to him.

"I hear him. He's alive, but I can't see him." Mark shifted in his seat and could see a compound fracture piercing Rick's lower leg. The tibia bone ripped out straight from his lower leg and his ankle was in an unnatural position.

Painstakingly, Mark unfastened the seatbelt and almost fell flat on the injured man. "His leg's broken."

"I think we've got a few fractured ribs up here." The pilot wheezed. "Can you open the door?"

"Yes." Somehow, Mark was going to get these men to safety. Lowering himself, he carefully checked the man's vitals. Weak but conscious, Rick winced and looked Mark in the eye. "You were right, dude. I saw her."

"I'm sorry. We shouldn't have gone up."

Rick put a shaky hand over his face. "I know. And I'll beat you up for that later. Just get me out of here first."

"I will." Mark crouched and crawled to the shattered door.

"And get the girl."

"We will. Close your eyes so you don't get any glass in them." With all the strength he had, Mark turned the twisted lever with his bloodied hand and threw his weight into the broken door until it opened.

CHAPTER 61

"What did she look like?" Z asked the store owner, Theo.

"She had this funny haircut. All short and dark except for long blonde bangs." Theo sat behind the store counter. His wife stood next to him.

"Is this her?" Z held out Bet's mug shot.

Theo shrugged. "Could be."

His wife grabbed the photo. "I didn't see her, but this lady has black and gray hair."

"She may have dyed it."

Theo took the picture again. "What happened to her face, it's all scraped up."

Z nodded. "She fell when the officer arrested her."

"You didn't do no police brutality to her?" Theo asked. "If this is her, she was a nice lady." He looked at the picture again. "Just down on her luck."

"That's why we need to find her. Her luck may be changing."

Theo looked at Z skeptically. "I don't like to see her all hurt like this." He held up the picture.

His wife smacked his arm. "What, now you're falling in love with a criminal?"

"She's going to pay me back."

"And you wonder why we work so hard when we should be retired?" His wife threw up her arms, exasperated. "Here, give all the people money. Go ahead. Maybe this nice policeman needs cash. Don't worry about me and my dream to go home to Greece." She stormed off, still muttering. "I'll go, but I'm not taking you. Maybe I'll find a nice criminal to take me."

She retreated into the back.

Theo handed the mug shot to Z. "If it's her, call me when you find her. She may need bail money."

"I heard that," his wife screamed.

"Don't hurt her again," Theo whispered.

"We're trying to help her," Z pleaded. "Wait." Z turned and grabbed a newspaper and slapped it on the counter. "We thought Bet Harper was dead. If she's alive she needs to know we may have found her daughter."

CHAPTER 62

Carson sat, stuck on a ledge that jutted from the side of the deep canyon. Every few minutes, the clouds would clear just enough for her to see the crash. The helicopter had landed at the bottom of the gulch. Walls of rock surrounded the craft, its blades broken and crooked like arthritic fingers. During brief glimpses, she hadn't seen any sign of life in the wreckage.

She'd climbed herself into a corner. The only way down now was a steep drop. The heavy clouds above her were too thick to see through to find another route.

Cold and shivering, Carson had no shelter. The rain would stop for a few minutes then start again. At least the lightning and strong wind had abated. She lay on her stomach and crawled to the edge. If there were survivors, how would they climb out of the canyon? "Hello! Is anybody there?" Carson yelled into the clouds.

Silence.

"Are you okay? Is anybody alive?" She kept talking to keep herself company.

At least the helicopter hadn't blown up into a fiery ball. Carson scooted away from the edge and wiped her muddy face with her muddier hands. *This is all my fault.* She started crying. *How can I live knowing people died looking for me? It's not fair.*

"I'm sorry!" she screamed to no one.

She heard a crunch of metal and a voice from below. "Carson, is that you?"

CHAPTER 63

Bet and Rox sat in McDonald's parking lot munching on hamburgers.

"I wanted a sausage and biscuit," Rox said as she sunk her teeth into a Big Mac.

Bet took a handful of French fries and stuffed them in her mouth. "We should call Shauna."

"I know, but there're no pay phones." Rox smeared her fries with ketchup. "I gotta place we can go to call. Crank might even be there."

"Where?"

"A friend of Crank's is a body artist." Rox smiled. "It's not far. But it's still kinda early for him to be up."

"Body artist?" Bet tried to envision a friend of Crank's that was creative.

"You know, tattoos."

"Oh," Bet said. She finished eating and put her trash in a bag. "Rox, do you want to call your mother to let her know you're all right?"

"No." Rox stared straight ahead. "She won't care."

"I'm sure she's worried." Bet pulled her long, bleached bangs behind her ears.

"No, she probably already drank all the beer Shauna brought and had her pills."

"Pills for what?"

"Her back. Or so she says." Rox pulled the visor down to check herself in the mirror. "My hair looks so cool."

"Where's your father?"

"Gone."

For the first time, Bet saw sadness or pain cross the girl's face. "Gone where?"

"What is this, twenty questions?" Rox glared out the windshield.

"Do you want to call him?" Bet prodded.

"I'm not allowed." Rox angrily pushed the visor up. "My mom said he was doing stuff to me, so the courts said I can't see him any more."

"Oh, Rox, I'm sorry."

"He didn't do nuthin'. Mom just got mad 'cause I wanted to live with him. It's no biggie. He has a new family now and doesn't need me. Mom doesn't need me either."

"I'm sure that's not true. A parent loves their child unconditionally and forever."

"Then why didn't he fight for me?" Rox's eyes glistened with tears. "Let's go." She started the engine and threw the car in reverse.

Bet held on to the dash as Rox sped off. "Rox, your mom is hiding in a shell of alcohol and drugs. After Carson's daddy died, I went into my own shell. The problem was I took Carson with me. She never had a chance to grow or grieve. Trying to protect her, I wound up messing up her life."

"Yeah, well at least you loved her."

"And your parents love you, too." Bet looked out the window. "Maybe it was easier for your parents not to take responsibility for you. You know, let you do whatever you want. I was the opposite, I smothered Carson." She swiped at a tear. "I never gave her a chance to live."

"I guess all parents are screwed up."

Bet smiled. "But we mean well."

"Carson's probably on a cloud in heaven spreading her wings." Rox glanced at Bet. "Aw geez, you're not crying again, are you?"

"Sorry." Bet used a ketchup-stained napkin to wipe her face. "I only wish I hadn't clipped her wings when I had her."

"I'll bet she was pretty happy," Rox said. "At least you cared." She pointed to a bank marquee's clock. "It's almost one o'clock, we'll wake Pinto up if we have to."

"The, um, body artist?"

"Yeah." She smiled mischievously. "Do you want to see my art?" She raised her shirt.

"Maybe later." Bet shook her head. What would she have done if Carson came home with a tattoo? *I'd love her, no matter what she painted or pierced.*

They headed to the outskirts of Deep Ellum, an arty-eclectic area east of downtown Dallas. Rox pulled into an alley and parked behind a graffiti-painted brick building.

"Pinto lives above the store. We can call Shauna from here." They got out of the car, and Rox pounded on a back door. "Pinto, open up. It's Rox."

After a few minutes, Pinto opened the door. Bet figured it was him by the etched Pinto scripted across is chest. He looked sleepy eyed. His shoulder length hair was disheveled, and he wore nothing but a pair of jeans. His lean torso was painted with various tattoos. Bet didn't see much natural skin left untouched.

"Rox Star. What's goin' on?" He rubbed his face and held the door open for them.

"Sorry to wake you up. Ya seen Crank?"

"Not for a day or so." He looked outside before he closed the door. "Hey, I heard the police are looking for you. What'd you do?"

"It's a long story. But I'm gonna have another charge against me for what I'm gonna do to Crank. Ya know where he is?"

They stood in a small room with chairs set up like an old timey barbershop. Paint splotched the cracked linoleum floor, and the walls were pasted with templates of tattoo designs.

Bet recognized a few of the designs from Pinto's chest.

"Rox, you need to stay away from Crank. He's into some bad stuff." Pinto stood, arms crossed with his hands under his armpits. "He's changed, gotten real weird. He must've come in to some money 'cause he's driving a new tricked-out car, and I think he's got a gun."

Bet turned to Pinto. "Is the car a Honda?"

Pinto smirked. "I think it was." He nodded at Bet and asked Rox. "So, who's your friend?"

"That's Mrs. Cleaver. She's helping me find Crank."

"Are you a cop or social worker?" Pinto asked Bet.

"No. Crank has something of mine as well. We both need to find him," Bet said.

Pinto turned to Rox. "I mean it, stay away from him." Pinto said. "He's not the same. He scares me now."

"Well, he doesn't scare me," Rox said. "Can I use your phone? I need to call Shauna."

"Yeah." He nodded toward a desk near the front door. "Dial nine."

While Rox went to use the phone, Bet looked at a small template of a dove. "Pinto, how much for this tattoo?"

CHAPTER 64

"Carson, is that you?"

The voice from beneath the cloud layer was music to Carson's ears.

"Yes! Yes!" She lay on the rock and scooched to the edge. "Are you okay? Is anybody hurt?" Thick clouds prevented her from seeing the person.

"Are *you* okay?" the voice asked.

"I'm on a cliff and can't get down."

"Are you hurt?"

"Not really." Carson's heart danced the Macarena in her chest.

"A few of the guys have serious injuries. I need to help them first. We're radioing for another rescue team, but we're having trouble getting a signal down here."

"Okay. I'm golden now that you're here. Is everybody, you know..." Carson didn't want to yell '*alive.*'

"Don't move. Let me help the others first."

"Okay." Carson wanted to wave her hands to move the clouds so she could see her hero.

CHAPTER 65

"Where's Rox?" Z glared at Shauna, who stood outside the beauty school

"I don't know." Shauna's acting skills failed miserably.

"Where's your car?"

"A...a friend has it," Shauna squeaked and wouldn't look Z in the eye.

"How did you get to work this morning?" Z took a step closer.

"The friend dropped me off." Shauna's knees wouldn't stop shaking.

"Who?"

"A friend." She tightened her smock belt. "I don't know," she whined.

Z crossed his arms over his broad chest. "This friend"—he raised an eyebrow—"that you don't know, did you color her hair last night?"

"You saw me last night. How could I?" Shauna took a nervous step back.

"Who was she with?"

"I don't know, mister. Now let me go, I have a perm setting."

"Why don't we go down to the station and talk."

"I didn't do nuthin'!"

"It appears your car was used in an armed robbery this morning." Z tried to hide the smirk when he said "armed."

"No, they didn't!" Shauna's jaw dropped.

"They?" Z leaned close to her. "Come on, you can ride with me to the station."

CHAPTER 66

Mark went to work helping the crew in the wrecked copter. His injured hand made it difficult to get the medic bag opened. The two in the cockpit were banged up pretty good but were alert. "Stay strapped in your belts for now. I don't want to hurt you more by trying to move you," he said, as he crouched in the rubble. "Let me check Rick's leg. He's losing blood."

The pilot nodded and whispered, "You know what you're doing?"

"Yeah, I have a little experience in medicine."

"At least you're good...for something." The pilot wheezed and fussed with one hand on the radio controls. The other hand he held close to his chest. "I can't...get a signal. We're...surrounded...by rock." His words sputtered between labored breaths.

"Keep trying," Mark said, as he cautiously crawled to Rick. Glass and metal crunched under him. He checked the man's vitals, which were weak but steady, then made sure Rick could move his arms and legs before placing a stabilizing collar around his neck. Mark laid him as flat as possible before securing his injured leg around a makeshift splint. "I want you to stay flat with your leg raised like this." He gently put his leg on a backpack before starting an IV of saline to keep him hydrated. Mark hoped another rescue team would get to them soon before Rick lost too much blood or his foot.

Mark cleaned Rick's cuts and brushed the broken glass off of him.

He was happy they'd found Carson. But he felt awful for

pushing these guys to fly in bad weather. He was determined not to lose anybody. He checked Rick's vitals again. "You're going to be all right."

"I better be, 'cause I need to beat you up for this."

Mark smiled. "I'll let you throw the first punch."

It seemed like forever, but when the radio crackled to life and the pilot gave their coordinates, Mark squeezed his eyes shut and whispered, "Thank you."

CHAPTER 67

Bet was surprised how quickly Pinto painted the small dove tattoo on her ankle. He even wrote "Carson" under it. It felt like someone had rubbed sandpaper over her ankle, but the pain was nothing compared to the hole she had inside without Carson.

They'd sat and sipped on delicious French pressed coffee while Pinto stuck his paintbrushes of needles in Bet's leg.

Rox sat in one of the chairs and stared out the window after hanging up the phone with the beauty school. "I can't believe the police came to see Shauna. I wonder where they took her." Rox absentmindedly twirled her short red-tipped hair. "She'd never leave with a perm setting. This is bad."

Bet worried the police were tracking them so close, but she felt this was the day to find Crank and get everything over with. Rox needed to go with the police to get her life straight, especially now that Bet had dragged her deeper into a life of crime. The money Bet would leave for her would take care of her for years, a lifetime if Rox learned how to invest well.

"Rox, let me go to Crank. Give me a head start, then turn yourself in," Bet said.

"I don't want to go to jail!" she snorted.

"You're young. The state will pay for your education while you're there." Bet checked out her tattoo in a mirror. "The police are the good guys. When you get out I'll..." she hesitated, "I'll help you financially."

"Are you going to get educated in jail, too?" Rox asked sarcastically.

Pinto, who'd been sitting in one of the parlor chairs, said, "I don't want any trouble here. It's hard enough to keep this place running." He looked at Bet. "Especially giving away free tattoos. The police will look for anything to shut me down."

Bet lightly touched her sore ankle. "Yes, thank you for this. I'm sorry for pulling you into this as well. We just want to find Crank and get on with...with things."

"Things?" Rox laughed. "Isn't that bad English?"

Bet laughed, too. A real laugh. It felt good. She raised her coffee cup. "A toast to all good *things*."

"Good things." Rox clinked her glass with Bet's.

Pinto jumped from his chair and ran to the window. "Oh, no."

Rox leaped up, too. "Is it the police?" She ducked behind a chair.

"No." Pinto turned to Rox. "It's Crank."

CHAPTER 68

Carson didn't want to be impatient, but she'd been waiting over an hour and could hardly stand not knowing what was going on. The clouds cleared, and she could see the wreckage. The mangled craft lay like a squashed bug in the canyon. Her hero was nowhere to be seen. He must've been inside the crashed helicopter, hopefully saving everybody else.

It was late afternoon, and the storm left the air sweet and clean, except for a few whiffs of gas and oil from the wreckage. The sky was a rainbow of colors with the sun still behind thin clouds. Carson sat on her ledge amazed at the beauty of the mountains.

Just then, a ray of sun flashed through the clouds, contrasting all the colors in the world, it seemed. The greens of the grass, the purple of the mountains, and the blues of the silver-lined clouds mixed into a palette of splendor. She breathed in the sparkling air and gave thanks for this moment, for being found.

Carson couldn't wait any longer. There were people down there that needed help. She was going to get off this damned mountain if she had to jump. She turned on her tummy, closed her eyes and scooted off the edge of the cliff.

I'm coming, Mom.

Chapter 69

I'm coming, Carson, Bet thought, as Crank pounded on the back door of the tattoo shop. She pulled her pant leg over her painful new "body art" and stood to go to the door. Now she had multiple marks of war. Her blade-sliced arm and her tattooed ankle.

Rox jumped ahead of her. "I'll get it."

"No, wait." Bet ran to get in front. "Stay here. Let me talk to him first."

"No way!" Rox pushed passed her.

Pinto blocked them. "Go upstairs. Crank and I have some business." He took Rox by the shoulders and turned her toward the stairs. "Don't make this harder than it has to be."

"You're not buying from him, are you?" Rox squinted at Pinto.

"Rox Star, you know me better than that. He...he makes me pay him. For protection. That's all."

"Protection from what?" Rox wheeled and face him.

Pinto sighed. "Sometimes, it's easier to give him a little cash to get him off my back." He pushed her again. "Go."

The door burst open, and Crank barged in with two of his henchmen. He sported two black eyes, and his nose still looked out of whack from Bet's punch. "Roxie! What a surprise." He scowled fiercely at his friends then said to Rox, "I thought we got rid of you and your old lady."

"No such luck." Rox stood her ground. "Give me my stuff back, and I'll quit lookin' for you."

"You mean this?" He pulled a mosaic box from his pocket. "It's mine now. It's my good luck charm." He shook it, and something inside rattled.

"Crank, c'mon, let's do this. Then you leave." Pinto stepped in front of Bet and Rox.

Crank shoved him aside and pushed Rox against the wall. "Hey, baby, looks like you two ladies were playing beauty parlor." He pushed his weight into her and tried to kiss her.

Rox turned her head and fought him off. "Stop!"

Bet grabbed his collar and pulled him off of Rox "She said stop."

Crank turned, surprised. Then he violently shoved Bet to the floor. She heard a funny clunk when her head hit the linoleum.

"I say when to stop." Crank kicked Bet hard in the gut, knocking the wind out of her. She lay like a fish out of water, gasping for a breath. "That's for breaking my nose."

Crank turned back to Rox. "I'm not done with you. You're coming with us."

"I wouldn't be caught dead with you, jerk." Fire spit from Rox's eyes. "You don't scare me."

He smiled wickedly. "You just might be caught dead with me."

"Crank. Stop." Pinto stood between him and Rox. "Any trouble, and the police will be here. Take the money and leave."

"I said I call the shots." Crank pulled a gun from his pants and held it to Pinto's head.

"No, Crank, no," Rox whispered. "No guns. You never did guns."

"Get the money. In fact, give me all your cash." He pushed Pinto toward the desk and then spoke to his friends. "You two take Roxie to the car. I'll take care of goldie oldie."

Unable to take a deep breath, Bet felt like a cement wall pressed down on her chest. She wondered if a few ribs weren't cracked and tried to catch enough air to fill her lungs. This was madness. She would not let Crank take Rox. Not after everything the girl had done for her. She closed her eyes and thought of Carson. Of missing her, of not letting her live life, of getting to heaven to see her.

Life.

It was a blessing. Just like that man in the convenience store said. *Life is good.* It was a gift. One that she was trying to thanklessly give back. Through the swirl of pain, Bet recalled an

Emily Dickinson quote: "Life is a spell so exquisite that everything conspires to break it."

Bet caught her first breath. Rox had given her a reason to live. Bet had learned more from this girl in a few short days than she'd ever known or taught Carson. Yes, life *was* a precious gift, one with a big floppy bow all wrapped with pretty shiny paper. The ache for Carson would always be with her, but this was not the way it was supposed to work. Bet would help Rox and let God plan the rest. *Oh, Carson, I'm sorry. I miss you so much.* Her insides filled with sadness for Carson, but a tiny ray of something—maybe hope, or of being needed—opened up, too.

She rolled over and, with every ounce of strength, pushed herself up. Supporting herself with a chair, she stood. She had to protect Rox. Holding her ribs, she tried to get past Crank. "Don't hurt her," Bet yelled to the two guys holding Rox. "Let her go," she gasped. "Leave before you get into more trouble."

Both men looked unsure as to what to do.

Bet's head jerked back as Crank pulled her short hair. She felt the cold muzzle of the gun on her cheek.

He grabbed her in a chokehold. She could hardly breathe with the pain in her ribs and pressure around her neck.

"Dude, this isn't what we signed up for." One of Crank's minions pushed Rox against the wall, and the two men sprinted out the back.

"Rox," Bet croaked. "Run. Save yourself."

The girl hesitated for only a split second before turning away. She ran out the door without looking back.

CHAPTER 70

Carson pushed off the side of the ledge, but muddy slime gave her nothing to hold onto. *I climbed down one mountain, I can climb...* She didn't finish the thought because, against her will, she began sliding, belly flopping against the mountain as she picked up speed. She grabbed and clawed, trying to stop herself from being hurled off the steep wet cliff. Panic seized her insides, and she couldn't catch enough breath to scream for help.

She felt like she was under water drowning, flailing arms, grasped at anything, but she had no control over her movements. Gravity dragged her faster and faster, and she fought to stay against the mountain, and tried to resist the terrifying pull of falling backwards. She raced by branches but missed them, reaching out a second too late. Her head bounced against the slippery slope. Her fight drained. *I give, you win.* She couldn't even cry. *I almost got rescued. I almost made it.*

She flew by a low-hanging branch and managed to grab it, slowing her descent just enough to catch a breath, and giving herself enough time to dig her toes into the wet, muddy rocks.

The scraggly branch snapped and ripped out of the wet mountain, roots and all. But the slowdown helped Carson turn sideways; she bent her knees and managed to mud-ski on her butt the rest of the way, still clinging to the branch like a skier's pole. The slope widened enough for her to balance. The rocks blended with dirt, now mud, gave her more purchase, but she was still flying too fast.

The bottom rushed toward her, and she twisted, landing flat on her back, the wind knocked out of her.

Put your arms above your head. Carson thought, but couldn't move. The broken branch lay on her chest; its twigs stuck her face and nose. She tried to suck some air, but her windpipe felt like a linguini and her lungs like flaccid balloons. She finally gasped a tiny breath, then another. She threw the broken branch off of her and gulped air.

On her back, she looked into the clearing sky at the mountain she'd just fallen from. A wave of vertigo overtook her, and she got a little sick to her stomach. Except for the muddy slope where she'd dug in, the descent was almost a sheer drop. How had she made it down alive? Maybe her guardian angel had stuck the branch out for her to grab. Carson looked at her scraped hands and bloodied fingers, and marveled that she lived through the fall. Her feet were mud boots and hurt like crazy from the wild ski trip. But she was still here! She tried not to pass out from shock. Today, she realized with astonishment, could have been the day she died.

CHAPTER 71

Crank's grip was like a vise around Bet's neck. She couldn't pull him off. She swam in and out of dizziness from sore ribs and lack of oxygen, but she was glad that Rox had run.

With the cold gun pressed to her face, Bet thought this was a crummy time to have a change of heart and want to live. Maybe this is the way it was supposed to be. She closed her eyes.

She was ready.

"You've gone too far, Crank."

Bet's eyes flew open at Rox's voice. The girl stood at the door holding the baseball bat from the backseat of the car.

"No, Rox. I can handle this," Bet choked out, her voice barely a whisper.

Crank sneered. "Hmmm. Should I shoot the old lady first or be sporting and kill a moving target?"

"Kill me, let her go," Bet pleaded.

Rox didn't stop. She charged toward Crank, swinging a grand slam. The first hit landed on his hip. He howled in pain and his hand jerked up.

The gun fired, and the wall in front of Bet splintered. Her ears hurt from the concussion of the blast. Everything sounded muffled except for a high-pitched ringing in her ears.

Bet grabbed at Crank's hand as he aimed the gun at Rox, but only knocked his hand away. Rox scrambled behind him. Bet heard a sick thud as Rox landed another swing on his back.

Crank grunted and lost his balance as he tried to turn and aim the pistol at Rox.

This time, Bet grabbed his arm and pointed it down. Rox

aimed again, landing a hard strike on his neck.

The gun discharged.

"The police are on the way," Rox screamed, swinging. The bat caught the gun. Through her brain fog, Bet heard a clink of metal and a crush of bones and watched the gun sail across the room. Pinto slid from behind the desk to retrieve the weapon.

Bet pushed Crank off her. A sharp pain twisted through her lower back. She could hardly move. Crank fell to the floor, and Rox slammed him again in the chest.

Bet held a hand out. "Rox, go. Give me the bat." With her ears still ringing, she could hear her own voice inside her head but wasn't sure Rox heard. Bet tried to take a step but felt disconnected, like her brain worked but her body didn't listen.

Rox looked up. "Z's on his way, I'm gonna turn myself..." Rox's face registered shock. "Mrs. C, oh no! *No!*"

Bet made a meager attempt to move. "It's okay," she tried to say, but slowly crumpled to the floor. In a distant haze, Bet heard Rox scream. "Mrs. C. you've been shot!"

CHAPTER 72

"Carson? Carson!" Mark screamed.

Carson tried to sit up but she hurt all over. "Here." Her voice came out a squeak. "Over here."

She heard the squish of his feet on the muddy ground. "I think she fell," Mark yelled into a mic clipped to his uniform. "I don't see her!"

It hurt, but Carson raised her arm over the brush, and waved. "I'm good. I'm okay, I think." She rolled onto her side and pushed herself up.

"Don't move." Mark was at her side. "You could have a spinal cord injury." He kneeled next to her and checked her face, her head and arms. "Lie down. Can you move your fingers and toes?"

"Yeah, I just sat up. I'm fine." *I'm rescued—I'm alive!*

"Does this hurt?" He pressed the left side of her abdomen.

Carson recoiled. "Everything hurts."

"That's where your spleen is. I hope it's not ruptured. Did you land on your side?"

"No, my back. In the mud and on all those stupid rocks." She pushed his hand away. "I'm okay, really."

He looked up at the trail marks she'd left on the side of the mountain. "You're sure you can move?"

Carson nodded. "I just got the wind knocked out of me in a major way."

He had her sit forward and checked her back. "Yeah, you're bruised and scraped up. You can move?"

"Yeah."

"I shouldn't be doing this but..." He scooped her up like a baby and carried her toward the crashed helicopter.

"No, I'm too heavy." Carson clutched his neck.

"Don't be silly," he said. "I just hope your back's okay."

Carson hadn't been carried like this since her daddy used to take her all sleepy and snuggly and put her in bed. "Your hand, it's all bloody," Carson said. "You're hurt. Put me down."

"I'm okay, but some of the crew's hurt. The pilot is trying to radio for a rescue helicopter." Mark held Carson close, not out of breath or acting like she was a load. "It's hard to get a radio signal in this canyon."

"Put me down, and I'll help you take care of them." Carson squirmed out of his arms when they reached the crash. Her muddy feet hurt when they hit the ground, but otherwise she could move.

Mark hovered over her like he expected her to fall.

Carson pointed to his hand. "You're bleeding."

"Yeah, I know. Can you help me wrap it up so I don't bleed all over the crew?" Mark grabbed a medic bag and dug inside. He pulled out a roll of gauze and ripped it open with his teeth.

While he quickly rinsed his hand with a bottle of water, Carson surveyed the damage. The helicopter lay sideways. One side was smashed in, the rotors snapped and crooked like broken insect wings. Shattered glass shimmered in the light of the late afternoon sun. Carson gasped when she saw a broken body inside the wrecked shell.

"Here." Mark handed Carson the gauze. He'd already wrapped his hand and needed Carson to cut the end. "It's my right hand. I need to do some emergency surgery on Rick." He nodded toward the body. "If you're sure you can move, maybe I could tell you what to do. You can be my hands."

"Surgery?" Carson peeped. "Like with scalpels?"

"Needle and thread mostly. His ankle is fractured and he's losing blood. We have to stop the bleeding."

"Ankle?" Carson recalled when, in Girl Scouts, she learned how to fashion a cool ankle brace for a sprain. For the life of her she'd never remember how to do it now. And, during the demonstration, there was no blood.

"Come on." Mark held the bag and jumped into the helicopter.

Carson took a deep breath and followed her hero.

CHAPTER 73

In his office, Z paced back and forth in front of Shauna, who sat whimpering and wiping tears from her face.

"Where were they going?" he growled at the girl. It hadn't taken Shauna long before she broke down and admitted that Bet and Rox had been right under his nose last night. He was relieved and angry at the same time.

"I told you already. They went to look for Crank, but I don't know where."

"Why did Rox kidnap Bet Harper?"

"Kidnap? I don't get it." Shauna's face was blotchy and wet. "They were together."

"How'd Bet's shirt get bloody?"

"Something happened with Crank. Like his girlfriend cut her with a knife. I don't know."

"Isn't Rox his girlfriend?"

"Not anymore. 'Sides, Rox wouldn't hurt or kidnap anybody." Shauna looked perplexed. "They both wanted to get Crank."

"Did Bet try to leave?"

"Nah. I mean, she told Rox to stay with me because she wanted to go do something." She scrunched her face and looked confused. "She did tell Rox to turn herself in."

"What did Bet want to do?"

Shauna shrugged.

"Did Rox let her go?"

"No, but the lady could've left any time. Rox didn't tie her up or nuthin.' When I told her you may've found her daughter, she got all freaked out, screamin' and everything." Shauna eyed Z.

"You didn't tell me her kid was dead."

The door burst open and the young officer that had told Z about the convenience store rushed in. "Sir, we just got a call." He stopped when he saw Shauna.

Z turned to him. "What call?"

The officer hesitated, then said, "It was Roxanne Mayhill. Bet Harper's been shot."

CHAPTER 74

Inside the helicopter was dark. Carson smelled blood mingled with gas and oil. The body moved when they came in. *Good, he's not dead.*

Mark squatted next to the injured man. "Rick. Hey, you awake?"

Rick waved his hand weakly but didn't open his eyes. His face was a weird gray color, like a figure at a wax museum; he looked real but dead at the same time. Carson tried not to look at the odd angled foot. *Was that a bone?*

"You guys okay up front?" Mark yelled into the cockpit.

"Weak, man. Help's on"—the pilot gasped—"the way."

Mark looked into Carson's eyes. "I need you to be my hands." He held up his bandaged hand, already saturated with blood.

Her own pain forgotten, she took the medic bag from Mark.

"Rinse your hands and put on the gloves," he directed.

Carson quickly opened a water bottle and scrubbed at the mud. Then she snapped on a tight pair of sterile gloves over her scraped hands.

"We can't do micro-surgery here but we're going to try to save his leg. There is a big artery that runs along the back of the leg, the popliteal artery. I clamped that off earlier. Now we need to repair some of the collateral arteries and unclamp it to get blood flowing into his foot again. Ready?"

Carson nodded, scared.

"How do you know so much?" Rick whispered.

"Medical school," Mark said as he handed Carson a bottle of medicine. He tore an alcohol pad open with his teeth and told her to wipe the top with it. "Draw up a syringe full of this. Try not to get any bubbles in it."

He turned to Rick. "We're going to inject some xylocain into your leg to numb you. Okay? It might sting a little."

"You're a doctor?" Carson asked, piercing the needle through the rubber top and pulling the medicine into the syringe. Her hands shook when Mark pointed to the place in Rick's leg he expected Carson to stick. She hesitated, holding the sharp needle over the skin, then semi-closed her eyes, put the needle above his leg, and stopped.

"You can do it," he whispered to Carson.

She did. But didn't push hard enough. Mark's left hand guided hers, and she felt the needle hit the skin.

"Medical school?" Rick winced when the needle went in. "You're a doc?"

"Yeah, sort of." Mark answered, then directed Carson. "Now here." Mark pointed to another place on Rick's leg.

It was hard to find the courage to stick a needle in someone, but having Mark there talking her through it helped.

"A little deeper."

Carson could feel the needle go through the top layer of skin, and she thought of sticking an orange instead of a real leg. She pushed the syringe plunger. Mark pointed to a few more places. Each time Carson stuck, it became a little easier.

"You should be numb by now."

"I'm cold." Rick started shivering. "Man, I thought you were just a flunky." His teeth chattered loudly.

Carson grabbed a blanket and put it over Rick's chest.

"Put new gloves on," Mark said, as he took a bottle of saline and squirted it over Rick's leg, cleaning the open wound. "Now, Carson, see that artery?" He took a set of hemostats and, with his left hand, carefully lifted a stringy piece of meat. "I need you to sew it back together."

It took almost thirty minutes before they heard a helicopter approach. Mark had successfully supervised Carson's scary attempt to get some blood flowing back into Rick's lower leg, and continually checked on the pilot and co-pilot.

It surprised Carson how tough the artery was; it was like sewing a piece of al dente spaghetti. Without the blue and red dye going through the bloodstream like in anatomy class dissections, Carson couldn't figure out how anybody could tell what part was what. Mark telling her the names of the body parts and talking calmly helped keep her steady, focused. And she didn't vomit once.

The late afternoon sun couldn't reach the inside of the canyon. The rescue helicopter hovered above while Mark talked to them with the mic clipped to his collar. A stretcher was lowered and dangled like a waiting ride at an amusement park. After a few attempts Mark caught the stretcher, his bandaged hand had a hard time gripping the metal edge. With his good hand, he managed to release the bed from the cable and it fell with a clank.

Carson ran from the wrecked helicopter and helped Mark carry the bed to Rick.

"His head and shoulders are heavier than his legs, but I should do the ankle. Do you think you can lift him?" Mark kneeled at Rick's broken leg.

Carson nodded. There was no way she was going to drop this guy.

They positioned the stretcher as close to Rick as possible, and on the count of three, heaved him on top. All of Carson's bruised muscles screamed, but she did not let go. Rick gave a sharp yelp and his face twisted in pain.

"I'm sorry," Carson cried.

Rick blew out some short breaths and gasped, "I'm good. You did good, Carson."

Blood soaked through Mark's bandaged hand, but it didn't slow him down as he secured the buckles around Rick.

The helicopter still hovered overhead, kicking up wind and small leaves. Carson was glad for the mud, otherwise they would have been fighting a major dust storm in the narrow canyon.

She and Mark scooted the stretcher to the door.

"We need to carry him over there." Mark nodded his head toward the dangling cable.

"I got it," Carson said and took hold of the side rail.

"On my count," Mark said.

They lifted Rick and ran. Adrenaline surged through Carson, giving her more strength than she'd ever known. Mark clamped the stretcher to the cable and gave the signal for the helicopter to go.

For a few anxious seconds, they watched Rick ascend, swinging, barely missing the sides of the mountain as the helicopter pulled him up. The waiting crew kneeled by an open door of the wobbly craft, hauled him inside and flew out of sight.

Around the roar of the engines, Carson couldn't hear what Mark was saying in his mic. But in no time, another helicopter flew over and lowered stretchers for the other injured men.

Even with his hurt hand, Mark had done most of the work. For the next hour, he and Carson unbuckled the pilots from their seats and gently carried them to the stretchers. Carson noticed the pilot breathing funny, like he had a hole somewhere in his body where air was escaping. While they waited outside for the rescue cable to descend, the pilot grasped Carson's hand and held on tight. She brushed broken glass from his face and held a water bottle for him to sip.

Mark secured the co-pilot on the stretcher and came over to the pilot. "Hey, don't drink anything. You'll probably need surgery." Mark buckled him in.

"I'm glad...we...found...you," The pilot gasped at Carson, he still clutched her hand.

"I'm sorry to be so much trouble." Tears filled Carson's eyes.

The pilot squeezed her hand harder. "This...was...fun." He gasped again. "But...*you* saved...*us*."

"Come on, let's get you out of here." Mark wrapped a blanket around the pilot, and he and Carson secured the cable to the bed. The air of the waiting craft swirled around them. The noise deafened Carson.

By the time both the pilot and co-pilot had been taken away, the afternoon sun slid behind the mountains, and the canyon was shrouded in deep shadows. Mark patched more gauze over his bloody hand. "We'll only have one chance to get out of here tonight. Otherwise, it'll be too dark. Another helicopter is on its way." He looked into the sky. "I hate to say it, but there's a chance we'll have to wait until morning."

A cool breeze caught her hair, and she thought of the cold night ahead. Carson sat wearily. "I'm okay. I've been out here for almost two weeks, I can stand another night." So close to going home yet she still had to wait. She shivered.

After the pilot and co-pilot had been taken, Carson heard the distant whir of the helicopter fading as it flew out of sight. *Don't leave me!*

Mark must have read her thoughts. "Carson, we had to get the others to a hospital first."

"Is everybody going to be okay?" Carson tried to keep her voice happy.

"I think so. How are you?"

"I'm fine now." But Carson started crying anyway. The tears on her cheek turned the crusty dirt to mud. "I am so ready to go home."

"I'm sure you are." His voice sounded tired, and he held his hurt hand close to his chest. "We were worried about you, especially with the fire and all."

"It was scary." Carson stood and walked to him. "Let me help you with your hand."

"I can wait."

But Carson started fishing into the medic bag, found some more gauze and Neosporin. "I'll just re-wrap it."

Mark laughed. "You're turning into quite a doctor."

Carson smiled. "Tell me what to do." She snapped on another pair of gloves.

Mark allowed her to cut the bloody bandage off. "I may need stitches." He winced as the last of the gauze pulled at the cut skin.

Carson tried not to gag after looking at his gashed and bloody hand. "It looks worse than it is," Mark said, but Carson could tell he was in pain.

"It looks pretty bad."

Mark poured saline on his hand. There was a long jagged cut along the palm and into the thumb, as well as scattered cuts like buckshot front and back.

Carson carefully smeared Neosporin over his hand and opened another package of gauze. As she wrapped, she asked, "Can you tell the pilots coming to get us to call my mom and tell her I'm coming home? Tell her I've missed her."

Mark looked away.

"Does she know you've found me?" Carson felt a nervous tingle. "She worries a lot."

"It's real hard to get a signal here." He suddenly became very serious. Too serious.

"Yeah, but you're talking to someone in that mic. I can give you her cell phone number. She always answers that." Carson wished he'd look her in the eye.

"Let's get out of here first." He'd gotten real busy helping secure the gauze.

"Has anybody talked to her?" Carson had a funny feeling that something was wrong. She figured her mom was at base camp driving everybody crazy trying to find her.

He grabbed at his jacket as his radio cackled. He looked to the horizon, now almost dark. "I don't see you yet," he said into the mic, but in the distance they heard a helicopter.

Carson looked to the sky, too, but didn't see the copter. The canyon walls echoed the noise so it was hard to tell which direction it was coming from. With the rain-washed air, everything above sparkled brilliantly in the last rays of the sun. She secured the wrap on Mark's hand and noticed that blood had already seeped through. "You need to get back tonight, otherwise you'll lose too much blood. I can wait another night." Carson tried to get him to look at her. "Can you please have someone call my mom and let her know I'm okay? She really worries."

Mark finally looked at her, smiled but looked drained. "Carson, we're both getting out of here tonight."

A nagging worry kept biting Carson. "Is my mom in Colorado?"

He shook his head. "I don't know, Carson. We're still looking for her."

CHAPTER 75

Bet lay on the floor but felt no pain, didn't feel much of anything really. She was all floaty and disconnected. In an odd way, she could hear and see what was going on, like she was looking into the room from a distance.

Rox was freaking out, screaming and crying, clutching Bet's hand. "Z's coming, an ambulance is coming! Don't die on me!"

Bet wanted to tell her it was all right, that she wasn't hurting, she was just a little cold and sleepy.

Bet tried to talk, to tell Rox to look in her back pocket and find the will she'd written. But she wasn't sure her lips moved, even if her head formed the words. She wanted to reassure Rox that this is what she'd wanted all along. To get to Carson.

It was a strange sensation, but a film clip of Bet's life flashed on. There was her favorite doll when she was a little girl.

Her mom and dad.

She saw her husband on their wedding day.

His kiss, his warm embrace.

His strength and light. The way his eyes crinkled when he smiled. Just like Carson's.

Being pregnant, sitting quietly and feeling the first tickle of movement of Carson in her tummy.

Carson as a toddler, laughing and running with outstretched arms into Bet's embrace. Hugging her neck, squeezing so hard, Bet felt it all the way to her heart.

Five-year-old Carson on spindly legs, kicking a soccer ball with her daddy.

Old Roady, her dear, loyal friend, lying by the kitchen window, thumping his tail on the floor when she came near.

And Carson, oh Carson, all the happiness they'd shared together like the light of rainbows and the smell of crayons.

And finally, toasting with Rox for "all good things."

Bet smiled.

And the world went black.

Carson, help me find the light.

CHAPTER 76

Carson jumped up from the rock she'd been sitting on and knocked the black medic bag over. "What do you mean you're still looking for my mom? Where would she go?"

Before Mark could answer, Carson heard the thump of rotor blades and saw another helicopter descend from the sky. She gathered the black medical bag and stuffed the things that had fallen back in, happy now she was going home, but worried about her mom.

Mark stood and waved the copter over them. "Leave the bag," he said and turned back to the approaching craft. A winch descended with a ragged bundle of belts on the end.

Carson threw the bag into the crashed helicopter and thought about her mom. Her mother was never away from her cell phone. She'd grounded Carson once because she'd called while Carson was on the bus and Carson hadn't answered, embarrassed that the other kids would laugh because her mommy was checking on her.

"We're still looking for her." Carson thought of Mark's words. She suddenly felt a gnawing fear. *Oh no. Knowing Mom, she went out in the woods looking for me, and now she's lost. What if the wolves or bears attack her? What have I done?*

Mark grabbed at the bundle and unhooked it from the winch. "Carson, here, put this on." Mark tossed her a vest of belts and buckles.

"Where's the stretcher?"

"No stretcher, just you and me." Mark had already put his vest on and managed to buckle most of it together before Carson could consider how they were going to be rescued.

"They're going to lift us with this?" She held the limp vest up. "What if it breaks or comes loose?"

"We'll be fine." Mark took the vest from Carson and helped her step into it.

She gulped. "Isn't there another way?"

"We can hike, but I'm not sure we'd get back tonight."

Carson looked at the bright red blood already saturating the new gauze around Mark's hand. "Okay, the helicopter it is." She took a deep breath. She had to find out about her mother. And it would be nice to wash the caked mud out of her hair—with really hot water. But the vision of the helicopter crash still haunted her. *What are the chances of two crashes in one day?* She didn't want to know.

Gulp. "Okay. I'm ready," she squeaked. Oh, man. If her mother could see her now.

CHAPTER 77

A huge puddle of blood congealed on Pinto's floor where Bet had fallen. Z paced while the other officers took pictures, collected evidence and cordoned off the area with yellow crime scene tape. He tried to calm down enough to talk to Rox, who sat handcuffed and sobbing in the kitchen.

But first, the police needed to get Crank out. Z got satisfaction seeing the big man cry in pain when the handcuffs snapped around his wrists.

"My back, man. Owww. I'm the one who's hurt. Lemme go," Crank whined the whole time he was being tethered. "Look what that lady did to my face."

Z strode over to him. "I've been waiting for this moment for too long. Enjoy the view on your way to the car, because it'll be the last time you see daylight without bars blocking your view."

"I didn't do nuthin." Crank sobbed like a baby. "Tell him, Pinto, tell him I'm innocent!"

Pinto stood behind Z, arms crossed, and shook his head as two police officers dragged Crank out.

Z turned to Pinto. "I wish we'd gotten here five minutes earlier. Just five stinking minutes." He punched a fist into his hand.

"Yeah. Better yet, none of this would've happened." Pinto stared at the congealing blood. "I gave the lady a tattoo this morning just before Crank showed up."

"Really? Bet Harper?"

Pinto nodded. "A dove with her daughter's name under it."

Z gave Pinto a pat on the back. "Thanks for your help with Crank." He blew out a breath. "I need to talk to Rox."

Pinto said, "She's cool. Really. She was trying to help the lady."

"I can see how much she helped." Z went to the kitchen.

"Z," Rox sobbed. "We were...buds...friends...we was..." Rox could hardly get any words out, she was crying so hard. "Is Crank dead? If not, I'll...I'll finish him off..." She wrestled with her handcuffs.

"Rox, stop." Z stood over her and tried not to feel sorry for the girl. "You are in a lot of trouble. I can't imagine what you were thinking."

"Me and Mrs. C, uh, Bet, were friends." Rox wailed. "I didn't hurt her."

"That's not what the evidence shows, Rox. I'm sorry, but I have to read you your rights." He put a gentle hand on her shoulder. "Then I suggest you get an attorney. The best one you can find."

CHAPTER 78

Carson wanted to get this rescue done. She was excited, afraid, and nervous about her mom, not to mention petrified about flying through the air on a teeny weenie cable.

She stood while Mark harnessed them together, helping with shaky fingers when Mark couldn't use his injured hand. When the helicopter flew over, the cable swung like a pendulum under it, Carson looked up at its massive metal belly. Her nerves tingled all the way to her teeth.

I didn't make it this far to crash now. This will be fun, yeah, a real barrel full of monkeys. There's no place like home, there's no place like home. Her brain tried to talk her down. *Calm, stay calm.*

The helicopter roared above, vibrating the air around them.

Mark yelled into her ear. "This is as close as they can come. They don't want the blades to hit the rock."

Carson nodded. Her knees fought to hold her up.

I could never do this for a living, no way, no how. Carson swallowed as she watched Mark grab the winch.

"You're scared, aren't you?" Carson's nerves were clanging again.

"Yeah, a little." He smiled and stood up. "Come on, we don't have much time."

"I don't know about this." Carson trembled.

"You're doing great." He brushed mud from her face. "Hey, don't cry now, you're almost home." He just about bit his tongue when he though of their home.

"My mom. Is she okay?"

He didn't answer.

"I'm scared," Carson whimpered.

"So am I." Mark smiled. "You ready?"

Carson nodded and prayed she wouldn't pee all over herself.

"Bring it on," Mark said into the mic. He looked Carson in the eyes and nodded. "Remember to breathe."

The roar of the helicopter's engine drowned out any other words. Mark grabbed the swinging cable, clamped it on to their vests and spoke in the mic again. Carson couldn't hear what he said, but suddenly felt herself being lifted off the ground. She screamed as they swayed in mid air. They almost hit the side of the mountain before pulling away from the canyon walls. Carson shut her eyes and screamed again, pressing her face into Mark's leather jacket.

Her stomach tickled so hard she could barely stand it. The harness squeezed her legs and chest. *Faint, that's all you have to do. Or just have a heart attack.*

"Breathe."

Carson heard Mark's calming voice. She took a deep breath.

"Look."

Carson opened her eyes and took another gulp of air. A feeling of exhilaration swept through her. This was so cool! She looked at the line of mountains as they flew over treetops. She saw areas that were blackened by the fire mingled in the lush green foliage. The deepening dusk cast everything in a blue and purple glow.

"Not a bad view," Mark yelled.

Carson laughed and nodded. The wind in her hair was sweet, and the sky smelled of evergreen and magic. The ride was thrilling.

As soon as they got over a flat grassy area, they began to descend.

"The landing might be rough. Hold on to me," Mark shouted.

Carson wrapped her arms around her hero as the ground rose to meet them.

Mark was right; the landing was rough. They both hit the ground running then fell. Carson landed on top of Mark. She tried to roll off him, but they were still connected. Mark fought to unhook the cable from their vests. He finally unclamped the winch, and Carson watched the helicopter fly away, pull the cable in, then circle back to land on flat ground.

After Mark unhooked them, they lay on their backs and looked at the emerging stars. Carson began to giggle. "Wow."

Mark laughed, too.

In no time, the rescue crew was there. "Are you okay?" One of the medics lay her flat and began checking her. Others surrounded her, poking all over. Mark stood, dusted himself off and backed away.

"I'm fine!" Carson tried to stand up. "Where's Mark?"

Carson was loaded on a stretcher and carried to the waiting helicopter. Mark boarded last.

"Sit next to me," Carson said, as he started toward the back. "Please." She grabbed his unbandaged hand as the craft took off. "How's your hand?"

"I'm fine." Mark smiled. "You did good today, Carson."

"So did you. Thank you." Another medic pushed in and stuck a needle in Carson's arm. "Ouch! A little warning please." Carson gave him a dirty look.

"Fluids, hon. You're probably dehydrated."

Mark put a comforting hand on her shoulder, and she relaxed. Carson looked out the window at the moonlit horizon. As they crested the edge of a mountain, she thought she saw a pack of wolves running along a ridge. She took a double take, and could have sworn she saw a silhouette of a Chihuahua howling at the full moon.

CHAPTER 79

The helicopter landed right on top of a hospital roof. *This is almost as scary as climbing the mountain,* Carson thought as she was rolled out of the craft onto the gravel-paved roof. She pictured the stretcher getting away from the paramedics and her falling over the side of the building.

"Stay with me," Carson begged Mark as he stepped back to let the others take over her care. "I need to call my mother."

"I'm right here." He ran behind the stretcher but didn't say anything about her mother.

"I can walk." Carson tried to sit up.

"Stay down. We're taking you to the ER," one of the paramedics said and tried to hold her down.

"I'm fine!" Carson pushed his hand off her shoulder. "You guys are all about the drama."

She was given the once over in the emergency room and got poked and prodded in all her sore places. The saline IV drooped from a metal pole.

"How am I going to shower with this on?" she wailed and wagged the tubing. The hustle and bustle of the busy room made her nervous, especially after the quiet solitude of the wilderness. Her bruises and cuts hurt from all the attention. "Can you turn out those bright lights? Where's Mark? Did he call my mom?"

"We're almost done." A nurse took her hand. "We'll get you cleaned up and to a quiet room soon." She put a cold stethoscope on Carson's chest. "Mark's waiting outside with your Outward Bound group. And a cute guy named Seth keeps asking about you." She smiled and squeezed Carson's arm. "You can visit with them later."

Her touch settled Carson.

An hour later, Carson was showered, her head stitched, her wolf bites scrubbed and taped, and her scrapes doused with ointment or patched with Band-Aids. She finally lay resting in a hospital room. She was exhausted and wired at the same time. Chicken broth had warmed her insides and a half-eaten container of cherry Jell-o filled her up. Mark sat next to her in a chair.

"So you're a doctor?" Carson asked.

"Still working on it. I sort of dropped out of my residency program because my dad and I didn't agree on things." Mark smiled wearily.

"So like even when you're older, your parents still screw you up?"

Mark laughed. "They try."

Restless, Carson tried to get comfortable in the bed. "The next time I run away, I'm going someplace with room service." She pulled the blanket to her chin, feeling entirely too exposed in the flimsy hospital gown. "I need real clothes."

"Why did you run away?" Mark scooted the chair closer.

Carson shrugged. "To prove something, to myself and my mom," she emphasized. "Speaking of Mom, did you get a hold of her? She's probably worried sick."

Mark stared at her, unsure how to respond.

"Why isn't she here? I figured she'd be the first one at the door. Is she out in the woods looking for me?" Carson sat up quickly, suddenly scared. "Is she okay? There are bears and wolves out there." Her lip began to quiver. "Mom?" she whispered.

Before he could answer, there was a knock at the door, and Dana, the leader from Outward Bound, stuck her head in. "Hey, how are you?"

Carson could see the group of campers standing behind her, Seth included.

"I'm not dressed," she whispered, and pulled the blanket even higher.

Mark stood and took off his cool leather jacket. "Here, put this on."

"Thanks, too bad you don't wear the same size underwear." She slipped the heavy jacket over her shoulders. "I'll give it back as soon as they leave."

"Keep it."

"What? No way"

"You earned it."

She didn't have time to protest again as the room filled with visitors. Seth immediately took a spot next to the bed. "Man, look at you! What a cool adventure. Did you really fly on a cable from a helicopter?"

Carson nodded. He looked so cute.

"We were all really worried about you." Seth sat in the chair Mark had vacated. "I was worried," he said a little softer.

Carson blushed.

Torey sat on the end of the bed, still as beautiful as ever. "Eww, what happened to your head? You look like Frankenstein, and hey, did you really get attacked by wolves? Lemme see the bite marks." She tugged at the blankets.

"No, don't." Carson held the covers tight. "I'm not dressed."

Seth took her hand, which still clutched at the blanket, and said, "Torey, don't you have an extra pair of sweats and a shirt? Let Carson borrow them."

Torey's face scrunched up like she was thinking the same thing Carson was. *Ain't no way I'll fit into them.*

"Yeah, you guys look about the same size," Seth said and squeezed Carson's hand.

Chapter 80

Mark took the elevator to the hospital lobby. His hand throbbed now that the Novocain had worn off. The gash along his palm had taken almost seventy stitches, plus a bunch of other small areas that needed to be sewn back together. Right now, his hand looked like a beginner's quilting exercise.

He stepped outside and called Coffey. The chilly air raised goose bumps on his arms. He missed his jacket, but he smiled thinking about giving it to Carson. She deserved it.

Officer Coffey answered quickly.

"It's Mark, sir. Carson's okay and is in the hospital."

"Yeah, I know."

"How's the rest of the crew?" Mark asked. He noticed the group of campers exit the hospital. Everyone except Seth. He smiled.

"They'll live. The pilot had a punctured lung and the guy with the broken ankle is in surgery now. He'll be okay, too." There was a slight pause. "I'm glad you knew what you were doing out there. He would've lost his foot. But we're going to get some heat for sending that chopper up in the storm, so get your butt back here soon."

"Okay," Mark said. "Um, sir, any news on Carson's mother?"

"Yeah, it's bad," Coffey said gruffly. "She got shot in some tattoo parlor. Don't say anything to the girl yet, and don't let her watch TV. It's all over the damned news. See ya at 0800 tomorrow."

CHAPTER 81

Carson sat on the hospital bed, Mark's leather jacket over her shoulders and wearing a pair of Torey's sweats, amazed that they fit her. Seth sat in a chair next to her.

"Are you sure my mom didn't show up at Outward Bound?"

Seth shrugged. "I haven't heard anything."

"She is such a major worry-wart; I figured she'd be at camp leading a patrol to find me." She folded a corner of the bed sheet. "I'm really concerned. I ran away to go to Outward Bound. She had no idea. I left her a note."

"You what? Ran away?"

"My mom freaks out about me doing anything. I wanted to prove to her that I could do something on my own."

"Cool! You're a fugitive."

"That's why I figured that as soon as my mom knew what I'd done, she'd be on a plane and making a huge stink at the camp. You're sure she didn't show up there?"

"Hey, you know how adults treat us kids. They don't tell us anything. I'm sure Dana's been talking to her." Seth hesitated. "Dana was acting weird about something that didn't have anything to do with the fire or your rescue. That space debris story."

"What space debris story?" Carson asked.

"Oh, yeah, I forgot. You've been incommunicado for the last few weeks." He leaned back in his chair. "A piece of a satellite fell from the sky and crashed to earth. Pretty cool, except some kid was killed."

"That's terrible."

"I think Dana knew someone or something about it. You know

grown-ups. Everything is a big secret."

Carson nodded.

"Your hair looks real pretty down."

Carson giggled and pushed some of her long blonde hair behind her ear. It felt good to wear it down. Different. "Thanks."

"You had a major adventure, man. I've done this camp for two years and haven't had as much fun as you."

"Fun?" Carson laughed. "I'm not sure I'd call what happened fun."

"Maybe next year, you and I can hike it together."

Carson felt a rush start in all of her sore spots and end in her cheeks. "Really?"

There was a knock at the door, and Mark stepped in. He shook hands with Seth, awkward with his left hand, then glanced at Carson.

By the look in his eyes, Carson knew something bad had happened. "What? What is it?" Carson asked, worry lacing her voice. "Did you hear from my mom?"

Mark fidgeted with his bandaged hand. "Carson, we need to talk."

CHAPTER 82

The next morning, Mark sat on a squeaky wooden chair outside Officer Coffey's office. He could hear voices and occasional barks of laughter behind the closed door. His father and Coffey.

While he waited, he unwrapped his bandaged hand and examined his patchwork of stitches. Cuts freckled the back of his hand and the stitched gash was turning a gross green-yellow color. He wondered if he'd lost any fine motor skills, wondered if he'd be able to do surgery again. He sighed. Maybe he'd get what he wanted after all. He'd be forced to quit his residency program for good. At least he'd have a good reason now, and his dad couldn't fight with him anymore about becoming a knee specialist. Something Mark found extremely boring. He'd loved working in the ER, but his father made it clear it was a lowbrow job. Mark needed to keep their good name and get into orthopedics like his dad and two brothers.

He wished they'd hurry so he could get back to Carson. Last night, he'd sent Seth out so he could talk to her. Mark had sat in the chair next to her bed. He noticed Seth had moved it closer. The look in her eyes still haunted him, and he hated to tell her what had happened.

"Carson, there was an accident at your house."

Tears filled he eyes. "Mom?"

"Your mom thought you were at home and..."

"Is she okay?"

Mark had been instructed not to tell Carson, but he didn't want her to hear it from just anybody.

"The day you left, a piece of a satellite fell on your house and destroyed it. There's nothing left." He looked at the floor. "Your mom thought you were there and had been killed." He explained how Bet had been arrested and escaped with a girl from the jail. "The police think she was kidnapped."

Carson's face was a mess of confusion and pain. "Kidnapped? Jail? My mom?" The words came out small and childlike.

"Carson, I'm so sorry, your mom was..."

His thoughts were interrupted when Officer Coffey's office door opened and Mark's dad and Coffey stepped into the hallway. Energy radiated from both of them, palpable in the narrow hallway. Mark stood, the wad of old gauze clutched in his hand.

"I'll let you two catch up. Then we have some work to do," Coffey said, looking at Mark. He turned to Mark's dad. "Doctor, it was nice talking to you." They shook hands.

His dad turned to Mark as Coffey went back into his office. His dad's military uniform was pressed perfectly, as usual.

"Mark." His dad clamped a hand on his shoulder and led him away from the doorway. "I heard what happened out there." He gripped Mark's shoulder harder. "I'm proud of you."

Surprised, Mark asked, "You are? I thought you'd be mad."

"Why would I be mad? You saved three lives, four including the girl." He removed his hand and continued walking. "Coffey is releasing you from your job if you want to go back to medical school." His dad sighed. "You can study what you want."

"Surgery? Emergency medicine?" Mark asked.

His dad nodded. "I just don't want to see you go to war. As a military ER doc, you'll be the first to get shipped out."

"I thought that's exactly what you'd want."

"What? No, that's the last thing I'd want. I've been to war. I wouldn't wish it on anybody, especially my own son." His dad stopped and looked Mark in the eye. "And I don't know what I'd do if anything happened to you."

For the first time, Mark saw a vulnerable side of his father and imagined him as a young man. Probably very much like himself.

He thought of Carson and felt a strong protective urge to help her. She needed someone in her life now, especially after what had happened to her mother.

CHAPTER 83

There's the light. Go to the light. Carson, I'm coming. Bet winced and tried to open her eyes. *Why do I feel pain in heaven?* The light was so bright. Bet struggled to reach it. She batted open her eyes and shielded them from the blinding radiance. She squeezed them shut again and waited for the warmth and love from heaven to engulf her.

"Mom?"

"Carson," Bet whispered. "I made it." She forced her eyes open and saw Carson. The most beautiful sight she'd ever seen. Carson. Her long hair was down and sunshine blonde, and her face was slim and tanned. "Oh, honey, you *are* an angel. I tried so hard to get here." Bet couldn't move. "Where are your wings?"

"Mom, what are you talking about?" Carson grabbed Bet's hand. "I was so worried."

Bet clasped her daughter's hand and held it to her face. She began crying. "You feel so real. I missed you so much." She wanted to jump up and hug Carson, to never let go. "Why am I hurting? I didn't think heaven would be like this."

"Heaven?" Carson sat next to her mom and hit a button. "Nurse, my mom's awake. Hurry!"

"They have nurses in heaven?" Bet looked around. "This looks like a hospital room." Confused, she realized she was in a bed.

"It is a hospital. You got shot, and they brought you here." Carson let her mother's hand go.

"I didn't go to heaven? I got shot? Where are you?"

"I'm here. Did you have a weird dream or something?"

"I don't remember...wait, Crank. He shot me, right?"

"Crank?"

"Yeah, and Rox. Oh my, how's Rox?" Pieces of her memory slowly slipped into place.

"Is that the girl they took to jail?"

"She's in jail? Why?"

"Didn't she try to hurt you?"

A nurse rushed into the room. "Mrs. Harper, it's good to see you awake."

Carson stepped aside and let the nurse examine her mother.

"I want to get up." Bet tried to shimmy off the bed. She felt a little dizzy and displaced. "Rox...Carson," she whispered, puzzled.

"Hang on, you need to rest. You have a big incision on your tummy." The nurse checked Bet's IV and raised the head of the bed a little. "Don't try to get up," the nurse said as she lifted Bet's hospital sheet and exposed her ankle. "It's time for your meds and to put Neosporin on this."

"A tattoo? Mom!" Carson bent to look closer. "When did you get that? And what's the deal with your hair?"

Bet stared at Carson. "Wait. If I'm in a hospital and you're here... I'm confused. A piece of space debris... You were home..." Bet stopped. Had she dreamed the whole thing? She touched her new hairdo, felt the sting of the tattoo and a deep pain in her lower abdomen. "Carson...the house...you called me from the house. That afternoon, after school, you called. Then the house was destroyed."

Carson sat next to Bet. "Yeah, I called you. Then I left right after we talked. I wasn't home. I didn't even know about what happened until a few days ago."

Tears stung Bet's eyes.

"I ran away to do an Outward Bound course in Colorado. I left you a note..."

"Oh, thank God!" Bet sobbed. "You really weren't home?"

Carson shook her head. "Then I almost got struck by lightning and got lost in the woods. I never knew what happened here."

"You got lost in the woods?" Bet tried to piece everything together. The fuzzy edges cleared a little.

Carson nodded. "For almost three weeks."

"I'm so happy, really incredibly happy." Bet smiled through her tears. "You're really alive? You're okay?"

Carson nodded.

"What happened to your head?" Bet reached out and touched Carson's face.

"I fell. And then I got attacked by wolves, and I was in a fire, and I got rescued by a helicopter, and I flew in the air on a cable."

Bet's eyes widened. "You did what?"

The nurse stepped next to the bed. "Carson can tell you about her adventure later. Bet, you need to stay quiet now."

"Sorry," Carson said. "I'm just so happy you're awake. We were really worried."

Bet didn't want to let go of her daughter. "This feels real, but part of me is afraid this is a dream."

"It's not a dream." The nurse stood over Bet, smiling, but holding a syringe full of medicine. "I can stick this in your arm to prove it if you want me to." She laughed then took the IV tube and injected the medicine in a rubber stopper. "But I won't. This is going to make you sleepy. You need to rest now. I'll keep an eye on Carson."

Bet felt the warmth of the medicine. "It seems Carson can take care of herself," she said, her words beginning to slur. She took hold of Carson and savored the heavenly feeling of holding her daughter's hand.

CHAPTER 84

After the nurse injected the medicine in Bet's IV, Carson watched her mother fight to stay awake. She didn't want to let go of her hand as much as her mom wanted to hold on to hers. In many ways, Carson felt like the earth had changed directions. She was home and her mom was going to be okay. That part was good. But her house had been obliterated to a crater hole, and all her stuff was gone. Every picture and video of her father was gone. That part sucked.

So much had happened.

She watched her mom sleep and remembered two days earlier, when Mark had come into Carson's hospital room and told her what happened. He said it didn't look good, that the doctors doubted her mom was going to survive.

Mark sat on the hospital bed and let Carson cry on his shoulder.

"I want to go home," Carson wailed into his sleeve. "I want my mom."

"I know you do," Mark said with genuine sympathy.

"I can't believe Mom was in jail and kidnapped..." She spoke between sobs. "And then got shot." Carson could barely see though her puffy eyes..

"We're working on getting you home so you can be with her." Mark hugged her tighter. "I'm sorry," he said.

But the doctors at the hospital wanted to keep her a little longer. She argued with them until they let her out.

"I just survived two weeks alone in the fiery woods eating two Snicker bars and some cruddy ferns." She winced at the memory of the slug. "I'm not sure I can take another day of hospital Jell-O. I want to go home and be with my mom."

"Okay." One of the doctors smiled. "We'll let you out of here after we finish a few tests and get some solid food into you. Deal?"

"Deal," Carson answered.

Later that afternoon, after Carson was released, Coffey allowed Mark to escort her home to Texas. She thought it was cool that had Seth stayed in Colorado so he could keep her company and fly back to Dallas with them. Since he lived in Austin, he said it was an easy commute to get home, say hi to his parents, then re-pack to hurry back to Dallas and be with Carson.

When they arrived, Carson was escorted through the airport, flanked by Mark and Seth, two hot guys, and everyone treated her like a real celebrity, especially since her story was on every channel in the universe. The airline even put them in first class.

Oh, man, the world really was rotating differently.

But in a good way, a really good way. Especially now that she knew her mom was going to be okay.

Carson watched her mom sleep, and she squeezed her hand.

CHAPTER 85

For the next three days, Bet was weaned from the medicine as she healed. The bullet had gone into her side and tore through some arteries. She went in and out of consciousness, but whenever she woke up she stared at Carson and smiled. "I still can't believe you're here. Everything is perfect except Rox being in jail. She needs to be here."

"I don't know, Mom. That police officer said that Rox forced you to leave jail. They have a video from the security cameras."

Bet shook her head and repositioned herself on the hospital bed. "I paid her to get me out. It was all my idea."

"My mom executing a prison break?" Carson sat on a lounge chair next to Bet's bed. "I just can't get my head around it."

"And what about you? Alone and lost on that mountain. Wolves, bears, and a fire." Bet started to cry. "To think I wouldn't let you take the trash out by yourself."

"It sounds like you've both had quite an adventure," a deep voice said from the open doorway.

"Officer Z." Bet waved and wiped tears away with the bed sheet. "How's Rox? Have you let her out yet?"

"No." Z strode into the room. "She's being held for kidnapping. Didn't she try to hurt you?"

"Rox? Heavens, no!"

Z took a seat on a chair near the window. "I shouldn't even be talking to you without your attorney present. And your doctors said you're not strong enough to make a statement yet."

"Well, if they'd quit giving me so much medicine, I'd be able to talk."

"I just wanted to make sure you were okay. It was touch and go there for a while."

"It's because of Rox I'm alive. She saved me."

"Wasn't she working with Crank?" Z asked.

"Rox was only trying to get something of hers from Crank." Bet looked at Z. "She needs to be let go. I'm the one who's at fault. She was helping me."

"She was helping you?" Z leaned forward. "Didn't she knife you, steal your purse and kidnap you?"

"Kidnap me? No! And Crank's"—she hesitated—"snarky girlfriend is the one who used the knife on me."

"Did you just say snarky?" Carson laughed.

Bet smiled. "I learned a few things from Rox." She looked at Z. "I coerced Rox to help me escape from jail. I paid her." Bet turned to Carson. "The reason I was incarcerated in the first place was because my only reason for living was gone. I thought you were at home when the house was destroyed." She grasped Carson's hand again. "I had nothing left and couldn't bear the thought of life without you." She looked at Carson tearfully. "My life was over. Then I met Rox." Bet looked at Z. "If it weren't for Rox, who knows what stupid thing I would've done. If anything, Rox saved me. We helped each other."

Z clasped his hands together and shook his head. "That's what she keeps saying, but not all criminals tell the truth."

"Let her go. She's not a criminal."

"You both have charges against you." Z ran a hand along his bald head. Then he looked at Bet and winked. "But the public is rooting for you and Rox."

"Every news station in the world is outside waiting to get an interview," Carson said. "I was told not to say anything because of some kind of national security."

"That would be Officer Coffey's doing," Z said. "He's really eating crow with that space debris incident." Z stood. "Look, let me see what I can do. You and Rox will have to deal with the criminal charges against you, so I suggest you get an attorney. For now, you rest and"—he hesitated—"don't get any ideas about escaping again."

"Don't worry. I have all that I need here." Bet smiled at Carson. "And Z, tell Rox we're in this together. I'll post bail and pay for an attorney. She needs to get out; today if possible."

"We'll see." He nodded at Carson. "I'm glad you're okay."

Carson smiled. "Thanks. It's good to be back." After Z left, Carson turned to her mom. "Mom?"

"Yes." Bet couldn't take her eyes off of her daughter.

"There's someone I want you to meet."

"Who?"

Carson blushed. "His name's Seth."

CHAPTER 86

Two days later, Rox sat with her leg slung over a hospital room chair, the TV droned in the background. "So Carson, did you really get attacked by wolves?"

"Yeah." Carson sat on the pullout couch next to Bet's bed. "It was pretty freaky." She raised her pant leg to show Rox the healing bite marks.

"That's pretty awesome." Rox smiled. "Maybe I'll have Pinto do a fang tattoo on my ankle like that if I ever get this stupid thing off." She raised her leg to show her ankle monitor. "I can't wait to be free again."

"It's a miracle we survived," Bet said, and held her side where the bullet had struck. "I'm ready to get out of here and start a new life." She lifted the shirt she'd struggled to get into that morning to look at the bandage. "Now that I have two belly buttons, maybe I'll get one pierced." She reached over and patted Carson on the knee.

Carson grimaced at her mother.

"Hey look, there's Shauna." Rox sat up straight and turned the volume up on the TV.

A reporter interviewed Shauna. "Rox Star and I have been best friends for, like, forever. She and that lady, Bet, came over and I helped them with a disguise. Did you see their hair? Wasn't it cool?" Shauna ran a hand through her own orange striped hair.

Rox laughed. "You go, Shanana!" She turned to Bet. "Did you hear she got a job in a salon in L.A.? A shampoo girl first; then she's gonna be a stylist to the stars."

"Hey, Mom. Did I tell you the *Today Show* wants me to go to New York and do an interview?" Carson looked at the TV. "I told them I couldn't go until you got better."

"Don't be silly." Bet turned to Carson.

"Why? Am I never going to get to travel again?" Carson crossed her arms.

"Of course you'll travel. Didn't you survive alone in the mountains for weeks?"

"Yeah."

"I think you can handle a trip to New York by yourself." Bet remembered the airline tickets she'd bought for them. "Maybe, soon, we can both take a trip there and you can show me all the cool places to go." Bet softened. "Grab life, honey. I'm sorry I held you back for so long."

The door opened, and Seth and Mark came in with armloads of flowers and balloons. "These were down at the volunteer's desk." Seth held up one box. "This is a bunch of baklava from some guy named Theo. There's a note that says you owe him sixty bucks."

"I need to pay him back." Bet laughed. "And I should buy him a very nice pen set, too."

"There are more flowers and packages downstairs," Mark said, unloading an armful.

"Oooh, chocolates!" Rox jumped out the chair and grabbed a box of candy. She opened the box, took one, and offered some to Bet and Carson.

"No, thanks," Carson said. "I've lost my sweet tooth for some reason."

Seth sat on the arm of the couch. "It's all the running you're doing now. Your body's a machine."

Carson smiled.

"Did Mark tell you we're going with my dad on a hike and climb trip in Colorado?" Seth asked. He looked at Carson affectionately. "You can come, too. It'll be fun."

Carson glanced at her mother. "No thanks. I'm not ready for any mountain adventures right now."

"Oh, you should go," Bet encouraged.

"I'm not into camping anymore," Carson said. "A trip with a nice hotel, hot showers and room service is more my speed now." She smiled at Mark. "And thanks again for everything."

Mark bowed. "I couldn't have done it without you."

"It worked out pretty well," Carson said, and squealed when

Seth grabbed her in a hug. "I heard the Colorado rescue team offered you a job." Carson settled into Seth's shoulder.

Mark shrugged. "I'm heading back to finish my residency. Then I might spend time in San Diego and get my old lifeguard job back in between semesters." He rubbed Carson's head affectionately. "My hand should be healed by then."

"Maybe we'll go to the beach," Bet said, excited. Then she hesitated. "I'm probably not going to be able to leave the state until I get the charges cleared, but you and Seth can visit Mark in California."

"Did that hair dye give you brain damage?" Carson asked. "Before, you'd never let me out of your sight, now you're trying to get rid of me?"

Bet slowly scooted to the side of the bed. "Carson, I still don't want to let you go." She looked at Rox chomping on chocolates. "But mostly, I don't want to hold you back anymore. I thought I'd lost you, and the pain was unbearable. But the whole time, I regretted that you never had the opportunity to see what the world had to offer."

"Does this mean I can walk to Starbucks by myself now?"

"Yes, as well as being able to drive there after you get your license."

"Cool!"

"Can she drive your pimped-out Honda?" Seth asked.

Bet laughed. "We'll see. I'm not sure what Crank did to it." She stood, shaky on weak legs. Seth jumped up to help her.

"Thank you." Bet let him assist her, and she sat next to Carson.

"Hey, Mark. Let's get the rest of those goodies downstairs." Seth and Mark went to the door. "You guys want something?"

"No, thanks," Bet and Carson answered together.

After they'd left Bet asked, "Rox, I've been meaning to ask you what was in that box you wanted so badly."

Rox wiped her chocolaty fingers on her jeans. "Bullets. But those weren't mine. Crank put them there. I just wanted the box back." She reached into her big purse and pulled out the small mosaic box. She gently rubbed a finger on the blue and white tiles. "Have you ever had one of those perfect days? You know, when everything went just right?" She looked at Carson and Bet. "My dad and I had one of those days a long time ago. He took me out for lunch, a baseball game, and to make this box." She held it up so they could see it. "He told me the tiles looked like an angel. I gave it to him to keep."

"Then why do you have it?" Bet reached toward Rox and took the box.

"His stupid new wife cleaned all my stuff out of their house and sent it to me." She shrugged. "He never asked for it again."

"It's beautiful," Bet said, admiring the small wooden box. "You know, Rox, in a big way you were my guardian angel." She handed the box back to Rox. "You've earned your wings."

"You keep it." The girl waved her hand at Bet. "You helped me, too." She looked as if she might cry.

"No, you went through an awful lot of trouble to get this. Give it back to your father. I'm sure he's wondering where it went."

"We'll see." Rox's lip trembled a little as she took the box back and stuffed it in her purse.

"Why don't the three of us go together and make a new one?" Carson asked. "That is, if you both aren't doing jail time."

"Look," Rox said, eyes glued to the TV news. "We're celebrities. They wouldn't lock us up now." She glanced at Bet. "Would they?"

"I hope not." Bet sighed. "Jerry thinks he can get us probation, considering everything."

"Jerry?" Carson raised an eyebrow. "Sounds like he's more than just your attorney."

Bet grinned. "He is rather dashing."

Rox shook her head. "There you go sounding like the Queen of England again."

"One day at a time," Bet said. "One day at a time."

CHAPTER 87

One Year Later

Bet helped Carson load the last of her luggage into her new SUV. Rox threw her backpack and overnight case into the backseat. The two of them were like oddball stepsisters. They'd become close, one needed to learn independence and the other needed a home.

"You looked beautiful at graduation yesterday." Bet held her daughter's hands and smiled. "You glowed on that stage." She brushed her fingers across Carson's forehead, which still bore a faded pink scar.

"Whatever." Carson slipped on a "Life is good" baseball cap, which partially covered the scar. "I'm glad it's over. Now on to a summer road trip, then college." Carson chose to go to Texas Tech in Lubbock, and Seth was going to USC in Los Angeles.

Bet was glad that Carson and Seth had found each other and had told Carson that she was glad she'd discovered love. "Open up and embrace it," she'd said to her daughter. "Yes, it will hurt if it doesn't work out, but in the long run your heart will be stronger and deeper for it."

Carson rolled her eyes, but smiled, too.

They seemed perfect together. Soon after Bet was released from the hospital, she and Seth had a few moments alone. They'd sat in a hotel lobby, the same hotel that Bet had left a month before. "Seth, it's nice to see Carson so happy."

"Yeah, she's awesome."

"Take good care of her. I held her back for so long, and the world's a big place."

"She can take care of herself," Seth said, laughing.

Bet loved that he laughed so much.

"You know, Mrs. C," Seth called her by her new nickname, thanks to Rox. "I used to be the fat kid, too. Even though Carson is amazingly beautiful, it'll be a while before she sees it." He got serious and looked away. "That fat kid doesn't just go away." He looked at Bet again and smiled. "I get it. I get how she is. We're good together."

Tears of happiness welled in Bet's eyes.

Now, standing by the car with Carson and Rox, Bet reached into a shopping bag. "Here, I got something for you two." She pulled out two dog tags. "They say, 'If lost please call,' and it has my cell number."

Carson smiled and pulled out a leather-strapped necklace hidden under her shirt. Nacho's worn dog tag hung on it. "I'll put it with this one."

Rox took hers. "Cool. Maybe I'll get a spiked collar to wear with it." She clipped it to her dangle of neck jewelry.

"And here." Bet pulled out two decorative wooden boxes. "I got one for each of you." She handed them to Carson and Rox. "But don't open them until you need them."

"Need?" Rox asked. "Is there money in here?"

"Not money. I stuffed them with kisses. Use as needed."

"Mom, you are so weird!" Carson said, while she admired the small box.

Bet gave each of them another big hug. "I'll miss you."

"Take care of the home fires," Carson said, looking at their new zero lot line home, courtesy of the U.S. government.

"I will. Now that I'm a free woman, I may take a trip, too." Both she and Rox had been on probation for a year. Even though they'd been treated like celebrities, too. Z had been a constant force in Rox's "rehab" and made sure that Crank stayed behind bars. "The church is sponsoring a few mission trips that sound interesting."

"Good. Just be careful," Carson warned, but smiled as she said it.

"I promised myself I wouldn't cry," Bet said, wiping a tear.

"It's okay. I might cry, too." Carson hugged her mom again.

"Oh, come on, you two missy mushy girls. I'm ready to hit the road." Rox stood by the opened passenger door. "I've been stuck in Dallas on probation for a year—I want to get out of Dodge, now!"

"Okay, okay," Carson said as she closed the hatchback.

Bet rubbed her hand across a dent in the bumper where Carson had hit a pole while driving with her permit.

"Here." Bet handed Carson a stuffed bear with an astronaut outfit on. They'd bought it at NASA when they got a VIP tour over the summer. "Take pictures of Nasee everywhere you go and email them to me."

"This is so corny." Carson took the bear and secured it in a seatbelt in the back. "Satisfied?" She pulled out a digital camera and shot a picture. "I'll make sure to take one in New Mexico and the Grand Canyon."

"And don't forget to take a bunch of you and Rox," Bet said. "What an exciting opportunity, a road trip to Los Angeles! Remember to take your time and see the sights."

"We will. Seth won't be at USC until the end of July anyway. He and his dad are taking a hike together in Colorado. Mark might even join them for part of it." She smiled. "We might see them if we decide to go that way."

"Mark seems to be enjoying finishing out his residency," Bet said.

"He'll be a good doctor." Carson tucked her long blonde hair behind her ear.

"And I'm glad you're thinking about going into medicine, too," Bet said, as she opened Carson's car door.

"I still haven't ruled out stunt-woman."

"Carson, that's not funny."

"Yeah, it is." Carson laughed.

"I think I just grew a gray hair. Let's go!" Rox complained. "Besides, I told my dad we'd be in Amarillo by tonight."

"Did he move there?" Bet asked.

"No, he's still in Houston. He just timed a business trip around our adventure, if we can ever get a move on. Then I want to be in LA before Shanana starts to do hair for that Johnny Depp movie. I *so* have to meet him." She clutched both hands to her chest. "Hey, Mrs. C, do you want me to give one of these kisses to Johnny Depp when I see him?" Rox pulled Bet's gift from her duffel bag.

Bet laughed. "Sure, there's a big wet juicy one in there somewhere."

"Mom!"

"Go Mrs. C!" Rox stuffed the box in her bag.

"Maybe you'll be able to work with Shauna, now that you've graduated with your cosmetology degree." Bet gave Rox a big hug and said to both the girls, "You two watch out for each other."

"Yeah, yeah." Rox accepted Bet's hug. "And thanks again for letting me stay with you and Cars.

"You're part of the family, Rox Star." Bet sniffed. "I can't believe you both are leaving."

"Don't worry." Carson got in the driver's seat and started the engine. "You can come visit."

Bet went to Carson's door. "You know, honey, you'll always be my baby."

"Oh no, not again." Carson raised an eyebrow at her mother.

"Have an adventure," Bet said. She closed the door and stepped back as they drove away. "And be careful," she whispered to herself.

Watching them drive away, Bet recalled an afternoon when she and Carson, who was then about five years old, had gone to a carnival. A big bunch of balloons had gotten loose and floated into the sky. At first, Bet felt a tinge of sadness as the colorful bunch flew away, but Carson started laughing, saying, "Look how happy they are!"

The balloons bobbed and whipped around in the wind, their ribboned tails swishing freely. Bet thought they did look happy, bouncing in flight—dancing balloons that looked like the image of laughter itself.

Through the back window of the SUV, Bet watched Carson and Rox, their two heads bobbing happily. Their fingers waved like ribbons as they drove over the hill and out of sight.

"I love you, Carson," Bet said, as she stood staring at the horizon, half expecting to see a cluster of balloons rise into the sky.

ABOUT THE AUTHOR

Jeanne Skartsiaris is author of SURVIVING LIFE a YA adventure story—a book that overprotected daughters will give to their mothers and worried moms will give their daughters. SURVIVING LIFE was an ABNA quarter-finalist.

A member of Romance Writer's of America and Dallas Area Romance Writers, Jeanne started writing to quell the little voices in her head. A worried mom, she worked as a medical photographer for a plaintiff's law from and saw too many photographs of accident scenes. She now looks at life as one big safety hazard.

Jeanne attended Creative writing courses at Southern Methodist University and lives in Texas with her husband and (overprotected) daughter. Currently she works as a Sonographer.

You can find her on Facebook at Jeanne Skartsiaris, Author and Twitter @jskartsiaris.

25522996R00149

Made in the USA
Charleston, SC
06 January 2014